DEAD BISHOPS DON'T LIE

A fast-paced, action-packed international thriller

ANDRÉ K. BABY

Thierry Dulac Thrillers Book 1

Revised edition 2022
Joffe Books, London
www.joffebooks.com

First published in Great Britain in 2012

This paperback edition was first published
in Great Britain in 2022

Cover art by Jarmila Takač

ISBN: 978-1-80405-459-8

PROLOGUE

March 6, 2005. 2.17 a.m. Saas-Fee, Switzerland.

Before he dies, he must suffer. The sentence still rang in Vasiliev's brain.

The dry snow squeaked under his burdened boots. It reminded him of Irkutsk. Sweat stung the corners of his eyes and trickled down his unshaven cheeks. His thick sealskin coat hindered his grip, and Vasiliev felt the man's limp body begin to slip.

"How much further?"

"Up a bit, past the Hotel Bristol," replied Kurganski.

Once more Vasiliev shrugged, strengthening his hold on the arm draped behind his neck.

As they crossed the town's small plaza, shouldering the unconscious priest between them, someone emerged from the darkness. The man headed toward them.

"Let me talk," whispered Kurganski.

"Grüezi," said the man in Swiss German.

"Ja, hallo," grumbled Kurganski, staggering like a drunk.

"Good party, *ja?"*

"Jawohl, now time to go home."

"Need some help?"

"No, we're fine," said Kurganski.

"Sure?"

"Ja." Kurganski straightened to his imposing height, his bulky fur coat adding pounds to his solid frame.

After a moment's hesitation, the man turned away and disappeared into the night.

"He saw your face," said Vasiliev.

"No way. I can barely see yours."

"I . . . Let's leave him here. In this cold, he'll be dead by morning."

"And if he isn't?"

Vasiliev didn't reply. There was no reply. The contract was clear: *Deliver and terminate. Before he dies, he must suffer.* Again, he strengthened his grip on the priest's limp arm and they pressed on.

"Almost there," said Kurganski.

Moments later, they stopped before the metal door of the Alpine Express cable car's entrance and put Salvador down. Vasiliev reached into his pocket and took out the passkey, as Kurganski shone the flashlight onto the door's lock. His hand shaking, Vasiliev inserted the passkey and tried to turn it. The key didn't budge. He jiggled it. Nothing. He removed it and tried again. "I'm sure . . . It's got to . . ."

"Here. Let me try," said Kurganski, handing Vasiliev the small LED light. "There." The lock clicked open.

Behind them, Salvador started to moan.

"Quick. Get the Desflurane," said Kurganski.

Vasiliev took out the small bottle from his pocket, opened it and put it to the priest's nostrils. Salvador fell unconscious again.

Slowly, they dragged Salvador up the staircase onto the platform of the Télébenne's landing area. In the darkness, Vasiliev could just make out a red cable car, its door ajar. They stopped and set Salvador down on the concrete floor, as Vasiliev tried to catch his breath.

"Get the rope," said Kurganski.

"Give me a second. What's the rush?"

"And have him come to again?"

Vasiliev groped his way to the far wall and took the coiled safety rope off its hook. Suddenly, he heard a loud metal clang and spun around.

"Damn," said Kurganski, clumsily picking up a ladder and carrying it to the edge of the concrete platform. He raised the ladder and rested it onto the thick metal cable. "There. Now we strip him."

They kneeled down and began removing Salvador's parka, when suddenly the priest struggled to free himself.

"Shit," Kurganski shouted.

As Vasiliev stared, too startled to move, Kurganski pinned Salvador down onto the floor and grabbed his wrists. "Relax, priest, you're going nowhere," he said. Releasing Salvador's left wrist, Kurganski punched him hard in the face once, twice, three times. Two uppercuts to the chin and Salvador lay still, eyes rolled back. "There. That's better," said Kurganski as he got up, rubbing his sore fist. He eyed Vasiliev: "Thanks for the help. Give me the rope."

"Sorry, I . . . I didn't . . ."

"Give."

Kurganski tied the rope tightly around Salvador's bare chest and threw the loose end around the cable near the ladder. They pulled him up until his head reached the cable, then secured the rope to the walkway's metal railing.

"Now the knife," Kurganski said.

Vasiliev groped in his coat pocket and took out a short, sheathed knife.

"The plaque."

Vasiliev took out the small wooden plaque, a small cord tied to both ends.

"Now, priest, time's up," said Kurganski. He hung the plaque around his neck and started up the ladder toward Salvador, half-naked, dangling grotesquely from the cable.

CHAPTER 1

Karen Dawson rose from beneath the cozy fluffiness of the duvet, stretched catlike and opened the hotel room's window. The view was stunning: Row upon row of jagged, white peaks as far as the eye could see, imposing their timeless serenity on the tiny village nestled in the valley below. She inhaled deeply, briefly shielding her eyes from the early sun's reflection off the slopes. *Another fantastic day.* Thoughts of insipid fellow teachers, humdrum classes, unpaid rent, lackluster sex life—all were quickly dissipating into the magic of the alpine air.

After a quick breakfast, anxious to enjoy that first crowd-free run, Karen grabbed her rented skis and headed for the Alpine Express base station. As she walked past the small Romanesque church in the town's plaza, she crossed herself discreetly. She was approaching the entrance of the base station, when the sudden wail of an ambulance shattered the morning's fragile silence. Karen started up the entrance steps, her pulse quickening with eagerness and excitement. *Strange — no line for once.* At the top, on the concrete landing, a handful of skiers had gathered and were staring at an object that appeared to be attached to the Télébenne's cable. Karen approached, curious.

Then it hit her. The 'object' was a man, hanging from the cable in the shape of a cross, bound at his wrists and arms, naked except for a piece of dark cloth around his waist, his mouth gagged with tape. His legs were tied and as she walked closer, she could see his face, eyes imploring, frozen in agony. His black hair was ruffled and a small icicle hung from his nose, his skin a translucent gray. On his right side, a slanted gash, from which blood had run down his torso and leg onto the concrete below. Something hung from his neck, too small to be identified.

Karen went numb.

She looked at the other skiers, her glance questioning: *Surely this isn't, can't be real? People aren't murdered in Saas-Fee?* The air of sadness, mixed with morbid curiosity of the man beside her, confirmed the opposite. She tried to turn away but couldn't.

"Is he . . . ?"

"Ja . . . dead." the man answered, almost mechanically.

She crossed herself. "God . . . Who . . . ?"

The man didn't answer. Moments later, two ski-patrolmen were closing off the area with metal gates, pushing back curious onlookers. A Japanese skier taking a video brushed past her, describing the macabre scene in a muted voice.

Karen shuddered. She felt dizzy. She dropped her skis and sat on the concrete floor. She willed herself not to be sick. Minutes later, two policemen carrying a ladder hurried by and set it on the cable, next to the dead man's body.

"Everybody out. The Télébenne is closed," shouted one of them, waving the skiers down the steps.

Karen got up, felt her knees weaken and grabbed the metal railing. *No way I'm skiing today.* Despondent, half dazed, she started trudging back to the hotel, skis on her shoulders. She barely noticed two drably-dressed men, one in a sealskin coat, tugging their suitcases through the narrow cobblestone street. As the horror and sadness of the moment sank in, that special thrill of linking those smooth turns quickly faded into irrelevance. Instead, Karen felt the dull weight of a man's

cruel death pressing on the hedonistic bubble of her surroundings, bursting it.

For Karen Dawson, Saas-Fee's magic ceased to exist.

Back at the hotel, she tried to read, but the sight of
the distorted corpse kept creeping back. She had to talk
to someone. Still too early to call her mother in Vermont,
and the hotel bar wouldn't open until noon. An hour later,
she walked downstairs to the small dining room decorated
in Swiss pastoral, where Frau Graf was already setting the
tables for lunch.

"Have you heard what happened at the cable car?" asked
Karen.

"Ja," answered Frau Graf perfunctorily, her rosy face
avoiding Karen's gaze and focusing on the dinnerware.

"Who was he?"

Frau Graf raised a shoulder in reply and continued
about her work.

Murder must be bad for business. "Have a great day," said
Karen, walking out in disgust.

CHAPTER 2

March 6, 8.25 a.m.

Chief Inspector François Besse of Sion's Cantonal police force had been called to the scene that morning by one of Saas-Fee's 'gendarmes', a retired ski guide known affectionately by the villagers as Willi. Besse's weekly trip from Sion to Saas-Fee usually took the better part of an hour. He would drive along the valley floor and slowly witness the daunting 4000-meter peaks invade his retreating horizon. By the time he'd reached the village, the mountains had encircled and trapped him inside a wall of granite and feldspar.

François Besse was from Geneva, where the faraway mountains were decorative, not threatening. From the beginning of his assignment at Sion, he'd noticed the stern, worried look of Saas-Fee's villagers: When they spoke, they often looked up at the peaks, not in admiration but in fear, as if to make sure the mountains hadn't suddenly decided to crush them. On August 16, 1965, the mountains had so decided, and hurled 2000 tons of snow and ice at the villagers below. Twenty-two had died, instantly entombed in their houses of wood and brick. The mountains had exacted a heavy toll for continuous trespass.

Today, Besse threw the little Opel from side to side, swerving, passing, darting in and out of cars at double the speed limit, all to that pathetic *Pin-Pon* of its siren. He made it in thirty-five minutes.

At the base station, the body lay covered on a first-aid toboggan. Besse approached, and Willi gave him a small plaque, the one that had hung from the man's neck. It read: "The Lion is dead, the Dragon is wounded."

"Grüezi, Willi. Terrible business, this. Who was he?" said Besse, looking quizzically at the plaque.

"Grüezi, Inspector. I'm not sure, but a woman said it was the bishop staying at the Hotel Tenne. She says she and her husband had breakfast with him two days ago."

Besse's relaxed gait, longish hair, thin lips under large and inquisitive eyes hinted at any profession except the constabulary. He looked permanently startled. The brown leather thigh-length jacket, tied loosely below his former waist, helped restore the authority partially dissipated by the look of surprise. So did his small-winged, brown bow tie.

Besse instructed the policeman to photograph the dead man, and as they walked briskly to the hotel, Besse began feeling increasingly nervous: Pickpockets, ski thieves, and drunks were his daily fare. He'd never headed a homicide case. His methodical mind raced, sifting to find—*Procedure — murder.*

"Grüezi, Phillipe. Do you have a priest or a bishop staying here?" asked Besse, of the hotelier busy drying the orange juice glasses.

"Ja, Inspector, we have Archbishop Salvador and his chauffeur. Rooms twelve and fourteen. The archbishop is in twelve and . . ."

"Is this the man?" said Besse, showing the hotelier the picture.

The hotelier froze, stared silently at Besse and nodded, his mouth slack.

Besse and Willi rushed upstairs; Willi pounded on room fourteen's oak door.

"What is it?" asked the sleepy, disheveled chauffeur, half-hiding behind the door.

"Police. Do you know this man?" said Besse.

The chauffeur dropped his eyes to the picture and recoiled in shock. He staggered back, clutching the door with both hands, then turned to the bathroom and vomited.

Besse helped the stricken man onto the edge of the bed. "Are you all right?"

"Yes, I think so. Who? Who could have done this?"

"I'm asking you," replied Besse.

The chauffeur slowly shook his head and broke down in tears.

François Besse knew he was out of his depth. He telephoned headquarters in Berne.

CHAPTER 3

Vasiliev glanced at his watch: 8.32 am. "We're making good time," he said, as he drove the Fiat rental off the Lötschberg Car Train.

The Saas-Fee assignment was Vasiliev's second, after his assassination of a Communist Party official turned too greedy for his own good. The new Russian oligarchs didn't tolerate violations of their strict code, as their fathers hadn't before them. This time, the contract was to be executed outside Russia, and Vasiliev had never traveled west of the Urals. Victor had been reassuring: A ski vacation in Switzerland would go unnoticed: Russians were everywhere, outspending each other in orgies of self-indulgence, making up for lost time. Victor's down payment had quashed any lingering doubts. Yet Vasiliev had not grown accustomed to his profession's acute side effects. After two years, the eyes of his previous victim were never far away, boring into his consciousness at the slightest occasion. He feared he would never forget the archbishop's final look of raw terror.

Suddenly Vasiliev felt Kurganski grab his forearm.

"Look out," Kurganski shouted.

Too late. Vasiliev's eye caught the young girl's look of terror, her raised right arm. He swerved to the right. The sickening thud of her body on the left side of the Fiat told him he'd hit her hard.

"Damn." He stopped, rolled down his window quickly and looked about. To his left, the girl's body lay twisted on the road, her legs sprawled onto the curb. At the intersection up ahead, a handful of people were waiting for the tram. Vasiliev's brain raced into overdrive, weighing his options. "If we make a run for it, and someone gets our plate number, we're dead."

"If we wait, they'll tie us to Saas-Fee. *Go, Go!*" said Kurganski, his right nicotine-stained hand signaling Vasiliev onwards.

As Vasiliev floored the Fiat, he caught a glimpse of the gesticulating onlookers in his rearview mirror. "Damn, damn, damn," he said, pounding the steering wheel.

"You were too close to the curb. If . . ."

"Fuck right off."

"We're still a half hour from the airport. Step on it." said Kurganski.

"Someone *must* have gotten our plate number."

"Those Swiss will be shit-fast at tracing the car. We've got to get rid of it," said Kurganski.

"But it's due back today. Hertz will get suspicious."

"We'll phone them and say we're extending for a couple of days."

"Our plane leaves for Moscow in one-and-a-half hours: we won't make it," said Vasiliev, hardly controlling his panic.

"We get rid of the car in Zürich and take the train to Kloten airport. Plenty of time," said Kurganski almost matter-of-factly.

"We don't even know the train schedule. We could . . ."

Vasiliev felt Kurganski's hot breath close to his cheek.

"Listen, asshole. *You* got us into this mess. *I'm* going to get us out. Go to the train station *now*," said Kurganski.

"Okay, okay, let me fucking drive. One accident is enough."

"Goddamn right."

Vasiliev parked the car in front of the Zürich train station and they rushed inside. Kurganski went to the ticket counter, while Vasiliev purchased a local newspaper: He breathed a sigh of relief: *Nothing on Saas-Fee.*

Beneath the arches of the station's glass-paneled roof, the dull gray of the cement walkways blended into the dark green of the railway cars. The morose look on the faces of the morning passengers only accentuated the atmosphere of daily dismal routine. Yet the minuted announcements of the train departures actually helped calm his raw nerves. He desperately needed to join, if only for a moment, the quiet predictability of Swiss life. After what seemed an eternity, they boarded the train, and Vasiliev tried to concentrate: *Calm down, breathe deeply, relax*, he told himself. *Such a stupid, stupid mistake.*

* * *

The ambulance rushed the injured girl to the hospital in Zollikon. The onlookers were talking excitedly when policeman Hans Gerhauer arrived at the scene, minutes later.

"Crazy bastards. The poor girl never had a chance," said the young man in a light gray overcoat.

"What make of car was it?" said Gerhauer.

"A dark-colored Fiat, quite recent."

"How many people on board?"

"Two, I think."

"Can you describe them?"

"No, they were too far."

"Did you get the plate number?"

"It started with ZH 10 something."

Gerhauer grabbed his microphone and growled the information to his dispatcher in Zürich.

* * *

Kurganski stepped quickly off the train at Kloten, Vasiliev following close behind. *Still an hour before our flight to Moscow. We'll attract attention if we reroute*, thought Kurganski.

In the airport's huge aluminum-framed departure hall, there seemed nothing unusual as passengers hurried about, searching for their gates.

"Take this and wait for me at the Lufthansa Lounge," Kurganski said as he handed Vasiliev his luggage.

Kurganski turned and walked to the phone booth across the passage from the Hertz reception desk and dialed their number. He turned cautiously, enough to see the young, bored-looking woman pick up the phone and put on her fake customer smile.

"Hertz, how may I help you?"

"My name is Berger; I rented a Fiat three days ago, due today."

Kurganski focused intently on the girl, watching for any unusual sign: a hand on the mouthpiece, a signal to a co-worker. Nothing. She continued looking at her screen. "I want to extend the rental for three more days," he said.

She paused briefly, fingers flying on the computer's keyboard with the ease of a concert pianist. After what seemed like a century to Kurganski, she said: "No problem, Mr. Berger. It's an extra sixty francs per day, plus insurance and taxes."

"Fine." As he hung up slowly, he watched for any hint from the girl. She seemed to share a joke with her colleague and continued looking at her computer screen. Kurganski breathed deeply: the gamble had paid off. Hertz hadn't been notified, and they were in the clear. *Otherwise that girl deserves an Oscar*, he thought, as he rushed upstairs and joined Vasiliev in the Lufthansa lounge.

"Everything is OK. We're clear. Now, we wait."

* * *

Later that morning, on-duty Inspector Pierre Schmidt, Zürich Police, had received the hit-and-run report and relayed the information to all cars: *Dark-colored Fiat, year unknown, partial plate number ZH 10, traveling in the general direction of Zürich. Two occupants minimum.*

Intercept and arrest.

Central Car Registry had been notified for any possible narrowing down of the list and had come up with three listings. At 3.45 p.m., Schmidt received a call from one of the patrolmen.

"Schmidt."

"Inspector, we have one dark blue Fiat here illegally parked on the Bahnhofstrasse," said the gendarme.

"What's the plate number?"

"ZH 10387 683."

"Any sign of the occupants?"

"No."

"Anything else?"

"It has a broken left headlight."

"*Merde.* Why didn't you say so? Stay there and arrest anybody getting into that car." Schmidt phoned Central Car Registry: The owner of the car was Hertz, Kloten location. Schmidt signaled the two adjutants to follow him: They jumped into the Volvo and descended onto the airport, siren screaming, blue lights flashing.

"Police. Let me see your file on your Fiat, plate number ZH 10387 683," said Schmidt to the Hertz supervisor.

"But sir, I'm, we assure our clients' confid—"

"Who dealt with the rental?"

"Ah. Sarita Dellinger, over there," said the supervisor, his resistance melting.

Schmidt glared at the young woman.

"Do you remember who rented this car?"

"No . . . well, yes actually, the man phoned about four hours ago, saying he wanted to extend the rental a few more days."

Schmidt turned to the supervisor and said:

"Get me a printout of your incoming calls this afternoon, from one-thirty onwards."

Schmidt knew the futility of his gestures, but procedure required them to be followed. He knew that his prey had already eluded him. He copied Berger's false driver's license and sent it out to the Swiss Federal authorities. He had it sent to all airlines, for a passenger list check. To no avail.

* * *

Aboard the plane, Vasiliev felt reborn. The package had been delivered, the contract executed, and their mission completed. Even Kurganski's gamble had paid off. *The man's brilliant*, he thought. He toasted Kurganski with vodka and cheap champagne. For a moment, he felt a tinge of remorse obscure his cheerfulness: He had a daughter and imagined the grief of the parents if the accident were to prove fatal. He hoped that her backpack had absorbed the blow. *Shit, nothing I could have done*. Now it was on to Moscow, to the safety of the Motherland, where he hoped his identity would dissolve into the milk of Russian humanity.

CHAPTER 4

Sion, Switzerland. March 7, 2005, 8.35 a.m.

Besse kissed his wife Bénédicte, hugged his three-year-old daughter Amélie on the doorstep of his two-bedroom flat on Rue des Cedres, and walked briskly along Rue des Pins, on his way toward the police station. As he approached, he could see the vans, their parabolic antennas aimed at the skies and the world's TV stations. He felt his stomach stir the remainder of Bénédicte's slightly burned croissant, as the thought of his upcoming, unwanted notoriety began to sink in.

"You have visitors," said the adjutant, as Besse hurried up the steps to the entrance. "They flew in from Paris this morning. The Feds in Berne confirmed it by fax. They're from Interpol: Inspectors Thierry Dulac and Daniel Lescop."

Besse struggled nervously past the gaggle of journalists, TV reporters and cameramen. "Nothing yet. *Pas encore.* No comment," he shouted to the angry horde. As he neared his glass-paned office, Besse saw a thin, brown-haired man, comfortably ensconced in Besse's chair, cigarette in hand, gesticulating and speaking intensely to a younger man in a blue shirt. As he entered, the thin man rose and extinguished his cigarette on Besse's favorite porcelain saucer.

"Thierry Dulac, Interpol France," he said, extending his left hand: "This is Daniel Lescop. So, Inspector Busse, what was the time of death?"

"Besse, François Besse," he answered, awkwardly grasping the extended hand. "I don't know. We don't have the coroner's preliminary report yet."

"When?"

"In a week, maybe."

"How about this afternoon?"

"What? I can't . . ."

"Perhaps if I call Berne . . ." Dulac grabbed Besse's phone and started to dial.

"Wait . . . I . . . I'll see what I can do."

Dulac put down the receiver.

"Where was he staying?" asked Dulac, now picking up the binder containing photographs of the dead man.

"At the Hotel Tenne. He had booked for a week."

"What about Forensics?"

"They went through the room yesterday."

"At what time?" said Dulac, moving closer to Besse.

"From noon to six."

"And before? Did you guard access to the room?"

"No, it . . ."

"So it was unguarded between the time of the discovery of the murder and noon?"

"It was locked by the hotel," replied Besse, looking up at Dulac's steady gaze and waiting for the hammer to fall.

"But not sealed."

"Ah . . . no."

"Splendid. Get me Forensics' report . . . by . . . ?" Dulac was smiling, his large concave frame bent threateningly close.

"Ah, I think we can get an initial by the end of the . . ."

"Day?"

"Really, I can't . . ."

"Do you have the roadblock report?"

"Well . . ."

"You *did* set up a roadblock."

"Actually, no. We were looking for witnesses."

"Excellent," said Dulac, drawing a deep breath. "Any sworn depositions yet?"

I really don't need this, this French asshole's crap, thought Besse. *Why didn't Berne send a Swiss?* Besse caught his thought in mid-air. *But of course, Salvador was French. Politics already.* "You must understand, we're a small police force here. This isn't Paris."

"Inspector, Paris doesn't have only *one* road leading out. It's easy to control the outgoing traffic. No?" said Dulac, looking at the photographs. "Unless of course you think they skied out over the mountains."

Besse felt his pulse quicken. The anger surged from his gut: "There's no need for your sarcasm."

"You're right. Sorry. Inspector, have your men check all departures from the hotels and pensions, yesterday and today. Let's go over them this afternoon, shall we?" said Dulac, his tone patronizing.

"But there are over 4000 beds in Saas-Fee: it'll take a week."

"Tell me, Inspector, does everything around here take a week?" said Dulac, his jaw set in confrontation. "These killers aren't having Swiss fondue, waiting for your gallant alpine-skiing policemen to knock on their door. A little more urgency on your part might help us catch them, *even. Am I getting through?*"

"Yes, of course."

"Good. Now, get me a map of Saas-Fee and we'll allocate streets."

* * *

By 4 p.m., Dulac and Lescop had finished questioning staff and clients from nearby hotels, restaurants and bars, and were driving back to Sion in Lescop's rented Opel. Dulac reread his notes: *"Rien.* Nothing. And you?"

"Afraid not."

A half hour later, they arrived at the Sion police station.

"What? Not even a preliminary report? Your coroner's had over a day." Dulac shouted at the cocker-spaniel-eyed adjutant behind the reception desk.

"I, I don't know. It's not my responsibility. I'm only . . ."

"Get him on the phone."

At that moment, one of the reporters milling about in the reception area recognized Dulac. In an instant, the reporter and his colleagues were swarming around him like angry wasps, poking microphones and cameras into his face: "Inspector Dulac, any initial suspects? How did they get him to the cable car? What is the possible motive of such a grisly crime? Is this a sex-vengeance thing?"

Dulac faced the onslaught with a virulent outburst of Gallic temper: "Back off, you, you bunch of . . ."

"Yes?" said the pimply brunette, microphone in hand.

Dulac bit his tongue and forced a smile: "Madame, I have no suspects yet. It's a little early in the investigation, don't you think? Don't worry, we'll keep you updated." Dulac turned to the adjutant: "Well?"

"The coroner doesn't answer."

"Great. Just pissing great."

Dulac retreated to the calm of Besse's empty office and shut the door.

A half hour passed when through the office's glass partition, Dulac caught sight of a short, rotund man with a smile that took half his face slowly approaching Besse's office. The man knocked and timidly opened the door.

"Inspector Dulac?"

"Come in."

"I'm Dr. Zubriggen, the coroner. You have been calling me?"

"Ah . . . Finally, Doctor."

"I have the preliminary report. Do you wish me to read it?"

"By all means. I'm all ears." said Dulac, putting his feet up on the desk and not bothering to offer Zubriggen the empty chair before him.

The rotund man sat down slowly, adjusted his bifocals and read the report in that strange sing-song tone of the Swiss Germans when they speak French: "Death occurred approximately at 6 a.m., because of asphyxiation caused by the crucifixion, hypothermia and shock. This was accelerated by the loss of blood. The incision was made between the fourth and fifth rib, with a very sharp knife, or possibly a scalpel. The parting of the tissue was extremely clean, with . . ."

"Tell me, Doctor, any signs of a struggle?" interrupted Dulac.

"Yes, I was coming to that. Yes. He has bruises on the face."

"Any traces of the attackers on his body, under his fingernails?"

"We did not see any."

"Drugs?"

"This will be in my final report. This will take more time, Mr. Dulac."

"Less than a week, I hope."

The little man, surprise on his oval face, smiled questioningly at Dulac. "What?"

"Never mind. Just leave the report here," said Dulac, as he rose and showed the doctor out.

Dulac glanced at the doctor's report. *A professional job.* The killers planned that Salvador would die slowly, before the opening of the cable car. They wanted to prolong the archbishop's terror of confronting his own death. *What could warrant such a cruel, horrific death?* As he awaited Besse's report, Dulac pondered the meaning of the plaque, the one found hanging from Salvador's neck. It was rectangular, of a heavy, dense, wood. The inscription, bearing burr marks, seemed to have been carved with a drill.

The Lion is dead. The Dragon is wounded. What could this possibly mean? Why a crucifixion? Why the ritualistic cruelty? Why the reference to animals? To whom was the message addressed? Dulac had sent the information to the research division of Interpol, and he knew the Crays' computers were already crunching, digesting, filtering and expunging, searching their huge data banks for information and leads.

Dulac felt a surge of anger, the kind of anger that fueled his desire to do battle. These killers were mocking him, silently flaunting their success. They'd killed methodically, boldly. Boldly enough to leave a message. He picked up the plaque, rotated it and studied it from all angles, and put it back on the desk. He swore he'd find them.

* * *

An hour later, Besse appeared. His investigation had fared no better. Dulac and Lescop returned to Hotel Castel, where after a quick supper, Dulac retired to the perfunctory sparseness of his minuscule room. Lying on the stiff bed, his mood morose, he watched distractedly the horrible pictures of Salvador's body on the evening news when suddenly the phone rang.

"Inspector Dulac?"

"Yes?"

"My name is André Beaulieu, the new head of Interpol Research in Lyon. We have the initial report from our computer search."

"And?"

"We've searched for all possible links with known groups, including Al Qaeda, and can't find a pattern or link. We don't have anything on recent crucifixions, but it's a method of execution in Sudan and Iran. Also, the 'Ndrangheta Mafia' has been known to crucify traitors."

"I doubt the archbishop qualifies."

"Just a minute," said Beaulieu, "Mr. Harris is on the line. He wants a word with you."

Mr. Harris! Yes, this guy is really new. Dulac cringed. The last person he wanted to talk to was Richard Harris, the General Secretary, a.k.a. his boss.

"So, Dulac: *Quid?*"

Dulac hated Harris's sophomoric use of grammar-school Latin, but played along. *"Nihil habemus."*

"What?"

"We have nothing, yet."

"Any word from the coroner?"

"We have his prelim, which only gives us time and cause of death. We can't do much until we have his final."

"How long?"

"If we're lucky, a week."

"Then let the Swiss carry the ball."

"Meaning?"

"Get back to Paris. There's been a new development. There's someone I want you to meet."

CHAPTER 5

Paris, March 8, 8.20 a.m.

That Thursday morning announced another dreary winter day in Paris. A day when the fog paints its limestone buildings a dirty monochrome beige and everyone's mood a dirty monochrome black.

"A what?" asked Lescop, his air a mixture of amusement and disdain.

"An animal mythologist." Dulac looked away from Lescop and signaled to the tall, coffee-carrying waiter.

"What do *they* eat for breakfast?" asked Lescop, making no effort to hide his disdain.

"Her name is Karen Dawson. *Dr.* Karen Dawson. She's American. She teaches at La Sorbonne."

"Ham and eggs, with lots of ketchup."

"Very funny. *Non, mais:* What will they think of next at that damn human robot factory to keep themselves busy and burn up *my* tax money?"

"Careful, *I'm* a graduate of La Sorbonne."

"I know."

"So whose idea was that?" said Lescop.

"Harris's. Who else? He's read some book of hers, and thinks she'll look at the plaque and, presto: instant killers." Dulac snapped his fingers, magician-like.

As Dulac looked in the mirrored wall across the table, he caught sight of the gangling waiter hovering to one side, his head swinging back and forth like an ostrich's: "*Monsieur?*"

Dulac turned. "Croissant and *café au lait*. And hot, this time."

"The same," said Lescop.

"*Évidemment,*" replied the waiter haughtily. He spun around and ordered to someone invisible behind the high counter: "*Deux réguliers.*"

Dulac looked distractedly outside at the already busy street: the Rue de Castries's stationary morning traffic was spewing its usual dose of oil and gasoline fumes under, over and around the *habitués*, sipping their espressos on the terrace. The waiter arrived with their orders, swinging the tray deftly onto the table in one smooth, fluid motion.

"She sounds smart." said Lescop, trying to brighten his boss's day.

"Frankly, I don't care if she's goddamn Einstein. I'm not into brain-heavy female intellectuals these days. Give me a good lay, that's all."

"Perhaps that, too."

After gulping down the remainder of his tepid *café au lait*, Dulac got up: "Come, let's see what we can find on *Dr. Karen Dawson.*"

CHAPTER 6

The day after the murder, Karen had tried to ski, but images of
the dead man kept haunting her. Sullen, tired and depressed,
she'd left Saas-Fee that evening, and was back in her office at
La Sorbonne the following morning. Among the many messages on her answering machine, her landlady had left three
of diminishing degrees of civility: The rent was long overdue
and if she didn't pay up, the heat would go off first.

Sitting down before her cluttered desk, Karen glanced
at the calendar: March 8. Five years. Already five years since
she'd received news that Joseph Campbell, Sarah Lawrence
College's Professor Emeritus, had accepted her Ph.D. thesis
in animal mythology. It seemed like only yesterday. At thir-
ty-four, unmarried and between men in her life, lost within
the labyrinth of the Parisian social structure, Karen Dawson
lived for her work. Her recent book, *Myths and the Hunt,* had
increased her notoriety within the narrow confines of the
world's mythologists, renowned and otherwise.

At 10 a.m., Karen's phone rang, and a dry, clipped voice
said: "Dr. Dawson?"

"Yes?"

"This is Chief Inspector Thierry Dulac. I'm with
Interpol. Could we meet at your office this afternoon?"

By the tone of his voice, Karen sensed that the man was not asking, but merely conforming to protocol.

"What is this about?"

"I'll tell you when we meet. How about 1 p.m.?"

"Ah, my schedule is quite full. Although I guess . . . How long will this take?" Karen's anxiety level grew rapidly, as the function of the persona at the other end began to sink in.

"About an hour. See you then, Ms. Dawson."

The line went dead.

She hung up slowly, her mind racing as she felt pangs of bottomless, pervasive, guilt invade her. *An Interpol inspector. Why? What could I have possibly done to trigger this? Is it my taxes? My status in France? Could it be the murder in Saas-Fee? No, I was just a passerby.* She racked her brain, to no avail. She couldn't eat lunch.

* * *

Dulac didn't appreciate being told by Harris to seek outside help. Even less in the guise of a female. Dulac had up till now been in exclusive control of his investigations, and prided himself in resolving them internally. His record spoke for itself: four murder investigations in his five years as chief murder investigator, and four successful resolutions.

Dulac approached the transparent door leading to Karen Dawson's office and her silhouette came into focus. Having equated *Mythologists, female* to *Retirement-age lab-rat technicians,* he smiled: Almond-shaped eyes behind oval black nacre rims, a pair of taut, curled lips, the dark blue, impeccably cut blazer contrasting with the auburn ponytail. *She looks like that model in the KPMG ad in* The Economist. *The one every man in Paris wants to see naked in his bed.*

"Good afternoon, Ms. Dawson – oh, I'm sorry, *Dr.* Dawson." He leaned over the messy desk and thrust out his left hand.

"'Ms.' is fine." She rose, smiled and awkwardly shook it. "Please sit down." She offered him the wooden chair, while she tried to rearrange some of the desk's clutter.

"Thanks." Dulac sat down slowly, all the while observing the svelte, studious-looking woman. He paused for a moment, savoring her noticeable uneasiness. He pulled out his pack of Gitanes. "Mind if I smoke?"

"I'd rather you didn't."

"Fine."

As Dulac put back the cigarettes in his pocket, he said: "You're obviously wondering what all this is about."

"Frankly . . . yes."

"Well, Ms. Dawson, this isn't my idea, but someone at Interpol seems to think you can help us."

A wave of relief surged, crested and broke over her anxiety. At first blush, she wasn't at the center of this visit. Her thoughts slowly turned from fear to curiosity. "Help doing what?"

"A man has been murdered; you may have read about it. Archbishop Salvador was murdered in Saas-Fee, last Sunday."

"I was in Saas-Fee last week—"

"Then you're aware of this grisly business?"

"I saw him being taken down from the cable car."

She cleared her throat as she recalled the unforgettable scene of the naked man slowly being lowered from his modern-day crucifixion.

"We believe you could help us in our murder investigation."

"Really?"

"We think a mythologist might find the meaning of this." Dulac thrust the plaque onto her desk. "It was around his neck."

Puzzled, Karen looked at it for a moment, then picked it up. It was heavier than she thought. Like a small tombstone around the dead man's neck, bearing an inscrutable epitaph. A shiver ran up her spine. She felt drawn into a shapeless abyss. Her mind raced in a thousand directions: Why the connection between an archbishop and a lion, other than the too obvious connection with 'Lyon' the city? Why the mention of a dragon? What was the connection between dragons and lions? Her brain raced: The enormity of the possibilities

27

was overwhelming: lions and dragons appeared in mythical cultures all over the world. Lions, the perennial symbol of force and supremacy, royalty, tyranny . . . rarely democracy. Dragons, sometimes benign, sometimes evil.

The various references to allegories of dragons and lions spanned centuries. How could one draw any inference to this crime with such scarcity of information? Besides, the plaque inscription could be making astronomical references to the Leo and Draco constellations.

Something bothered her, but didn't register consciously.

Dulac continued: "We can arrange for a leave of absence, 400 euros per day plus expenses. You would report directly to me."

"I, I don't know . . ." Karen sat dumbfounded. Here was a policeman, blustering into her office and on a day's notice, requiring a major professional shift and a commitment. She enjoyed the comfort of the teaching world, its predictability and its set hours. The exchanges with students and alumni were intellectually satisfying, yet remained shrouded with the knowledge that everything they discussed was safely in the past, over and done. He offered the present: Action, applying her knowledge to the struggle of life and death. The thought frightened yet fascinated her.

"I'll have to think about this. First, I'd have to check with my department head."

"I already have his authorization."

"You certainly don't waste time."

"Murderers usually don't give us much. So we can count on you?"

Karen hesitated for a moment, and then retreated behind the safety of her academic walls. "No, I really don't think so. I've never been involved in something like this. I wouldn't know where to begin. Besides, I have my classes, my students. Believe me, Mr. Dulac, that's plenty challenge enough. In any case, this plaque has, maybe hundreds of interpretations."

Dulac was ready to go beyond simple persuasion. It was time for the heavy artillery: "I see. I know this is all rather sudden, but perhaps you could give the matter a little more thought before deciding. With your knowledge and experience, you could save us a lot of time. Besides, an opportunity like this must be quite rare for a university professor. Call me if you change your mind. Here is my card." He rose to leave. "Oh, by the way, Ms. Dawson, don't forget to renew your residency visa. It expires next month."

Karen felt she'd been kicked in the stomach: The French often reminded one of one's non-Frenchness, sometimes subtly, sometimes not. She didn't need to be told that she was barely a guest in France. Residency visas were like condoms: Necessary but humiliating to obtain. The visa people had godlike authority, and always let you know it. Among the ex-pats at La Sorbonne, horror stories animated many a lunch conversation at the cafeteria: The slightest character slur could complicate matters enormously. Behind this thinly veiled threat stood the specter of numerous delays, even a refusal to renew her visa. Dulac had done his homework. *I've got to placate this jerk.*

"How long would this take, that is, if I accepted?" she said, trying desperately to regain control.

The Howitzer had scored a hit. He had the labyrinthine, unpredictable French bureaucracy to thank for it.

"I don't know, perhaps a couple of weeks."

"I might be able to manage that. Let me speak to my department head and get back to you."

"Perfect. Glad to see we understand each other, Ms. Dawson."

You arrogant French frog, she thought, barely conscious of the generalization. *There will be payback.*

"By the way, if you accept, I'll want a study plan of the permutations and combinations of lions and dragons in cultures and societies past and present, with your assessment of their applications and meaning to our case. You will be informed of any new facts coming through our department. You will be given an encrypted cell phone only for use in this context. Do you have any questions?"

Karen suppressed a smile at Dulac's requirements. *This jerk has no idea of mythology's processes.* "I must keep my undergrad classes. My postgrad supervision can be postponed."

"I'm sure we can work around that." Dulac replied.

"I'll let you know tomorrow."

"In case you don't catch me, leave a message. I'll be in Lyon."

CHAPTER 7

March 9, Lyon, Cathedrale St Jean's presbytery.

Dulac didn't like presbyteries. They reminded him of his school days at Lycée St Stanislas in Montpellier, and St Jude's presbytery. The memory of that sweet smell of incense permeating Father L'Ecuyer's worn, dirty cassock, came back to him as he walked up the steps of the Archdiocese at St. Jean, adjacent to the cathedral. In retrospect, he had spent far too much time confessing sins, real or imaginary, to Father L'Ecuyer, a short man with the vivacity, odor and color of a corpse. Dulac remembered waiting patiently for absolution, as L'Ecuyer would ponder interminably on the severity of Dulac's penance. At last, Dulac would hear: "Four Hail Marys, morning and afternoon, for the next two weeks." The sentence didn't vary, regardless of the magnitude and variety of Dulac's sins.

"Mr. Hudak, I presume," said the bent, wiry little man, behind a warm smile and bird-like eyes.

"Thierry Dulac. Monsignor Dorlot?"

"Yes, please come in."

Dulac entered the parlor, and the smell, *that* smell, invaded him again. *Must be the unspent testosterone*, he thought.

"Please," said a convivial Dorlot, inviting Dulac to sit beside him on the worn, leather couch facing the large, now empty, oak desk. "Who could have done this? Why?"

"Monsignor, if we knew . . ."

"Yes, yes, of course. Forgive me." Dorlot wrung his hands nervously.

"Monsignor, there are questions you may not like, but that I have to ask. Are you sure you're up to this? I can come back if you wish."

"No, please go ahead. I'll try to help in any way I can."

The telephone rang.

"Sister Emilie, please take my calls," shouted Dorlot impatiently, to the nun somewhere in the adjoining room.

Dulac spoke, "Tell me about Salvador – sorry, *Monsignor* Salvador. Did he have any enemies, anyone you can think of?"

"Enemies is perhaps too strong a word. Not enemies, but detractors, yes. Quite a few."

"Detractors?"

"He had a brilliant mind, but he tolerated no unsubstantiated opinions. He could turn you into intellectual jelly if you didn't back your opinions solidly. I saw it happen more than once with the younger *curés*."

"So, tact wasn't his strong suit?"

"Correct."

"Was he insulting? Insulting enough for a humiliated person to strike back?"

"No. He always did it so that the injured party would laugh at his own stupidity."

"Someone didn't have quite that sense of humor."

"Yes, you're right," said Dorlot, looking suddenly morose.

Dulac paused for a moment and took a deep breath.

"Monsignor Dorlot, did Salvador have a sex life?"

"Inspector, I . . ."

"I have to know."

"I wasn't aware of any."

Dulac looked intently into Dorlot's sullen face, for a trace of hesitation.

"I, I guess I was quite close to him. He was a friend and mentor."

"I see." Dulac paused.

"Don't even think of it, Mr. Dulac. It wasn't so."

"I didn't say a word."

"Your silence was enough."

"Did he have any potential rivals, someone who could aspire to his position?"

"Impossible. That's not the way it works. The Vatican will send a Pontifical Nuncio, a legate, to oversee his replacement. It's the bishops and priests of the parishes who suggest a replacement, but the Vatican has veto power. The Holy See ultimately decides."

"What about his correspondence?"

"I've gone through it and found nothing unusual."

"Did you see all his mail, incoming and outgoing?"

"Most of it. Although he would write the occasional memo longhand and send it himself."

"Any hate mail?"

"None I'm aware of."

"What about meetings, groups or what you do call them — synods?"

"Yes, synods. But I'm not the person to ask. You'll have to see the other archbishops. He was a member of committees at the Vatican. The Legate will know more."

"Monsignor, how do you think the assassins knew of Salvador's whereabouts and vacation plans?"

"I've been racking my brain. It was I who sent him to Saas-Fee. Someone must have overheard, but whom? There's only Sister Emilie and myself here. She's been here for over thirty years."

"They must have used a wiretap, but there's none now: We checked. Monsignor, does the plaque we found on him mean anything to you?"

"It's the final insult to a brilliant man."

Dulac knew Dorlot was taking the plaque at face value: *The Lion is dead* equals *the Archbishop of Lyon is dead.*

"Monsignor, I won't take any more of your precious time. I know you have a lot to do these days. Have the Legate contact me when he comes." Dulac rose and walked out of the musty room, but the smell would stay with him for three days.

The following morning Dulac returned to his office in Paris, where Lescop handed him a large brown envelope, sent express post from Sion. Zubriggen's final postmortem report had been sent well within the proverbial Swiss week and yielded only the slightest of clues: The doctor had found seal hairs on Salvador's body, probably emanating from one of the assassin's coat or hat. He'd also discovered a minuscule bit of foreign human tissue on Salvador's nose.

Besse had left Dulac a message on his answering machine, stating he and his policemen had started investigating the hotels, bars and restaurants, to see if someone could identify a person, somewhere, wearing a sealskin coat or hat. Besse would copy him on his report.

Probably in a week.

CHAPTER 8

Karen spoke to her department head and confirmed his permission to accept Dulac's offer. Her call to the inspector was less than enthusiastic. She tried to apply her structured mind to the task. *Where to begin?* Lions, through archetypal time, were not usually connected to the Catholic Church, except incidentally. How did the killing of an archbishop relate to the killing of a lion? On what archetypal plane could the killing occur? Had a lion been killed, metaphorically, in a struggle with . . . which dragon?

Were there any references in mythology to such a battle, and if so how did it apply here? Was the killer making a bold political, religious or other statement? If so, to what audience? Or was this a personal vendetta? The thought struck her that the same killing could represent a killing of a lion on one plane and the wounding of the dragon on another. Even, why was the assassin bothering to advertise this event so obscurely, instead of making his demands known clearly?

This must be Dulac's job, not mine. She began her search in earnest.

Karen's office phone rang.

"Dr. Dawson?" The voice was high-pitched, childlike.

"Yes?"

"My name is Archbishop Paolo Fiore. I'm the Vatican envoy concerning the replacement of Monsignor Salvador. I'm told that you're collaborating with Mr. Dulac in the investigation?"

"I'm doing some research for him, if that's what you mean."

"You are the mythologist?"

"Correct."

"I'm in Paris for a few days, and I'd like to make your acquaintance. Would that be possible?"

Karen was all too familiar with the European need for personal, face-to-face contact. "I have a rather busy schedule."

"I won't take much of your time. We could meet for coffee, yes?"

Fiore's insistence wasn't going to be softened by any of her academic constraints. *Might as well get rid of him quickly.*

"I have a break at three this afternoon."

"Perfect. Where do you suggest we meet?"

"At the Café Étudiantin, at the entrance. Do you know it?"

"I'll find it. How will I recognize you?"

"Ask for the manager, Charles."

* * *

"Good afternoon, Ms. Dawson?" said the man in a brown suit, standing at the counter, incongruous among the students.

"Monsignor Fiore?"

"Yes, thank you for coming on such short notice."

She approached the extended hand, only to clasp a small, sweaty, sponge. She wasn't sure what to expect in the way of the representative of the Vatican, but Fiore wasn't it. A full head of dark blond hair, youngish with horn-rimmed glasses, dressed in a well-cut suit, and save for the clerical collar, he could have easily passed for a patent lawyer at Coudert Brothers. *Obviously, the Church is still recruiting successfully, at least in Rome*, she thought.

"Let's have coffee, shall we?" said Fiore.

36

"Fine."

As they ambled toward the always-busy dining room, Karen noticed an almost imperceptible limp in Fiore's otherwise assured gait. He found an empty table, and offered Karen one of the uncomfortable, straight back chairs.

"First, let me properly introduce myself. I am the Pontifical Nuncio, sent by the Vatican to oversee the succession of Archbishop Salvador — the late Archbishop Salvador, I mean. I am also the contact with Interpol in this horrible business."

The high-pitched voice started to irritate her.

"When I was told Mr. Dulac hired you, I thought it would be useful to meet you. The Vatican is extremely upset about all of this, yes, very concerned, and wants to find answers quickly."

"When you say the Vatican . . ."

"The Pope, if you prefer."

"I see."

"We are worried about the repercussions on the Archdiocese. Also, is this an isolated incident, or will these assassins try again?"

"It crossed my mind also."

He slouched forward slightly and looked intently into her gaze.

"Do you have any idea what the plaque means?"

"Not yet. I don't have much to go on: The plaque is pretty enigmatic."

He relaxed, looked away, reclining a bit and said:

"I know, I know. I have some vague notions of mythology myself; I studied Greek history at the seminary," he said, obsequiously trying to strike a sympathetic chord.

Karen noted the Legate's body language. She couldn't help thinking: *What was the attraction, for a handsome, intelligent and personable man, in about his mid-forties to join such a sterile, suffocating organization as the Catholic Church, especially in the Vatican? Was it unshakable faith? Was it power? Was it the will to bring about change? Or all three?*

Fiore finished his coffee and rose to leave: "Again, Ms. Dawson, the Vatican is extremely pleased that you've accepted to help us. Feel free to communicate with me directly if I can be of help. You can reach me through the Secretariat of the Vatican."

"Yes, of course," Karen said, feeling ill at ease with Fiore's offer. Why should she contact him? She reported to Dulac. *The last thing I need is to get between Vatican-Interpol politics.*

CHAPTER 9

March 11, Zürich, 9.00 a.m.

Inspector Schmidt of the Zürich Police had ordered the Fiat towed into police custody: It was now material evidence in his crime investigation and would be gone over with the proverbial Swiss meticulousness, for any fingerprints or other clues as to the true identity of the occupants. Forensics in Berne had discovered the well-crafted counterfeit of Berger's driver's license. Since he was now a fugitive from the Swiss authorities, the event had taken an international turn, requiring registration at the Registry at Interpol under the Swiss–Interpol Cooperation Agreement.

Fate, through the untimely death of a Swiss schoolgirl, would now intertwine Schmidt's and Dulac's paths.

The report read:

Head investigator: Pierre Schmidt.
Rented Hertz Fiat, plate ZH 10387 683 involved in hit-and-run on Kleiner Strasse, corner Littoff Strasse.
Driver: Alias Christian Berger, registration number 60756-90876.

Analysis:
-No fingerprints.
-Four cigarette butts, no prints.
-456.6 km odometer reading from Kloten airport.
-Seal hairs found between front seats and dashboard.
-Minimum two occupants, no description.
Onboard GPS indicates car traveled through Sion, Saas-Fee, Zermatt, Sass-Fee, Zürich.

Later the same morning, Lescop was waiting in Dulac's office on Place de la Concorde when Dulac arrived, disheveled, unshaven and wearing the same shirt, tie and jacket as the day before.

Lescop gave him that knowing smile. *"Patron,* you *must* see this: It's a report from the Swiss authorities on a hit-and-run near Zürich."

"Yes, yes, more of the same shit." Dulac, exhausted by the previous night's extracurricular activities, sat down heavily and read the report. Suddenly his eyes grew wide, he sprang up, his face suddenly aglow with anticipation. *"Get Schmidt on the line, now!"* he barked at Lescop.

"This is Thierry Dulac, Interpol."

"Yes?" said Schmidt.

"You have a rented Fiat involved in a hit-and-run?"

"Exact," said Schmidt in an effortless French.

"I want your people to make a DNA analysis of the seal hair contents."

"No problem, but why?"

"These men may be involved in the Archbishop Salvador murder case."

"I see."

"When can you have the results sent to our Lyon office?"

"It might take a few days."

At least it wasn't a week, thought Dulac. "Any information on the occupants?"

"Not yet. We're looking at the Kloten videotapes: The car was rented under the name of Christian Berger. The driver's license is a fake."

"Send me the tapes as soon as possible," said Dulac.

CHAPTER 10

The task was bewildering, Karen thought: How could one go on examining cultures that spanned centuries, hosting lions and dragons? How did this relate to the crucifixion of an archbishop in modern times? The message had to be deciphered, better sooner than later. Lions had enriched and nourished the imagination, folklore, art and mythology of mankind since the dawn of civilization. As depicted by the Paleolithic paintings and drawings of Lascaux, Chauvet, Bernifal, through Assyrian, Greek, Semitic and Egyptian cultures, lions had given courage, strength and wisdom to the heroes that vanquished them, often bestowing mythological immortality.

Karen had been moved by the early cave drawings and paintings, witnessing man's preoccupation with his passage to death, through ritualistic depictions of offerings and sacrifices. On her tour of Irak's sites during her summer semester, the dramatic, beautiful Assyrian bas-reliefs showing lion hunts had tweaked her curiosity about Assyrian mythology and history. She had made her career choice early.

The Old Testament's reference to lions in Genesis: 49.9 was the most known in Judaic traditions: The Lion of Judah symbolized Christ, descendant of Abraham, Judah, David and Solomon. Passages in Isaiah: 11.6.9 referred to lions as a symbol of unification of opposites and eventual peace on earth. Surely, there was no application of such myth here. Karen knew there was a paucity of lions, in the history and mythology of the Catholic Church. A winged lion sat triumphant, illuminated in the Book of Revelations, better known as the Apocalypse according to John. The apocalyptic vision of its author had metamorphosed the four Synoptic Evangelists into animals, the first of which had been a lion representing St. Mark.

How could this relate to the killing of Archbishop Salvador?

Biblical scholars inferred that the lion's den, in the allegory of the Lion of Judah, supposedly foretold of the Inquisition, the purification arm of the Church to convert the rebellious Albigensians in 1233. A.D. The many references to lions in the Torah made analysis even more complicated. She needed more facts.

CHAPTER 11

Dulac slouched slightly at the keyboard of his baby grand Steinway, inherited from Clara Fournier, his concert pianist mother. He labored at the difficult spreads and chords of the Brahms Rhapsody number 2, opus 79 in G minor. Since the accidental death of his wife, killed in front of his eyes by a drunken taxi driver in Athens, he'd found refuge and solace from the somber world of international crime in his childhood passion, his piano. He was mainly self-taught, and the limitations of his lack of technique hindered progress. The speed and dexterity of earlier times were all but gone, to the extent of relearning works that had seemed so easy in his teenage years. The frustration and distraction contributed many false notes. To minimize mistakes in the fast passages, he borrowed a trick from older concert pianists: he would improvise an uncalled-for *ritardando,* giving the impression of slow, thoughtful expression, instead of the superficiality of brilliant technique.

If Ivo Pogorelić can get away with it, so can I.

Regardless of the increasingly disproportionate work-reward ratio, the Steinway's unique, crisp sound drew him back, again and again, as an addiction.

His day had gone well: The DNA test results of the seal-skin hair in the Fiat matched those found on Salvador's body.

He made an appointment with Karen for next morning, and actually looked forward to meeting her. Until lately, he hadn't given much thought to more serious forms of female companionship, preferring the occasional, impersonal release of the one-night stand.

Now, Brahms removed him from the world of subterfuge and murder, and thrust him into a world of melancholy, honesty and beauty. For a moment, he wished he could share the experience.

* * *

The following morning, Karen strode briskly into his office and sat down. Her tousled hair framed that high forehead and almond eyes sensuously. Her light blue blouse, opened slightly suggestively, confirmed Dulac's earlier impression: Fit, verging on desirable.

"I'm afraid I don't have much to report, except a bunch of hypotheses. Oh, by the way, I met a Monsignor Fiore yesterday. He mentioned he already talked to you about meeting me."

Dulac felt uncomfortable. He would have preferred to be the only contact, but found no reason to object to Fiore's request.

"Yes, he told me he would phone you. So, what have you found?"

"I don't see the ancient lion-dragon myths applying: The religious background of the crucifixion and the death of an archbishop make me think that any lion or dragon mythology prior to the Greek and Judeo- Christian traditions is just not going to lead us anywhere."

"That sounds plausible," Dulac said.

"Don't get your hopes up: There's a lot of mythology involving lions and dragons in that period of history, but let's start with the most commonly known lion myths: In Greek mythology, Heracles — our Hercules, the Greek demigod and son of Zeus — was given first the task of killing the

Lion of Cithaeron. But later, to repent for the killing of his own sons by mistake, he was given twelve tasks. If he were successful, he would no longer feel the pain and remorse. The first task was to kill the Lion of Nemea, which he did with his bare hands. Now, his second task was to kill the Hydra of Lerna, a gigantic dragon with nine heads, which keep growing back when they're cut off. With the help of Iolaos, God of the wind, Heracles finally killed the dragon."

"I'm sure you're about to tell me what all this means, right?" said Dulac, smiling.

"In mythology, you've got to think in terms of transposition: If the assassins impersonate Heracles, and see themselves as liberators from the Catholic Church, the killing of a lion is only one of many tasks, possibly killings."

"And the dragon?"

"The wounding of the dragon symbolizes the wounding of the Church, as it replaces severed heads by growing others."

"Then why kill at all, if the dragon-Church keeps replacing severed heads?"

"Yes, I know, but don't forget that Heracles eventually kills the dragon."

"Isn't Greek mythology quite remote—?"

"I thought I should mention the theory, anyway," interrupted Karen.

"You don't look very convinced."

"Yes, well, another lion myth is the so-called Lion of Judah. Scholars have interpreted this as a symbol and prophecy of the coming of Christ, as a descendant of Abraham, Solomon and Judah. This could fit with the crucifixion of Salvador, representing a modern-day Christ in the eyes of his murderers. The Lion's den in that allegory represents the Inquisition, launched to convert or kill heretics, like the Albigenesians."

"Are you suggesting this is a revenge of some early Christian sect?"

"It's not impossible."

"You're reading too much Dan Brown. This is still pretty far-fetched."

"Not necessarily," replied Karen. "The closer myth in time is the one in the Book of Revelations, or if you prefer, the Apocalypse according to John: He represents the four Synoptic Evangelists, Mark, Matthew, Luke and John, as animals. The first is Mark, represented by a lion."

"I still don't see the connection with our case."

"Not at first blush, but again, the lion has been seen by critics of the Apocalypse as Christ also, because they say Mark was the most Christ-like of the Evangelists. I know these myths are diffuse and distant, but I need more information to—"

"I don't have any more to give you, other than we've traced the assassins' rented car: They traveled through Kloten."

His meeting with Karen left him with mixed feelings. The elusive, allegorical world of mythology did not sit comfortably with his rational, Cartesian way of thinking. He was used to cold, factual and scientific analysis, not ancient, vague allusions to long-gone myths, personages and deities. He was starting to wonder if she would help at all in his investigation. He caught himself wishing she wouldn't, to break the bond of professionalism that now forcibly restrained him.

Later in the day, Dulac contacted Besse again in Sion, in the hope that the tracing of Berger to the Hotel Tenne and the interview with the hotelier, bartenders and waitresses, would help him come up with composite pictures of the killers. The Kloten videotapes were blurred and inconclusive, but a man fitting Berger's description had taken a Lufthansa flight to Moscow, the day of the hit-and-run. Dulac had sent the tapes to the Interpol National Central Bureau in Moscow, and no match had been found in their database. Meanwhile, in Paris, pressure from the French Minister of the Interior and Minister of Justice was mounting steadily, along with public outrage. Daily references to Salvador's murder in the press kept reminding him of the slowness of his progress. France did not take lightly the murder of one of its archbishops.

CHAPTER 12

The train left the grayness of Milan and wound its way through the Italian countryside toward Stresa, and Archbishop Alberto Conti's spirits lifted, buoyed by that essentially tender, homogenous green of all of nature's verdure in early spring. His mind reveled in the anticipation of the sights, smells and sounds that awaited him. He'd been coming to the Borromeo Islands, on Lake Maggiore, every other year in spring for the last six years, replenishing and invigorating his being. Archbishop of Milan, he headed one of the largest and busiest archdioceses of Italy. At sixty-two, he had distinguished himself during the last Synod of Bishops, by his eloquence on matters of the Eucharist and priesthood celibacy.

The conductor announced, "Next stop, Stresa," and Conti reached overhead for his suitcase, and signaled to his bodyguard Piero. Since Salvador's murder, the Vatican had insisted that all archbishops travel with bodyguards. As he prepared to disembark, he walked by and glanced at two pale-complexioned men, their whiteness contrasting with the olive-skinned Italian passengers: *Definitely not Italians*, he thought. *Probably East Europeans on their way to Rome.*

Conti and his bodyguard took a taxi to the Hotel Palma, and Conti asked for his usual room facing the lake. He entered, opened the curtains, and took in the breathtaking view. The sun was casting its late afternoon rays on Isola Madre, the largest of the Borromeo Islands, an emerald set on a bed of turquoise. Behind, the Lombardy hills crouched silent, ominous and gray. He strode out onto the balcony, stretching and smiling at nature's grandeur. He would get up early the next morning, he told himself, to fully enjoy these treasured moments. To ease his conscience, he'd grabbed a perfunctory amount of correspondence before leaving, and decided to sift through it, to see if any pressing matters required his immediate attention. A dissatisfied priest's request for transfer, an interpretation of procedural matter under Canon Law, an unmarked envelope, sealed.

He opened it: It was from Salvador. As he read it, feelings of sorrow and anxiety overwhelmed him:

My dear Alberto,

During our last discussions, you asked me to give the matter more thought and get back to you. After many sleepless nights, and notwithstanding the risks, I have come to the conclusion that the long-term benefits of acting now outweigh the short-term benefit of remaining silent. We know those who will oppose us. Inaction leads to condoning the idea that the end justifies the means: I cannot accept this. We have seen what this did in Italy. Only a solid front will resolve the matter, in light of the power and pervasiveness of these people. We need to gather support quickly.
Please call me at the nearest opportunity: these matters are best dealt with in person.

Yours affectionately,
Antoine

Archbishop Conti had not slept well: The disturbing letter drove home the reality of his predicament, as a partner in Salvador's dilemma. For the moment however, he felt he could do nothing. It was getting late, and he would just make the eleven o'clock Mass at St. Ambrosio, the small neoclassical church in Stresa.

After lunch with his bodyguard Piero, having enjoyed his favorite half-bottle of Amarone, the two men strode to the dock and embarked on the small passenger ferry to Isola Madre. As the ferry approached the island's minuscule landing, a blushing pink azalea bush drooped almost to the water, to welcome him to this earthly paradise. They alighted, and Conti noticed the mauve rhododendrons had already carpeted the soil with their lush petals. Deep-green pines, magenta hibiscus, wisterias, white camellias, clusters of yellow mimosas slowly engulfed them: *We're caught on the palette of a Sisley painting*, Conti thought.

Flaubert had declared this island 'the most sensuous place on earth,' and Conti couldn't fault him.

They wandered slowly, pheasants and iridescent peacocks crossing their path. Conti stopped to film the immodest display of colors. He paused, mesmerized by a pink rhododendron, a huge puff ball resplendent before its green backdrop of subtropical pines. The intermingling of scents from flowers and trees —now the sweetness of cedars, now the pungency of the begonias — made him giddy. He had brought his missal and sat down on a wooden bench. He read intensely, and eventually dozed off. Piero continued walking toward the small fountain and lit a cigarette.

CHAPTER 13

Isola Rossa, Caribbean Sea

The disciples of Pistis Sophia had had a long, secretive and uneven history. Born in early Christian times, later rekindled by Abbot Bernard de Clairvaux in the twelfth century, The Tradition had been marginalized and persecuted by the Catholic Church. It had barely survived the Inquisition, later been forgotten and dormant for many centuries and had recently found a new breath of life. Its belief in and accentuation of the Divine Feminine attracted primarily women, impatient with the lack of progress of their stilted status within their religions. The simplicity of its Gnostic origins, features and practices attracted members of various faiths, frustrated by the archaic, oppressive restrictions of their churches. Four years ago, The Tradition had welcomed another celebrity into its fold: The Lady Sarah Litman, Marchioness of Dorset. One of the richest women in England, heiress to a tea fortune.

The sun sank glowing into the cauldron of the undulating sea. Above, a long ominous gray cloud filled the horizon, its orange edges suffused by the water's reflections. Alone on the balcony of her hotel-sized mansion, Lady

Sarah absorbed the ineffable view, though the cloud looked foreboding.

The Caribbean island of Isola Rossa belonged to Lady Sarah; it had been two laborious, strife-ridden years since her contractor had started the building of a huge open amphitheater, a scaled down Ephesus, to be integrated into the hillside between the mansion and the ocean. Now, she finally savored the realization of her dream.

The red globe finally eclipsed itself. The chant of a women's choir singing a Bach motet rose effortlessly from behind the center of the amphitheater and filled the Caribbean air with its classic serenity. *Even from here, the acoustics are amazing,* she thought. Lady Sarah, dressed in a white translucent robe, descended from the balcony and walked blissfully down the short path toward the amphitheater. On each side, cypress trees pointed their lance-like silhouettes into the dusk.

As Lady Sarah approached, the choir fell silent. She joined the five women dressed in flowing red robes, and together they walked toward center stage, each holding a large candlestick. They deposited them on the altar and faced the scala. Behind the altar of rose alabaster, a large icon hung from a wooden crossbeam supported by two marble columns. Of late medieval, early Renaissance inspiration, the icon pictured a winged and haloed woman in white, flanked by two smaller figurines, on a lower plane. The angel-like woman appeared to smile slightly, seated on her golden throne. Above, an eagle adorned a small inscription in Latin, and underneath, the head of a bull carried a sunlike disk between its horns. On one side of the figurines, strode a blue lion, *passant,* and on the other sat a seven-headed red dragon.

Lady Sarah seated herself on a small wooden chair beside the altar. She signaled the women to begin the ceremony. The five women stood still as a young man in his teens, dressed in a toga, brought a small white lamb, legs tied, and set it on the altar. The audience, sparsely spread amongst the expansive hard granite strada of the amphitheater, waited in expectant silence. The third woman from the right stepped up to the altar, arms stretched upwards in an imploring V, and began a long incantation, her voice rising in intensity and pitch.

The woman then seized a short sword from the altar, held it up above her head, then started to swing it downwards. A cry rose from the audience. At the last instant, she turned the blade on its flat side and rested it on the lamb's head. The symbolic gesture drew a murmur of relief from the audience.

The woman chanted loudly:

"Agnus Dei, qui tollis peccata mundi, miserere nobis,
Agnus Dei, qui tollis peccata mundi, miserere nobis,
Agnus Dei, qui tollis peccata mundi, donna nobis pacem."

Another woman, third from left, intoned with the audience the Pistis Sophia Credo:

Let us pray:
Pistis Sophia, Mother of Knowledge, Ground of All Being,
we rejoice in you and you in us. Help us live by the examples
of your bridegroom Jesus Christ, of Buddha, and of the
Prophet. Help us be filled with thoughts of inclusiveness of
all inanimate and animate matter, and to seek the power
of knowledge in all mankind. Let us share in your infinite
compassion and love. Let us discover you, through our under-
standing of others and of ourselves. Give us courage and
strength to oppose and convert your enemies."
We believe in our expanded consciousness after death, in
reunification with you. We rejoice at the thought of basking
in your eternal light, Amen.
Let us now share a sign of our mutual compassion."

The members of the audience and the six women exchanged embraces. The choir concluded with the chorale of a Handel Cantata, and the disciples slowly dispersed in a blissful unity of spirit.

CHAPTER 14

Kurganski and Vasiliev had seen Conti and his bodyguard leave Stresa on the ferry. They hurried back to the dock and boarded their small motorboat. They circled the island, found their preselected landing spot and hid the boat. The sun had already lengthened the elms' shadows as the two men strode nonchalantly along Isola Madre's labyrinthine paths, almost oblivious to its tropical plants and exotic birds, anxious for time to pass. Later, they walked past Conti, seated on a bench, snoring, his missal fallen beside him.

They circled back and took position behind a large juniper bush. Kurganski had counted fifteen visitors during their walk. From where he sat, crouching, he could see the dock and the shuttling back and forth of the open-deck red ferry boat, its white waterline cutting a swath through the turquoise water. Twelve had left; none had arrived. It was getting late. Soon, the Archbishop would leave and the opportunity would be lost. They would have to start all over again. Rescheduling murders was difficult, and expensive.

"We must do it now," whispered Kurganski to Vasiliev, and looking at the bodyguard. "Three tourists left: Check where they are and get back here."

Kurganski looked at the target: *Slightly built, for a bodyguard*, he thought.

The war had taught him that size was irrelevant. Some of the toughest, biggest Russian soldiers had wept like babies under the Taliban mortar attacks, slinking back to the barracks in near shock.

He himself had barely survived an attack from a lightly built adolescent. Hiding behind a wall, the boy had jumped out, and with Kurganski at point-blank range, the boy's gun had jammed. He dropped the gun, drew a knife and pounced on Kurganski with the speed of a hungry cheetah, slicing at his arm and shoulder. Kurganski had managed to get his pistol out with his other hand and fired at the adolescent's face. The boy that fell on him like a skinny, tall doll was only half his weight.

"No one," reported Vasiliev.

"Are you sure?"

"Positive. The others must have left on the ferry."

As the sun started dipping below the hills, igniting the Lombard sky with a soft orange flame, Vasiliev took out the small bottle of Desflurane and a cloth from his beat-up brown suitcase and handed them to Kurganski. Vasiliev unsheathed the knife and ran the blade across his fingernail, removing a sliver: *Deadly sharp*.

They crept up toward the thick, dwarf pine tree, behind the fountain where the bodyguard sat, puffing his cigarette, looking at the sunset.

Kurganski looked at Vasiliev, his glance inquisitive. Vasiliev nodded.

Kurganski leaped from behind the bush, cloth in hand and stuffed it to the bodyguard's face. The bodyguard lunged forward, simultaneously kicking backward with his right foot, hitting Kurganski in the groin. The Russian gasped in pain. The bodyguard turned, only to meet Vasiliev's knife with his stomach. Vasiliev thrust once, twice, then sliced upwards, the man's abdominal tissue and shirt parting easily. The bodyguard didn't utter a word, letting out a sickening gurgle as he slowly dropped to the ground.

Vasiliev stood for a moment, looked around: *No one.* They grabbed the man's convulsing body and dragged it behind the dwarf pine. Vasiliev wiped the knife with the Desflurane-soaked cloth, careful not to cut himself.

Now they crept slowly, purposely toward Conti: He was still bent over, dozing peacefully. *No struggle this time*, thought Kurganski, as he grabbed Conti's head and shoved the cloth over his mouth. Conti looked up quizzically, took two breaths and fell unconscious.

They dragged him behind the small bushes, the soft cooing of pigeons announcing the impending finality. They waited and heard the sound of the ferry leaving the island.

* * *

Conti awoke in pain, his wrists and arms taut and burning. His left side hurt atrociously. He looked left, then right: His wrists and arms were bound to the pergola's crossbeam, and his feet couldn't reach the ground. In the distance, he could see the mainland's distinct shoreline. He could hardly breathe. He tried to shake his head, but the duct tape over his mouth didn't budge. He looked down at his naked torso and saw the blood.

Desperation set in: *Where is Piero? He must come.* He started to shake uncontrollably. *My God. Piero . . . I will . . .* Suddenly he heard voices coming from along the path. The voices grew stronger: They were approaching. He felt a surge of hope. Contorting his face, he tried to wet his lips. A minuscule air passage was forming at the left corner of his mouth. He started to yell, but the sound stayed locked in the antechamber of his gullet, the veins and arteries of his throat ready to burst. He writhed in pain, trying desperately to loosen a limb, any limb. His shaking had stopped. He saw two men approaching and renewed his muffled grunts. They halted a few yards from him.

He couldn't believe it: They seemed to barely notice him. *They're ignoring me!* Conti's frustration turned to anger. One of them lit a cigarette. They spoke to each other nonchalantly, as if he weren't there. When they turned and walked away, he recognized them: The men on the train.

The weight of his body pressed on his lungs, as each breath became more and more painful, harder to exhale. He was suffocating.

Dear God, send Piero, he prayed. *I mustn't die. I have so much to do*. Time passed, with no sign of Piero. *They must have killed him*. He thought of Salvador. *We've failed, Antoine*. Conti began to cry. Moments later, he prayed for his soul and asked forgiveness for his sins.

On the shore, the lights of Stresa were beginning to blur, veiled by his eyes' watery mist. He felt dizzy, and his shaking started again. Cold, he was so cold. He knew he was lost and resigned himself to the inevitable. At the last instant, he panicked: He couldn't breathe. Then, darkness fell.

* * *

Early the following morning, the ferry driver walked nonchalantly, humming a popular song, enjoying the day's awakening. The fresh dew reflecting the sun off the hibiscus leaves caught his eye. He paused for a moment, breathing in the sweet scent of cedars. *Another gorgeous day*. He looked at his watch. He had ten more minutes before driving his ferry back to Stresa. He strode along until he reached the small clearing.

Suddenly, a man's lifeless shape came into focus.

The ferry driver froze in disbelief.

He saw all the blood and realized the man must be dead. He grabbed his phone and called the Stresa police station.

* * *

At 9.15 a.m., Inspector Andrea Calvino of the Milan Questura Centrale and three policemen piled into an Alfa Romeo and drove down the Autostrada toward Stresa, siren blaring.

Twenty minutes later, Calvino ordered that all ferries to Isola Madre be canceled, and commandeered a patrol boat.

They rushed to the pergola and cut loose Conti, wrapping his body in blankets. *Why such a horrible death?* Then Calvino saw the plaque: 'The Ox has fallen, the Dragon is wounded,' and the picture of Salvador's crucifixion hit him.

"He looks like . . . I think it's Archbishop Conti," said Calvino to the policeman.

"Yes."

Calvino heard a small commotion, coming from behind a large juniper bush: Two of Calvino's men had discovered a second man, inert, lying in his blood.

"Get the men to check nearby hotels for any missing persons. Start questioning the ferry drivers," said Calvino.

Soon, Stresa was astir with policemen. Visitors crammed the little ferry dock, cordoned off by the police: Two men had been murdered on Isola Madre. It seemed all the more improbable that such a glorious day beckoned.

"Will the ferries run to the other Borromeo Islands?" asked a tourist.

"No, not for now," said a policeman.

Calvino got a call from one of his men. "Inspector, Archbishop Conti has not been in his room this morning at the Hotel Palma. He didn't have breakfast there, as he usually does. His bodyguard is missing."

Calvino didn't speak. He rushed to the hotel and had the clerk open the door: The bed had not been slept in, and a note had been slipped under the door. Calvino read it: 'The Ox has fallen, the Dragon is wounded.' Calvino showed the photograph of the crucified man to the hotel manager, and Conti's identity was confirmed.

* * *

The *Corriere della Sera's* blood-red headlines shocked Italy:

Assassins strike again: Archbishop Conti and bodyguard murdered on Isola Madre.

58

Calvino's phone was ringing constantly, his office inundated by reporters.

He held an impromptu press meeting, declaring he had no suspects yet, but that Interpol had been brought into the investigation.

* * *

Dulac received Calvino's call early afternoon, and had his worst nightmare confirmed: *Serial killings with a political-religious agenda.* He took the afternoon flight to Milan and arrived at Calvino's office before dark.

"What do you have?" said Dulac, his tone and attitude implying he was taking charge.

"The coroner's preliminary report indicates time of death around 1 a.m. Cause of death is asphyxiation, and shock caused by loss of blood. They found a trace of Desflurane on his mouth. Here is the plaque we found on the body."

"This fits the pattern of Salvador's murder," Dulac said. "Anything on the killers?"

Calvino strode forward and thrust the document in Dulac's hand.

"We found this letter in his correspondence, on his desk at the hotel."

Dulac read it. "Make me copies. Anything else?"

"No, except that a fisherman rented a boat to two tourists a couple of days ago, and they returned the boat last night, but didn't pick up their thousand-euro deposit. He found that strange and reported it to the Stresa police."

"Good. Our composite picture specialists will interview him. In the meantime, you have the composites we've developed on the Saas-Fee killers: Send the pictures out now and put your border guards on red alert. They may be the same ones. These assassins are making a run for it as we speak."

* * *

Vasiliev and Kurganski had brought the boat back the previous night to the fisherman's dock, and had taken the night train to Milan, their grisly task accomplished. Their plane had left Milan for Tallin at 10.30 p.m. that night.

The next morning, at their hotel, the Estonian television news didn't mention the murders, and their plane to Moscow was, surprisingly, on time. They expected to collect their bonus from Victor. The next day, they met him in St. Petersburg.

"Any problems?" The tanned, stocky man barely cast them a glance as he flicked tiny, imperceptible motes off his dark blue suit.

"This time, none," said Kurganski.

"Did you deliver the message?"

"As instructed."

Victor handed them each a brown envelope.

"Well done. Now you must stay in St. Petersburg for a while."

"Why?" asked Vasiliev.

"Interpol has contacted the FSB. They are looking for you in Moscow."

Victor knew more: His contacts told him that Interpol had found DNA traces in the rented Fiat and were developing composite pictures of the Saas-Fee killers. These composites would only get more accurate when they got the reports of the Borromeo killings. He knew that Vasiliev and Kurganski's usefulness was fast coming to an end, and that they were living on borrowed time. He had already planned their 'retirement'. An inside job had already been contracted; their accidental deaths wouldn't even make Pravda's obituary columns. He couldn't afford to have the FSB arrest them, especially under Interpol supervision, and linking him to the crimes. Their fates had been sealed when they had accepted the second contract. Besides, the client had paid for their "retirement plan" in advance.

CHAPTER 15

All hell had broken loose in Calvino's office: The Minister of Justice, Minister of the Interior and the Prime Minister's office all had sent their representatives. All wanted answers Calvino couldn't give them: *Who and why?*

Calvino passed the phone to Dulac.

"Mr. Dulac, this is Archbishop Fiore."

"Yes?"

"Could you meet us tomorrow at the Vatican?"

"I'm available."

"It would be preferable if Ms Dawson could also join us."

"Why?"

"We will call her," replied Fiore. "Someone will meet you at the main entrance, St. Peter's Square, at 9 a.m."

"As you wish."

* * *

It was a gray, rainy morning in Rome. The drizzle heightened the somber atmosphere surrounding St. Peter's Square, where hundreds watched for signs of activity, special announcements, possibly a papal appearance.

The Vatican's message in *L'Osservatore Romano*, its official newspaper, had been short:

> *The terrible deaths of Monsignors Salvador and Conti fill us with sadness and consternation. Such unacceptable acts of violence against the Church are also felt by all of civilized humanity.*
> *We pray for the souls of our archbishops: May they find everlasting peace.*

As Dulac and Calvino strode up the stairs, a young priest dressed in a black cassock met them and led them to Fiore's large, richly decorated Venetian-style office. Karen, having come in on the morning flight, sat waiting, next to two prelates.

"Good morning," said Fiore. "Let me introduce you to Cardinals Volpe and Legnano. Cardinal Volpe is Secretary of State of the Vatican."

"Good morning," said Dulac perfunctorily, as Calvino chimed in and shook hands with the prelates.

Fiore took command: "Mr. Dulac, where does your investigation stand, now with this horrible development?"

Dulac felt threatened. Now, two murders: He felt the uneasy, unpronounced reproach of the inquirer: *Couldn't Interpol have prevented the second murder?*

"We have evidence linking two suspects — we think they are Russians — to the murders," said Dulac. "We've made composite pictures of them and are running them through Interpol, Swiss, French, Russian, and now Italian police data banks. We will refine the composites with new information gathered by the Stresa police. We have no leads yet as to who is behind this, but clearly the assassins' message hasn't been understood by its intended recipient. The question is: Who? Has the Vatican received any threats, recently?"

Volpe pounced: "M. Dulac, the Vatican receives dozens of threats, recriminations and ultimatums monthly, most of which are known to Interpol. You separate the harangues from the possible real threats. You tell us!"

Dulac's face turned crimson, and Calvino came to the rescue. "Our border guards are on highest alert for these murderers and are communicating with the Russian FSB. Their borders are on red alert. The assassins will not pass those borders," he added with a bit of Italian bravado.

"Dr. Dawson," said Cardinal Legnano, trying to defuse the animosity, "do you have any idea what these messages mean?"

"At this time, I can only offer theories."

"Of course, please go ahead."

"The naming now of the ox ... I think they are referring to the Book of Revelations, and the Synoptic Evangelists."

"But the names of Antoine . . ."

"Yes, I know, but please check the birth certificates of Monsignors Salvador and Conti."

"Why?"

"They may have other names that match those of the Evangelists: Mark and Luke."

"I will have them by end of morning." Legnano signaled to the secretary.

The room fell silent, as everyone realized the possible implication of a name match: There could be at least two more targeted bishops.

Calvino spoke: "We can't protect every bishop that may have a name of one of the Evangelists!"

"This isn't a coincidence," Dulac said. "The assassins probably have a religious motive, such as revenge, and are bent on destroying people, either as a symbol, or for more direct reasons. Monsignor Volpe, do you have any idea what Salvador meant in this letter to Conti?" Dulac showed Volpe and the others the letter. Volpe paused, and shook his head. "None."

The other prelates concurred.

"Were they in committees or organizations together?" asked Dulac.

Cardinal Legnano said, removing his glasses, "They were both, I believe, on the Liturgical Review Committee, before and during the last Synod, along with other bishops and archbishops. They also attended the Celibacy of Priests' Committee."

"Please have the names of all the members of both committees drawn up and sent to my office, along with their birth certificates. Let's see if we can narrow down the list," said Dulac.

"Dr. Dawson," Legnano said, "what do you make of the mention of 'The Dragon is wounded' in both cases?"

"I haven't looked into it very deeply, but my first reaction is that it refers to the Church. The Hydra of Lerna's severed heads grew back, the dragon was only wounded; the Church will replace its archbishops. The assassins wanted to make the point that they will keep wounding the Church. The reference to dragons could be chosen for their mythical hoarding of treasures: The assassins might point out that the Church also hoards treasures."

"What do these people want?" said Legnano.

Karen turned and looked at Dulac, who said, "The killers have one of the typical profiles: They like to play cat and mouse with the police. They want us to guess their motives and identity, while they stay one step ahead of us. Eventually, we catch up, when they make a fatal mistake. Right now, we are close to identifying the killers. Finding them is another matter. We think these were hired assassins. In that case, we have to find their contract. Any one of a host of organizations opposing the Church could be the enemy."

Dulac knew that the same people, if they were sophisticated, wouldn't try again. But then, human greed often overrode caution.

* * *

Dulac and Karen flew back to Paris.

"Let me buy you supper," he said. "That's the least I owe you."

"Actually, I'm a bit tired," replied Karen.

"I'd like to continue the discussion while it's still fresh. You have to eat somewhere."

"Twist my arm," she replied, capitulating.

Dulac wouldn't admit the real reason: He'd noticed that the prelates considered her opinions. He needed every ally he could get.

Later that evening, Dulac picked up Karen at her apartment in the sixteenth *arrondissement*. The contrast of the late fifteenth-century and modern furniture gave it a surprisingly warm, welcoming feeling, and Dulac felt immediately at ease. She had impeccable taste. Her beige silk blouse and matching pants blended with the soft eggshell and faded green colors of the apartment. *She looks stunning*, he thought. He was relieved not to see animals, mythological or otherwise, in the decoration: She seemed to know better than to impose her work on others in her home surroundings.

The reservation had been made for 8 p.m., and the maître d' steered them to a discreet table.

"Fine," said Dulac.

They sat down, Dulac sensing a slight discomfort on Karen's part. "You're probably wondering if an Interpol investigator comes often to the likes of *Chez François*."

"Well, yes," she admitted, looking embarrassed.

"Don't report me," he implored mockingly, "but I feel the taxpayers' money is well spent. A great meal now and then leads to great ideas."

"I won't." Karen smiled as Dulac chose a modest Bordeaux off the voluminous wine list.

"How about some calf brain? They do a reasonable job of it here."

"I'll pass," said Karen. "I think I'll have the chicken."

The maître d' opened the bottle, and Dulac expertly twisted the taster's glass and swirled a small amount of nectar in his mouth.

"*Pas mal*. I think you'll like this."

Karen shrugged. His forcefulness was becoming annoying.

"By the way, what did you think of the monsignors' reaction to Salvador's letter this morning?" asked Dulac.

"They were taken by surprise."

"That was the intent: I got the impression they know more than they are letting on."

"Hard to tell."

"What do you make of the sign-off?"

"You mean, 'affectionately yours'?"

"Yes."

"Maybe a sign of friendship?"

"Hmm," Dulac intoned, a little wryly.

"You're not suggesting . . ."

"No, of course not."

As the evening progressed, Karen felt intrigued by the man behind the persona.

"How long have you been at La Sorbonne?" he asked.

"Three years, counting my residency. And you?"

Dulac looked surprised.

"At Interpol, I mean," said Karen.

"Since my graduation from Montpelier Law School."

"You're a lawyer?"

"I've never practiced."

"So how does one become an Interpol agent?"

"Good ancestry helps."

"What do you mean?"

"My father was a diplomat."

"You mean you had *piston?*"

"I prefer the term 'personal appreciation.' It sounds less nepotistic."

"Same difference."

"We French like our nuances."

"Obviously."

"So why on earth does one become a mythologist?" he asked, as if she had chosen her career over grave digging.

"And why not?"

"I'm sorry; I admit I don't know much about it," said Dulac.

"Most people don't understand the role of myths. Have you read anything on their meaning, recently?"

"*Touché, Mademoiselle.*" He bowed slightly forward, glass in hand, toasting her with his eyebrows. "By the way, I hope you've forgiven me for that reference to your visa."

"Not yet." She felt the blood rush to her face.

As he was pouring the last of the Château Peyron into her glass, Dulac's cell phone rang.

"Mr. Dulac, this is Archbishop Fiore: We have the birth certificates, and they read: 'Antoine Pierre Marc Salvador, born in Metz on July 8, 1958.' Then: 'Paolo Luca Giovanni Alberto Conti, born in Naples on April 20, 1944.'"

"Send them to my office. How soon will you have the others?"

"By tomorrow."

"Any thoughts as to what Salvador was referring to in his letter?" queried Dulac.

"No," answered Fiore. "It's quite puzzling."

"I may want to question the others, once you have their certificates."

"I understand."

Dulac hung up, and turned to Karen:

"You were right: The birth certificates match."

* * *

The following day, Dulac got a call from Moscow.

"Inspector Dulac?"

"Yes?"

"Sergei Petrov, from FSB Bureau in Moscow. I contacted Russian National Central Bureau of Interpol, and I have good news."

"Go ahead."

"We have analyzed your composite pictures. We checked files from the Army. We have a match with two ex-soldiers, Sergei Vasiliev and Andrei Kurganski."

"How high is the reliability?"

"Seventy per cent. We need fingerprints or DNA samples from you."

"We don't have them, at least not yet. These killers were very meticulous about not leaving traces. Can you track them?"

"Difficult: If they work for the mafia, they change identities often."

"Keep in touch." Dulac hung up.

Dulac knew it was a race against time: If the Russian mafia found out that FSB had discovered the identity of the killers, chances were slim that FSB or Interpol would find them alive.

CHAPTER 16

The letter was short, handcrafted, beautifully calligraphed and illuminated in the Renaissance style, beginning with a hand-drawn and -painted letter "W," in bright colors of gold, royal blue, beige and magenta; a miniature work of art.

We, daughters of Knowledge, beseech thee, your Holiness:

We have stood silent long enough. We shall no longer witness, passively, the continuing hypocrisy of the Church. How many young lives in the villages of Alepa, Adjibian and Mogadishu, will be lost this week, this month, this year, while the Vatican sits comfortably, luxuriously, idle? How many young African lives are your Titian, Veronese, Botticelli and Rafael paintings worth? None? Did Christ not say: "Leave all, and follow me?" We require immediate exemplarity on the part of the Vatican: We require you sell the following paintings, through Christie's of London, on the following dates of this year:

Daphnis and Chloe, *by Titian, on or before July 15,* The Annunciation, *by Veronese, on or before August 30,* St Sebastian, *by Tintoretto, on or before November 1.*

The proceeds shall be publicly donated through UNESCO to the benefit of the needy villages, in Somalia, Darfur, Senegal and Ethiopia. We require your commitment by the June 10, the sign of which shall be the announcement of the Titian's impending sale.

We commiserate with you the unfortunate deaths of two of your Evangelists, Archbishops Salvador and Conti.

The letter was unsigned.

* * *

The Holy See had immediately summoned the inner council of the Roman Curia, the Vatican's Board of Directors, to discuss the letter's implications. On their orders, Fiore had convened Dulac and the head of the Italian section of Interpol, Inspector Romano Belli, along with the Minister of the Interior's representative. Fiore, Legnano and Volpe had been joined by the Head of the Swiss Guards, Commander Romer. Fiore had requested Karen's presence during the deliberations.

Volpe chaired the meeting, as Fiore and Legnano sat on either side. Volpe started, glancing now and then at his short notes. "Dr. Dawson, your worships, gentlemen, we are here to discuss the possible implications of the letter we have received last Thursday, a copy of which you have before you. We have received similar letters in the past, which we have put aside. However, in the present context, we cannot underestimate the portent of this letter. I am instructed not to leave this meeting without a recommendation to our Holy Father. But first, I ask that you all sign this oath of secrecy."

He leaned forward and handed Dawson a one-page document and a ballpoint pen. "Let us first address the issue of the letter's form. We have with us Dr. Giuseppe Franchi, expert in medieval calligraphy, to help us identify the author, or authors, of this letter. Dr. Franchi?"

A short bald man with a long nose, on which sat a pair of glasses the thickness of a telescope's lens, said: "The illumination is inspired by early medieval motifs, and the writer has used the *Batarde Miniscule* lettering style, popular mainly during the fourteenth to the sixteenth century. Today, not many calligraphers are good at it, and the ones that come to mind are from the Russian Orthodox school."

"Can it be imitated by others?" interrupted Dulac.

"Not without years of practice. This document was done by a master, probably good at other types of skillful, detailed and meticulous artwork."

"Such as forgery?" said Dulac.

"Possibly. Unfortunately, one doesn't earn a good living doing only calligraphy or illumination, these days."

"Can you be more precise as to the source?"

"I guess there are a half dozen calligraphers that could have written this. However, the heavy rough vellum paper indicates that the source is middle European — again, possibly Russian."

"I want the names of those calligraphers, Dr. Franchi," said Dulac.

Legnano turned to Karen. "What do you think of the illumination?"

"It resembles the main icon of the Pistis Sofia mythology: The Divine Feminine, adorned by the eagle, supplanting the ox, and—"

"My God, of course," exclaimed Legnano. "This resembles icons on letters we have received over the years from that group: Demands for the ordination of women, change of the basic liturgy, public recognition of papal fallibility, abolition of the teaching of the resurrection of Christ, modernization of the Credo, etc. Why didn't I think of it?"

"Let's get back the purpose of the meeting," said Volpe. "It is quite probable that the reference to our deceased bishops means that the writers of this letter are the assassins, that if their demands are not met, they will execute other bishops."

"Extortion," interjected Legnano.

"Perhaps."

"Perhaps?" said a surprised Legnano.

"Monsignors," said Volpe glancing at his notes, "please consider another perspective. You are all perfectly aware that for centuries, popes have enjoyed surrounding themselves with art, including the many paintings which hang in our magnificent museums. Popes Sixtus IV, Julius II, and the art of Michelangelo, Raphael, Titian and Bramante, come readily to mind. This passion for the beautiful, and the showing of religion through the eyes of great masters, was beyond any form of moral reproach.

"On the contrary, the Vatican encouraged artists, many of whom would not have created the masterpieces we now enjoy without papal support. As you all know, it was also part of a well-established social structure, making work for poor artists and artisans."

Volpe reached for his glass of water, paused briefly and continued:

"But the Church became the victim of its good intentions: These paintings, bought for mere pittances at the time, have acquired tremendous value. We are perceived now as rich owners of another private, priceless collection. The moral dilemma brought to our attention by this letter, is: Can we stand on high ground, and argue that generations will continue to enjoy these treasures in their proper setting in the Vatican, while our African parishioners die of hunger, sickness and thirst, *en masse*, and we do little or nothing about it? The dilemma is real, even without the threat of further assassinations. I must tell you that this subject has been discussed before within the Curia, without any looming threats. There is far from unanimity on the subject, as my colleagues will attest. Please don't misunderstand me: I don't for one instant condone these acts of madness: These assassins are completely reprehensible, and they should be brought to justice. At the same time, I cannot see how we can ignore this letter, and risk the lives of our bishops."

The prelates sat silent, embarrassed, looking furtively at each other for the first response.

"But the Church does contribute financially to aid the poor in those countries," said Legnano.

"Apparently, not enough," replied Volpe. "I'm trying to obtain from you a solution to this crisis. Right now, we in this room, and the Holy Father, are the only persons who know of this letter."

"You're not suggesting we sell the paintings?" asked Legnano, incredulous.

Volpe replied.

"Albert Einstein was once asked, "If you were escaping from a burning house, and you could only save either a Picasso or the cat, which would you choose?" Einstein answered. "The cat: Life is priceless.""

"I see," said Legnano, "but if we agree, we risk that these people will ask for more. Besides, are we absolutely certain that the murderers wrote this letter?"

Dulac listened, dispassionate at the exchange between the prelates, contemplating the *rapport de forces*. Volpe appeared to be in command, and Dulac couldn't fathom why Fiore was so subdued. He seemed in admiration of Volpe, nodding in approval now and then at Volpe's comments.

"To answer your question, Monsignor Legnano," said Dulac, "the writer of this letter has cleverly written it with enough ambiguity, to leave you the choice of deciding whether or not he is the assassin."

"Precisely," said Volpe. "If we can conclude that the letter is but a request, a timely reminder of a moral obligation that the Church should fulfill, we could take the position that we are abiding to a just cause. Besides, the writer is not benefiting personally from this request."

"Except that if Pistis Sophia ordered these murders, we are agreeing to being blackmailed," Legnano replied.

"Are you willing to accept and live with the fact that if we do nothing, other bishops will die?" said Volpe.

Legnano turned to Dulac for help.

"Mr. Dulac, can we be reasonably sure that Interpol will prevent further assassinations?"

"We are in the process of narrowing down the list of possible targeted bishops," replied Dulac. "We will give them maximum protection. However, I must tell you the assassins may change the rules, if they find out we're onto them. We're working with our underground contacts in Moscow, but we must buy more time."

Karen sat quietly, dumbfounded by what she was witnessing. Here were the most senior representatives of the Catholic Church, discussing the possible sale of its most valuable treasures: *To appease assassins*? She had thought — naïvely, she now realized — that if any organization was beyond bent morals, it would be the Church, her church. She felt disappointed and deceived. Yet she remembered that during her first visit to the Vatican's museums as a student, many years back, she had felt a mixture of awe, embarrassment and finally guilt. Her sense and appreciation of beauty had been in direct conflict with the values of her strict Catholic upbringing: Wasn't the essence of Christianity being compromised? Weren't the masses of Catholics, witness to this display of riches, being misled in their religious emotions and spirit?

Was it not too much to ask of any witness to these treasures, to make abstraction of the fact that they were owned by the Vatican, and admire them purely for their art?

Wasn't the message contradictory? You must follow Christ and live in modesty, but we in the Vatican, the higher caste, deserve to see, live, touch this luxury and be inspired by it, every day.

Deep inside, she felt a low-lying conflict and resentment that she had buried long ago under the guise of a certain fatalism, being rekindled and brought to the surface, for eventual resolution. She couldn't help but feel certain sympathy toward the writers, if indeed they weren't the murderers. Could one rationalize that the mere condolences mentioned in the letter were just that, and not a threat? She knew deep down that it would be an impossible sell.

It was late in the evening, after many cigarette breaks, when Dulac finally spoke. Tensions had mounted between Volpe and Fiore on the one hand, and Legnano, whose opposing views received weak, discordant support from other members of the assembly.

"Ms. Dawson, your worships, gentlemen: I sense we cannot resolve the dilemma along the clear-cut lines of either the commitment to sell the art, or to simply ignore this request. I do feel we cannot allow the Church to be blackmailed, but at the same time, I can't stand by idle while the lives of bishops are put at risk.

"I suggest the following: The Church will make a public commitment to give UNESCO another ten million dollars this year, to be distributed to the needy villages in Somalia, Ethiopia, Darfur and Senegal. If the writers of this letter are sincere, they shouldn't care if the funds come from the Vatican's Treasury or otherwise."

Dulac's timing had been perfect. A sense of welcomed relief permeated the assembly; the impasse had been avoided. All those canvassed agreed with the proposal. Volpe had his recommendation.

CHAPTER 17

Isola Rossa, Caribbean Sea

The island had been bought in the late 1880s from the British government by Sir Thomas Litman, the tea magnate. After a scandalous affair, he had married the eventually widowed Marchioness of Dorset, and their great-granddaughter Sarah had inherited both title and fortune. True to her great-grand-father's liberal disposition, unfettered by social mores, she sported a long history of affairs with married nobility, unmarried gardeners and chauffeurs, and recently a divorced cousin, the Earl of Salisbury. She also had fought and won a personal battle with drugs, and publicly attributed her success to the discovery of her new faith, Pistis Sophia. Liberated from her Anglican guilt, she enjoyed publicizing her views on Gnostic Christianity. Coincidentally, the faith gave full license to the few unexplored depths of her middle-aged sexuality.

* * *

It hadn't been difficult for Dulac to convince Karen to join him on his forthcoming trip to the Caribbean. A few days of sunshine on Isola Rossa would be a welcome change from the grayness of Paris, even if overshadowed by the investigation's pall. Dulac felt Karen's knowledge of Pistis Sophia was indispensable to the upcoming meeting, and that her presence would soften its tone.

The meeting had been arranged through the British Embassy in Paris, under the guise of an informational visit to the Pistis Sofia *haut lieu*. The Marchioness had agreed to meet Dulac, his assistant Daniel Lescop and Karen, but on home turf.

Dulac felt the humidity increase in the chartered jet, announcing their impending arrival. As the jet slowly taxied down the boiling tarmac and came to a stop, Dulac saw a white-gloved chauffeur dusting a light blue Bentley parked near a small hangar.

"Welcome to Isola Rossa," said the chauffeur in a strong Caribbean lilt.

The Bentley glided quietly up to the top of the winding dirt road, when suddenly a mansion surged into Dulac's view. The rays of the setting sun were warming the limestone of the Parthenon-inspired façade to the color of crème caramel. With its Doric columns flanked by late-Edwardian style adjacent wings, Dulac thought it looked curiously out of place amidst the untamed Caribbean landscape. The perfectly trimmed cedar bushes, forming a French labyrinth, only added to the incongruity.

Karen, Lescop and Dulac were led up the expansive steps and through the high-arched entrance.

"The Marchioness will meet you in the library at seven," announced the self-effacing *portier*, as they crossed the pink Italian marble hall.

Dulac cringed. He felt control of the situation slowly but inextricably being whittled away from him by the sumptuousness of the décor.

"This way, please," the *portier* said as he led them up the grand, granite staircase to their rooms.

Dulac couldn't help but stare at the lush landscape paintings adorning the walls of the entry hall, and thought he

recognized a Vermeer and a Holbein, flanked by the proverbial, ancestral turn-of-the-century British portraits.

At five minutes before seven, a muted knock on Dulac's
door announced the meeting with the Marchioness, and the
portier led him, along with Karen and Lescop, to the library.

"Good evening, Mr. Dulac," said a pert, attractive red-
head in her early fifties, her long, full hair held loosely by a
silver *broche*, thick curls wandering onto her naked shoulders.
"How good of you to come." Dressed in a pale pink, reveal-
ing *djellaba*, the Marchioness rose from her sofa and glided
gracefully across the room. She extended a regal, down-
turned hand to Dulac.

"Good evening, Marchioness; it is I who thank you for
receiving us in such beautiful surroundings," said Dulac,
quickly establishing equality of rank as a nobleman, by the
contresens des nobles return of the compliment.

"This is Karen Dawson from the Sorbonne, and my
assistant Inspector Lescop."

"Hello," said the Marchioness, as she gave Karen a quick
inquisitive look and summarily dismissed Lescop with barely
a glance. "Why don't we sit here?" She led them across the
lustrous silk carpet to the huge leather ottomans in the middle of the room.

Dulac felt at ease with the practiced attitudes and manners of nobility. He knew that Lescop was not, and sensed
Karen was struggling. He couldn't guess that the smell of old
books and the vastness of the library had helped relieve her
initial discomfort.

As she gazed at the endless rows of leather-bound col-
lections, Karen's wonder caught the Marchioness' eye. As
if to anticipate her question, Lady Sarah said, "A little overwhelming at first. It's probably the largest library of Gnostic
works in existence today," she said, matter-of-factly. "My
great-grandfather was a Manichaean."

"Impressive," replied Karen.

"And what is your profession, may I ask?"

"I teach animal mythology."

"How unusual. Come to think of it, we have works here on early Chinese Chou dynasty serpent rites that might interest you," she said coyly.

Karen felt the probing thrust of the Marchioness' razor-sharp intellect, and deftly parried the blow. "Yes, the Chinese were one of the first cultures to un-demonize the serpent through elaborate sexual interspecies rites, including men and women with serpents," she said, unblushingly.

"Quite." Lady Sarah chuckled, embarrassed at having been so obviously caught in her own trap.

Dulac interjected, looking annoyed and impatient: "Lady Sarah, thank you for receiving us on such short notice, but this is not a purely social visit."

"Of course, I apologize for the digression," she replied. "Surely you have more serious matters you'd like to discuss."

"We're investigating the murders of Archbishops Salvador and Conti, and have reason to believe Pistis Sophia members might be involved."

"Really? I must say that I find that extremely unlikely. We're a peaceful, meditative tradition. Why would a Pistis Sophia member want to kill archbishops?"

"The Vatican has received this, bearing one of the motifs of Pistis Sophia in the illumination," Dulac said, as he bent over toward her and showed her the letter.

"What makes you think it comes from our membership? Surely the motif can be easily copied," said the Marchioness.

"We've had the color particles of this letter chemically analyzed with a gas chromatograph, and they match previous Pistis Sophia letters to the Vatican."

"I see. But how is this letter related to the deaths? The authors commiserate with the Pope."

"Do you *really* think so?" said Dulac. "The context here is quite different. We found these plaques with the bodies of the bishops. We're treating the letter as a threat."

"'The Lion is dead, the Dragon is wounded. The Ox has fallen, the Dragon is wounded.' Most enigmatic, but I still don't see the connection," said the Marchioness.

Karen stepped in: "The given names of the dead bishops include Mark and Luke. These animals are the apocalyptic references to the Evangelists Mark and Luke. These are also part of the Pistis Sophia motif."

"I have often wondered where these animals came from," said the Marchioness. Then turning to Dulac: "Surely you don't think *I* have anything to do with this?"

"Of course not, Lady Sarah, but perhaps you can help us. For instance, have any of your members proffered threats recently, or spoken of their hatred of the Church?"

"No, not that I can think of. As you are probably aware, Pistis Sophia is not an organization in the traditional sense: In true Gnostic tradition, we are a community of faithful, but we have no hierarchy. I have little knowledge of what happens outside this island. We have — and I hate the association the term implies — many small 'cells,' each grouped on a very local geographical basis. I have absolutely no link, control or responsibility for the cells, which are autonomous. I am only a host, for those members wishing to practice their faith in our rather unique surroundings. Their contributions help defray our expenses."

"Who wrote these?" Dulac showed her previously written letters addressed to the Vatican bearing the Pistis Sophia motif.

"I have no idea," she said, with a slight curl of her lower lip.

"The letterhead was traced to your printer Karl Mittenwald, of Vienna."

"Perhaps, but all of the members staying here have access to our stationery," said the Marchioness.

"I want to question some of your key staff. This recent letter was signed, "Your ladyship's most trusted servant.""

"Excuse me, Madam," interrupted the butler, "dinner is served."

They arose and Lady Sarah took Karen by the arm, squeezing it slightly. She led the group through the wide, vaulted corridor. "Forgive my faux pas," she said to Karen.

"I should rid myself of the habit of testing my guests in such an obvious manner."

"That's quite all right. I do it myself sometimes," said Karen.

Dulac followed the ladies, his attention being drawn to a large room to his left, where a varied mix of people were dining, seated around a long, richly decorated table.

"I usually dine with the faithful, but I thought this would be more appropriate," said the Marchioness, showing them to a small room.

Again, Dulac noticed a Vermeer and two small Brueghels, surrounded by heavily brocaded blue satin drapes adorning high windows. *Nothing like the soothing warmth of the Dutch Masters*, he thought.

"Please be seated," said the Marchioness, as she sat facing Dulac, Karen at her left, Lescop at her right. "Shall we have some red with the pheasant entrée?" she said, almost rhetorically.

Dulac nodded approvingly.

The butler slowly decanted the 1995 Château d'Abzac, and Dulac couldn't help but think the mood was quickly changing from the interrogatory to the convivial. But a Frenchman couldn't refuse the opportunity of discovering one of the lesser-known Chateaus, and an exceptional year, to boot. *Might as well enjoy.*

* * *

During the dinner's progression, Karen felt a slight hesitation when the Marchioness's warming gaze would leave hers, to address Dulac or Lescop as she expanded on the history of Château d'Or.

"Sir Thomas had the limestone imported from the Loire Valley — Blois, to be exact. He was fond of saying the Caribbean climate would help his Château outlast Fontainebleau."

The evening waned, the Marchioness's gaze grew more insistent, and then Karen felt it: An almost imperceptible, fleeting pressure of the Marchioness' left leg on her right knee. At first, she thought it accidental, but moments later, the leg persisted. Karen knew she had one split second to react: Sublimated by the ambiance, the audacity of the move, the wine and the exquisite setting, she let herself be engulfed by the rising pressure in her loins and didn't move. Her heart raced, and trying to retain her composure, she looked straight in front at Lescop. Slowly, the pressure ebbed, and Karen breathed heavily. She felt her nipples harden against her now cumbersome bra. Dulac's conversation was becoming more and more remote, difficult to follow, and she suddenly felt a deft, probing hand caressing her leg, slowly squeezing the knee, reaching down into the softness of her inner thigh. She felt the increasing tingling and titillation of arousal and desire, heightened by the secrecy, as the Marchioness calmly continued to eat dessert, then sip her coffee, and converse with her guests.

"Let's have a *digestif* on the terrace, shall we? I never tire of the view at this time of the evening," said Lady Sarah.

As they followed the Marchioness to the terrace, Karen felt relieved and embarrassed, wondering if Dulac had noticed her arousal.

The view was astonishing, as the floating diffuse ball of fire slowly sank between the cypress trees framing the amphitheater below. For a moment, Karen regained her composure, as the fresh evening breeze revitalized her and cleared her thoughts. *What am I doing? I'm supposedly helping in a murder investigation, not here to explore my sexual curiosity.* The back of the Marchioness's left hand grazed the top of Karen's buttocks, as she gathered close behind her.

"Sublime view, isn't it?"

"Yes," said Karen, clearing her throat and feeling the surge arising in her again.

After more cognacs, Dulac, Karen and Lescop wearily turned in for the evening. The Marchioness bade them goodnight and reclined in her deck chair, taking fresh breaths of the cooling air.

* * *

Karen's room exuded quiet luxury: A faded green hue, Louis sixteenth furniture, ancestral paintings and a bathroom the size of her mother's garage in which a large onyx bath completed the tasteful setting. At last, she could relax, and once again try and gather her wits. She couldn't believe this was happening and swore significantly at herself. Apart from a fleeting, awkward teenage exploratory experience with a female college roommate, all of her sexual adventures had been heterosexual. She couldn't have imagined how easily she could be tempted to vary the menu. She poured the bottle of Hermes mousse and ran the bath, colder than usual, to help calm herself. She dimmed the light to relax her frayed nerves, set the whirlpool, and closed her eyes, as the cognac pounded her head and breast.

Suddenly, she felt a soft hand reach from behind her and slowly slide down her stomach, onto her mound. Startled, she tried to rise, only to meet the Marchioness's hungry mouth. The Marchioness's nude, slim body turned, slid down on top of hers, her hands probing, massaging Karen's taut breasts, grabbing her arching back with her left hand, her other hand now exploring deep, deep inside, now gently squeezing, now caressing, now rubbing her rhythmically.

Karen searched for Sarah's mouth, exploring deep with her tongue the softness of the lips, and entwining Sarah's tongue in a rising dance of desire. Karen reached around Sarah's mound, tugging, separating her firm buttocks, then inserting deft, fondling fingers.

As she climaxed, Sarah let out a long, guttural cry. Karen stiffened, and the release shook her taut body uncontrollably. After a unison of convulsion, Sarah led Karen to the *baldaquin* bed, where they both lay replete, wet, side to side on the now-soaked satin mauve sheet.

Sarah whispered: "A new Karen, am I right?"

"Very perceptive."

Later, Lady Sarah rose lasciviously and wearily from the *baldaquin,* and stretched her sculpted, toned arms.

Great body, for her age, thought Karen.

"Sweet dreams, my dear." She kissed Karen and slipped into her silk nightgown to leave.

* * *

The following morning, Karen awoke to the gentle warmth of an insistent sun ray on her neck. She felt queasy, angry, confused, as myriads of conflicting thoughts raced through her mind. She tried to piece together the circumstances of what happened, and how. Was it the wine, the cognac, or did she have an underlying, hereto unavowed lesbian penchant? Or was it an *erreur de parcours*? She felt angry that whatever the reason, she had compromised her professional integrity. How could she assess the Marchioness's implication objectively, if indeed she was mixed up in these murders?

"Good afternoon," said Dulac, as Karen joined the already-assembled threesome for breakfast.

"Good morning," she replied, looking ever so briefly at the Marchioness and finding refuge in Dulac's sardonic smile.

"I'm trying to convince these gentlemen to join me for a swim after breakfast," said the Marchioness. "Care to join us?"

"Actually, I'd like to spend some time in the library," answered Karen stiffly, barely glancing at the Marchioness. Time on her own is what she needed, desperately.

"Of course," said the Marchioness.

"Lescop and I want to interview some of your staff," said Dulac, sipping the *café au lait*. "Can you make them available this morning? We'll start with your administrative assistant, Miss Lee."

"Yes, I'll make sure she's available," replied Sarah.

At that moment, Dulac's cell phone rang. "Inspector Dulac please."

"Speaking."

"Sergei Petrov, FSB. We caught Vasiliev."

Dulac's quandary was quickly resolved. On the one hand, there was something too pat, too well prepared in the Marchioness' attitude and answers. She had been overly explanatory. He wanted to probe, to find a chink in her armor; her detachment from the whole matter irritated him. But that could wait. Questioning Vasiliev couldn't.

"Lady Sarah, I must return to Paris. Some urgent business." He certainly didn't want the Marchioness to know Petrov had called.

Dulac phoned for the jet. "I'll be leaving this afternoon," he announced.

"I trust you will stay a few more days," said the Marchioness, turning to Karen.

"I teach classes the day after tomorrow, and I'd like to get a lift back to Paris with Mr. Dulac." She felt vulnerable and alone and of no use to Dulac.

"As you wish," answered Lady Sarah, disappointment and resignation in her voice. "Let's at least enjoy the morning at the seashore."

Dulac pressed on. "First, I must talk to Miss Lee."

"My, my, how tedious. *Le devoir avant tout,*" said Sarah, summoning Lee on the intercom.

"Miss Lee, this is Mr. Dulac, from Interpol." Sarah introduced her assistant to the policeman. "He would like to have a few words with you concerning those grisly murders. You know, Monsignors Conti and Salvador."

Miss Lee, a beautiful Indonesian woman in her mid-thirties, nodded briefly at Dulac and looked quizzically, almost intimately, at Lady Sarah, seemingly not understanding why she would be questioned on the issue.

"Miss Lee let's go into the parlor here. We'll be more at ease," said Dulac.

As she sat down, he couldn't help but notice the necklace and pendant between the cleavage of her well-formed breasts. It was a replica of the Pistis Sophia icon, in gold.

"I'm told you have control of the computers and the stationery here. Is that right?"

"Yes."

"Please make available all your computers to my assistant M. Lescop. He will be staying on to look at their contents."

"I would have to ask the Marchioness."

"I'm sure she has nothing to hide. Any findings will be kept confidential. By the way, have you had any requests by guests for some stationery recently, say in the last two weeks?"

"No, I don't recall."

CHAPTER 18

Vasiliev's future had looked brighter. Alarmed by the bustling noises outside his apartment, he escaped through the roof only to find himself ordered to surrender by two FSB security force snipers, a sitting duck in the crosshairs of their 9mm VSS Vintorez gas-powered rifles. The odds of survival had simplified his decision.

Born of peasant parents in the Siberian town of Irkutsk, the Afghan war interrupted his medical studies at the University, and what noble fire he nurtured to save human lives was relentlessly extinguished by the ferocity and cruelty of the war. He had survived hand-to-hand combat twice. He witnessed the unimaginable: Adolescent Russian soldiers, dismembered limb by limb, castrated and left to die in the scorching Afghan desert sun. Completely disillusioned, he vowed never to return to the bleakness of the Siberian countryside. He had paid his dues, and life owed him more than that.

Today, however, he would've gladly accepted the alternative. He knew that, once the word was out on the street that he'd been taken captive, his days were numbered. He knew too much. He had to survive long enough to bargain with the FSB, to protect his daughter, Nicola.

* * *

Dulac had dropped off Karen in Paris. The jet refueled, he endured a bumpy ride to Moscow, which reminded him of why he so hated flying. Petrov met him at the airport in one of the old black Zil limousines, a relic of the KGB era and a tribute to the robustness of Russian manufacturing. It was Dulac's third time in Moscow, and the city looked radiant: That special crackling Russian blue sky enveloped the Kremlin buildings in Red Square, like toy houses in Gargantua's playpen. Even Lubyanka prison's pastel limestone shone in monarchial splendor.

Lubyanka: The name still strikes terror in many a Muscovite heart. The prison was emblematic of Stalin's darkest days; thousands died there, including many innocent Soviets, after unspeakable tortures, for being 'undesirable toward the State.' Many of its victims had furnished the medical schools of Moscow with their body parts, some supplying fresh beating hearts to their cardiovascular research departments. A few dissidents, including Solzhenitsyn and Sakharov, had miraculously survived to later decry the atrocities. Longtime headquarters of the Cheka, NKVD, and KGB, it now housed the administrative offices of the FSB, Russia's main intelligence agency. Lubyanka's long corridors and endless rows of cells were now empty, except for the occasional prisoner under current interrogation.

Dulac entered, and immediately felt the imprint of sorrow and despair left by the thousands of lost souls, still haunting the drab gray marble of the entrance hall. He wanted to leave.

Petrov had ordered that Vasiliev be brought to the interrogation room, near his office, so Dulac could witness firsthand any confession.

"We have been questioning him for three days," said Petrov. "You must understand that his army training makes him a tough customer."

Dulac saw that although there were no physical signs of abuse, Vasiliev couldn't hold out much longer. His eyes were lifeless, hollow beyond hope, and resigned to their impending destiny. A ghoul would have looked healthier. Dulac knew that Russian techniques, although more humane than in Stalin's day, fell far short of the Vienna Convention.

* * *

After another night of sleep deprivation, Vasiliev caved in: "I want to make a deal," he announced to Petrov.

"Wait behind the one-way glass," said Petrov to Dulac, and went into the interrogation room. "We don't make deals with criminals."

"Listen, my life is over. Then I die silent. You choose."

Petrov knew he wasn't bluffing. Nor could he afford to lose his prime witness and suspect. He also knew that part of Vasiliev's army training was self-suffocation if he fell into Taliban hands.

"I am listening."

"I want a ticket to Cuba and two million US dollars. Also I want twenty million dollars a year, for Nicola's lifetime. I give you name of my partner, and my boss."

"We already know your partner's name. Anything else?" Petrov exclaimed, outraged. "Didn't you forget a dacha on the Caspian and the chalet in the Urals?" Petrov's usually pasty white face turned crimson to the tip of his oversized ears. *The gall of this murderer.*

He stomped out of the room and glared at Dulac. "Very big imagination, criminals in Russia, yes?"

Dulac hunched and smiled laconically. "In France, those demands would be impossible."

CHAPTER 19

Since her return to Paris, Karen had tried to bury herself in her work. She couldn't close the gap of incomprehension between her students and herself, losing her emblematic patience, responding brusquely to their inane questions. The unprepar- edness of her lectures was becoming all too apparent, even to herself, leading her to cut short any pertinent discussions. Her mind was definitely elsewhere. In their hurried departure from Isola Rossa, Dulac had asked her to do more research on Pistis Sophia: Did the group have a history of violence? Did it have enemies? Any documentation on its 'cells'?

Dulac's request coincided with Karen's growing curi- osity. She was intrigued by the lack of formality and the openness: Decidedly not a sect, with all the pejorative, doc- trinaire aspects she had come to associate with the term. Hidden within the enclaves of the Sorbonne's main library, she plunged into the Gnostic publications and books of the Pistis Sophia tradition. She found a reasonableness of beliefs that mirrored, and gave concrete meaning to, her own. Pistis Sophia had, from the beginning, refuted the tra- ditional Christian, anthropomorphic God. The *Unnamed, Indefinable, Unknowable,* were terms it used in its preaching. The revering of the Divine Feminine was purely a symbolic, mythical necessity, not an actual belief. The tradition rejected the doctrine of the physical resurrection of Christ, believing the correct interpretation of the Gospels to be that of a reborn mankind. The tradition rejected the Catholic Credo, proclaimed by the First Council of Constantinople in 381 AD. It had developed its own. Pistis Sophia opened its doors to members of all religions and found the same response: Enlightened faithful wishing to see beyond the exclusive teachings preached by their predicators, and willing to enter into a new, inclusive manner of thinking, accenting the commonalities rather than the differences of the great religions.

Karen found no history of violence in Pistis Sophia, in sharp contrast with the tortures and murders committed by the Roman Catholic Church.

Along with the other Gnostic traditions, Pistis Sophia had suffered rejection and ridicule through the texts of early Christian writers such as Iraeneus. It had later been marginalized, then persecuted for centuries by the ever-growing Roman Catholic orthodoxy. Its lack of hierarchy, the cornerstone of its practice, had led to its downfall. Its modern-day resurgence intrigued her.

Karen also wanted to know more on Lady Sarah, Marchioness of Dorset.

Sifting through the many newspaper articles, she didn't envy the spotlight focused on her by the merciless British tabloids. *Another chauffeur, another lover?* read the headline of the *Sun. Sarah and Caroline, common taste for common men,* read another. *Marchioness of Dorset finally weeds out the gardener: Will she ever learn?* exclaimed *the Mirror.*

Marchioness of Dorset battles heavy cocaine habit had brought to an end what was left of her privacy, to quench the public's thirst for scandal. She had fought back with acts of philanthropy and generosity: *Lady Sarah gives 500, 000 pounds to children's leukemia research center.*

And then Karen sat up, bewildered at what she read. She reread, slowly, the headline and small article: *Marchioness tells bishops: 'Sell your rings and help the sick.'*

The *Daily Express*, on June 7, 2004, had cited Lady Sarah at a reception for the Leeds Muscular Dystrophy fund, which she chaired, as saying: "We don't see exemplarity from our churches: If our bishops were to sell their precious rings and golden staffs, we could raise another 400,000 pounds."

She rushed outside the entrance, grabbed her encrypted cell phone and rang Dulac: "There's a newspaper article on Lady Sarah you should see. I'll email it this afternoon."

CHAPTER 20

The three prelates had widely diverse backgrounds. Cardinal Eugenio Volpe, the aristocrat, descendant of the last Duke of Ferrara, claimed lineage to Lorenzo di Medici. He had the acumen, sense of organization and all- grasping intellect of a corporate CEO, and he applied his skills to the multitude of tasks assigned to him by the Holy See. He had chaired various synods, the Banco Ambrosiano Fraud Investigation, and some of the sex scandal investigations into the American Church.

He was tough, ambitious, and played the Vatican political chess game to the hilt. He chose his allies carefully, strategically. Once publicly called a snob, he had replied cuttingly that, quite to the contrary, he *was* nobility, and explained to his uneducated detractor that, according to some interpretations, 'snob' was a contraction of *Sine Nobilitas*, the Latin expression for 'without nobility'. This was inscribed on a plaque hung from those dormitories at Oxford, reserved for the sons of commoners. He had recently been named Secretary of State. Now, he felt history could give him a push: Secretaries of State often became popes.

Legnano was the son of a modest Tuscan wine grower. The Holy Father had, on many occasions, recourse to his earthy common sense, deep moral values and unwavering rectitude. He was oblivious to Vatican politics, and considered his nomination as cardinal to be extraordinary and unmerited. He had left his Archdiocese at Lucca with sadness and regret, to answer the call of duty, the call of the Holy Father. He missed the daily contact with his parishioners, the rolling hills of his beloved Tuscany, its soft-dry climate and fresh air. Whenever his schedule allowed, he returned to the family house near Capannori, and alongside his brothers, put his hand to tending and nursing the precarious, parsimonious vines.

Fiore was the youngish upstart. Possessed of a quick intelligence coupled with thinly disguised ambition, he carried a significant chip on his shoulders. He had hardly known his father, an alcoholic who died when Paolo was thirteen, leaving him rudderless until his uncle, the parish priest, had taken an interest in his education. Young Paolo had seen in the Church first a refuge, then an opportunity, to develop his ambitions and to escape at all costs the anonymity, boredom and absurdity of his small village. His slight limp, the result of an unattended and badly-mended broken ankle at age nine, had curtailed his sporting activities and made him further resent his father for abandoning him. Fiore's limp had degenerated and affected his back, earning him the cruelty of his playmates, who nicknamed him 'Quasi,' short for Quasimodo. It had left him with a deep psychological scar, disproportionate to the physical impediment.

He had shifted his efforts into the scholastic arena, graduating *summa cum laude* from his classical college and majoring in theology and history. His stay at the Jesuit seminary in Rome had been punctuated by the occasional prank: Wrongly accused of stealing croissants from the kitchen pantry, he had injected castor oil in the remaining batch and caught the villain the next evening, moaning in pain in the lavatory.

His rapid rise within the Church hierarchy had rendered many an older colleague envious, waiting for an eventual faux pas to bring Fiore down from his evertowering perch. He had found in Cardinal Volpe, though, a willing mentor.

CHAPTER 21

Kurganski knew the rules of the game, but couldn't believe he was already in it. For Victor not to return his three phone calls meant only one thing: Hunter had become prey, the assassin the victim, the wolf the lamb, being readied for the slaughter. He had played a deadly game of tag, and now he was 'It'.

He had to move fast, as Victor had probably already sent his contractor to do the job.

He knew that, as of today, he had no friends and many possible Judases. He could trust no one. Returning that night, he checked once more the talcum powder on the door handle of his two-room flat. Still unsmudged; he could enter. He packed quickly, his mind already racing ahead along the preplanned route of his lonely, desperate escape. He would become invisible, without habits, without fixed domicile, until the heat wore off.

He had money: 63,000 US dollars in Russia could sustain one for a very long time, if one lived long enough to enjoy it.

He secured the AK-47 on its bipod, rigged the trigger to a wire connected to the door, pointed it at the entrance, and locked the door. Throwing the brown suitcase to the ground, he climbed out the kitchen window.

CHAPTER 22

Dulac read Karen's message that night, weary and uncomfortable in the depressing, dark yellow room of his Moscow hotel. He whistled, after pumping the last bluish puffs from his Gitane. The article mentioned 'exemplarity'. So did the Pistis Sophia letter. *Coincidence? Unfortunate choice of words? Or pattern? Not much to go on,* he thought, *but it's a start.*

He clicked on Lescop's report on the birth certificates of thirteen bishops whose names included the Evangelists John and Matthew. Seven had participated in various committees with Salvador and Conti. Legnano had headed the Liturgical Review Committee, and the dead bishops had also been members of the Vatican Financial Investment Committee, headed by Fiore. *Odd: Why didn't he mention it at the meeting?* Dulac was being pelted by emails from the French Ministry of Justice and the Ministry of Interior. What progress had been made in the investigation? Suspects? He had leaked the identity of the Russians to the press, hoping to quench the public and political thirst for blood. Not enough. Now, inferences and innuendos were beginning to surface: Was he the right man for the job? Public opinion wanted quick, complete retribution. He guessed that the Vatican had also contacted his boss, the General Secretary.

CHAPTER 23

Late dusk painted the low meringue-like clouds a bluish orange, as the light evening rain moistened the cobblestone streets. Below them, a man in a black coat advanced, following Olga Ledova at a discreet distance, as she stepped out from the subway station and started her long walk toward Lubyanka Square and the prison.

He knew she had chosen the 10 p.m. to 3 a.m. shift to allow her to do other cleaning jobs during the day: Her four girls ate her out of every ruble, every month. As she approached the east entrance, the man quickened his pace and suddenly was upon her. He grabbed her hair from behind and with one swift, well-aimed stab, plunged the stiletto into the carotid. The second jab went through her heart. She fell without a sound, her lifeless form sprawling over her large handbag. He moved swiftly, dragging the body away from the entrance light to the wall alongside. He turned her on her back, pulled her right thumb, tightly, and severed it at the palm joint. As the blood drained, he pulled a small, heated thermal gel pack from his left pocket. He inserted the thumb. The digital thermometer read: *97.5 Fahrenheit.* He dropped the stiletto beside the body, rummaged through her handbag, found the key to the side entrance and entered.

* * *

Oleyev had heard about Vasiliev's capture through his sources inside FSB. He knew he was being tortured and would eventually crack. He couldn't let that happen. He didn't know where in the huge prison Vasiliev was being held.

Oleyev's helicopter had been equipped with the latest Thermionics heat-image sensing equipment from the military, used for tracking Taliban rebels in their mountain hideouts. The infrared laser could pick up and position a rat two feet underground. As he flew over Lubyanka, his electronics engineer had no difficulty picking out and locating Vasiliev's thermal image, as he was the only overnight visitor. Oleyev transmitted Vasiliev's GPS longitude-latitude coordinates to the hit man.

He had to move fast, as the gel pack would keep the thumb warm enough to work the two imprint-activated gates for only thirteen minutes. He took the thumb out of the pack and pressed it against the thermal imprinter of the first gate. The gate opened. He pressed the stopwatch function of the GPS. To his left, he saw the metal detector and took a deep breath as he strode quickly past. Silence: The boron shield on his GPS had deflected the intrusive x-rays. He pressed the soft gray thumb again, and the second gate opened. He set Vasiliev's GPS coordinates and the small electronic map indicated the path to his cell.

The hit man was now running along the endless corridor, looking for the staircase to the third floor. At last, the staircase appeared: *Four minutes gone, it's going to be close.* He ran up the staircase two steps at a time, arriving at the third-floor landing. He stopped to gasp for breath and take a GPS reading: He was nearly there. He sprinted down the corridor. Faraway, he could see the side rays of dim light along the metal-gray barred cells. He slowed, looked at his watch: *Seven minutes, nineteen seconds gone.*

Before drawing alongside the cell, the hit man pulled out a ten-inch gray tube from his right pocket and removed the protective caps.

Vasiliev heard a rustling, looked up from his book, and saw a tall, bald man in a long black coat, with hands outstretched, aiming a small object at his face. He heard a *phtuu!* felt a sharp pain in his neck, and the bald man was gone.

The hit man was running hard, jumping three steps at a time down the staircase, back along the corridor, throwing away his dart gun and overcoat to ease his stride. Sweating, slowing, he took the thumb from the gel pack and pressed it on the second gate actuator. The gate opened as he saw the pack's thermometer: *97.2 Fahrenheit*. Running again down the hall, he almost dropped the pack, then looked at his watch: *Eleven minutes*. As he slowed to pass the metal detector, suddenly the alarm sounded. *Damn*, he thought, as he fought off a surge of panic. He looked at his GPS: The boron shield had fallen off.

He ran to the last imprinter, pressed the thumb. Nothing! The gate didn't move!

He was trapped. Bells were ringing; the night guards would soon be on top of him, and here he was, like a rat in a cage, weaponless, ready for the picking. *Mothering fuck!* He tried the thumb again: Nothing. *The metal detector: It's locked the gates.*

Then he looked at the thermometer: *97 degrees even the thumb isn't warm enough! It can't activate the gates.* Between the intermittent ringing of the bells, he heard the sound of metal-clad army boots, echoing on the granite corridors. *How do I get the goddamn thumb warm?* Then, as he asked, a faraway thought slipped into his consciousness. How did children keep their thumbs warm? There was only one way to find out if the gate still worked. With a shudder, he put the thumb in his mouth, under his tongue, and waited.

The clanging of the boots was getting louder. The hit man waited a few more agonizing seconds, pulled out the thumb and pressed it on the gate's imprinter. The gate opened.

As he ran down the last corridor, one of the night guards crashed into him from a side aisle, and both men fell. A swift twist of the guard's neck, and the man went limp. The hit man continued his race, and the side door appeared. He crashed into the bar latch, and the door opened onto the drenched street.

He was free.

* * *

Vasiliev felt his body slowly, tightly shrinking around him.

He had difficulty breathing, as the toxin quickly spread throughout his autonomous nervous system, destroying it methodically, inescapably. He started to fall. He grabbed the edge of the sink and the tube of toothpaste. On his hands and knees, he could breathe easier. Then the toxin seized his brain in a horrid, vise-like grip. He screamed in pain. As he felt life leave him, he thought of his childhood, his always smiling mother, his intolerable wife, his little daughter . . . and finally, the happiness that could have been. In a last effort, he unscrewed the tube's cap and painfully wrote on the cement: *Nicola*.

* * *

The next morning, the phone's persistent ring dragged Petrov from his usual, comalike sleep.

That piece of shit recorder. It didn't catch again.

"It's Dimitri," said the meek voice.

"What the hell is it?"

"I have bad news: Vasiliev is dead. So are the night guard and the cleaning lady."

"I'll be over in ten minutes. You'd better have answers."

Twenty minutes later, Petrov, livid, summoned the night adjutant and the guards to his office.

"Explain, now."

"He used the cleaning lady's thumb."

Petrov walked briskly to the prison cell, looked at Vasiliev's sprawled body, still clutching the tube.

"Get me Dulac."

* * *

"Dulac."

"It's Sergei Petrov. They killed Vasiliev."

Dulac sat down on the bed, speechless. After a moment: "We were so close."

"That's what the mafia thought. He wrote his daughter's name, Nicola."

After a perfunctory breakfast, Dulac hailed a taxi. "Lubyanka prison," he growled.

In Petrov's office, the guilt and embarrassment weighed in pregnant silence. *How could this happen in the toughest, highest-security prison in Russia?* thought Dulac.

"We're trying to locate Nicola," said Petrov.

An officer interrupted: "We found her: She lives at thirty-five Podvony. She is there, now."

Dulac and Petrov piled into the chauffeured Zil and roared off, lights flashing, into Moscow's midmorning traffic.

* * *

"Good morning. I am Petrov, FSB, and this is Inspector Dulac, Interpol."

"I have been expecting you," replied the young, frail-looking woman standing in the doorway, staring at Dulac with tired, sad eyes.

Petrov and Dulac looked at each other quizzically.

"How is that?" exclaimed Dulac.

"Your being here means my father is dead."

* * *

Vasiliev had had a premonitory dream. He'd seen himself high above the earth, circling effortlessly over his broken body, over which prayed his dutiful daughter, dressed in the expensive dark blue dress she had always wanted, but which he could never afford to buy her. She had blown him a kiss before closing the lid of his modest, walnut brown coffin. He thought the room resembled the inside of a vault. He had a friend at FSB, an ex-soldier also from Irkutsk. He had carried Vasiliev's letter to Nicola.

Dear Nicola,

I am a prisoner of the FSB, and have no time left. I have many regrets, mainly not seeing you grow up, or making you proud of me. Life has not dealt me the good cards. I have no time, and so much to say. Maybe in the next world. Take the key. It opens a safety deposit box at the Vinogourov Bank, account 3805. 50,000 dollars are yours. Here is my authorization for the bank. The letter names the person who hired me, who will kill me. I know too much. The FSB wants him. Don't give them the name, except if they give you pension of 20,000 dollars. When you get the money, leave Moscow or they'll steal it back.

Goodbye. I love you,
Sergei.

Nicola felt no sorrow, no anger, but perhaps a touch of pity.

She had long ago learned that any feelings of anger or resentment toward her father only limited her, sapped her energies and dispersed her focus. She couldn't afford the waste. She needed every ounce to work herself through medical school.

Dulac spoke. "Mademoiselle, please accept our sympathies. Yes, your father is dead. If it's any consolation, his last thoughts were of you. Before dying, he wrote your name in his cell. We're here because we think you can help us identify his killers."

"As far as I'm concerned, my father has been dead for years. I buried him a long time ago."

"Perhaps," said Dulac, "but his killers have committed other murders. They will kill again."

"Sorry, I can't help," she said, crossing her arms in distrust. She shrugged in feigned ignorance, a bit too obviously for Dulac.

Petrov said, "I remind you of your duty as a Russian citizen, to cooperate and not withhold any information."

"Ha," she answered.

Dulac added, "If you know anything about these men, your life is in danger. They play for keeps."

"Gentlemen, unless there's anything else?" She walked toward the door and opened it.

As they left, Dulac turned to Petrov, who anticipated his comment: "I'll have her followed."

CHAPTER 24

Upon his return to Paris that night, Dulac had found a phone message from the Minister of the Interior's secretary, ordering him to meet the Minister the following morning. Dulac had barely slept. A summoning by the Minister of the Interior was unheard of, as it bypassed the General Secretary, his immediate boss. He didn't foresee it being the most enjoyable of experiences. A reprimand at best.

"Good morning, Dulac," said the short, lean man with a rubbery face, its jowls slackened by too many obsequious, politically perfect smiles.

"Good morning, Monsieur le Ministre."

"I will be blunt: The Élysée is not at all pleased with the archbishops' file."

The Minister cast a copy of *Le Monde* across his desk.

"Here, read at page five."

Salvador, Conti murders: Chief of Interpol still grasping for straws.

Dulac countered: "That's incorrect. We were—"

"I don't give a damn if it's correct or incorrect," interrupted the Minister, "it's the perception that counts. Need I remind you that we're in an election year, with the polls only four months away? Public opinion is fueled by the press. Go convince some reporters of your progress, if you have any. I'm giving you fair warning, Dulac. Unless you get results, tangible results within the next two weeks, there will be changes. Do I make myself clear?"

"Very."

"Bonne chance."

Dulac sat for a moment and hesitated. Both men knew that the Minister's comment was in direct breach of Interpol's Charter, which insured freedom from political interference. *So much for that theory, thought Dulac.* To bring it up now would hasten the end of his involvement in the case. It was his word against the word of a minister. The Minister rose from his desk, and Dulac knew they wouldn't meet again unless he came up with some dramatic piece of new evidence.

* * *

Karen's phone rang.

"Dulac."

"Yes?"

"The mafia killed Vasiliev."

"Wow! Serious people."

"Anything else on the Marchioness?"

"No, not really."

"How about lunch tomorrow, say noonish?"

"My schedule is a bit tight, but I could manage half an hour."

"Perfect. See you at *L'Express* at noon."

Karen put down the receiver. She welcomed the opportunity of seeing this man alone, after the uncomfortable breakfast at Isola Rossa. As she hung up, Karen felt a tingling, pleasurable sense of anticipation.

She had had time to think of her life and the recent turn of events. She caught herself enjoying the challenge of this new life-and-death game, and felt awakened, alive, as she hadn't felt in a long time.

As they sat down for lunch at *L' Express*, Karen felt drawn to the slightly silvering temples, the high forehead, the gray-blue eyes, aquiline nose ... and yes, those slender, elegant, aristocratic hands. She finally admitted to herself that she had a hand obsession, and that one of the first physical traits she looked at in a person was the hand and its gestures. Too thin: Boring intellectual. Too thick: The lineage of hard physical work was usually not far upstream the genealogical river — probably the son or daughter of farmers or machinists. She was willing to give the person a chance, but awaited, predictably, the first sign of ill-breeding or vulgarity.

She was rarely mistaken: *Next*. Hands were a sign of character, or the lack of it. A soft, fingers-only handshake, horror of horrors, indicated a noncommittal, insincere, even dangerous person. A firm, generous, trustworthy handshake was always welcome. Karen had few close friends, whom she cherished intimately. They had good hands.

As Dulac sat down, she sensed a certain vulnerability she had not witnessed in him before; the condescension had come down one keynote. As the waiter left with their order, Dulac turned to Karen, his gaze intent, hands clasped, his elbows on the table supporting his hunched shoulders.

"I need your help. I want you to go back to Isola Rossa."

"What?" Karen was incredulous.

"Without me."

"If this is your idea of a joke, it's in bad, bad taste."

"I'm not joking."

"Why on earth should I?"

"I will put the cards on the table, as they say."

"Please do."

"I think that you and the Marchioness ... well, how shall I say, got along quite well."

"That's none of your bloody business." Her face reddened and her body stiffened at the intrusion.

"But it is, you see; any connection with these murders is my business. The Marchioness will definitely refuse to see me. She will, how you say, clam up."

"But I'm a mythologist, not an investigator."

"Yes, I know, but you could do some research in her library, no?"

"Wouldn't that be a little obvious?"

"I'm sure you can be quite persuasive."

"Why should I get involved in this?"

"Try conscience, thirst for justice, civic duty. Frankly, on that front, you're my only hope. I'm trying to tie up loose ends. Of course, we would send an agent down with you."

"How considerate of you. Very comforting. Pray tell: What the hell would I be looking for?"

"I think the Marchioness knows a lot more about this Pistis Sofia letter than she's letting on."

"What makes you say that?"

"We've spoken to the engraver, Mittenwald. He says he never saw the letter. He mentioned that the Marchioness's private stationery was handcrafted elsewhere. We think the Pistis Sofia letter comes from the illuminator that does the Marchioness's personal stationery."

"I see."

"Yes, but to prove she ordered its writing is another matter. I must also be honest with you. You are talking to a man close to losing his job."

"Really?"

"I was summoned by the Minister of the Interior yesterday and the message is clear: Without news, I will be sacked. It's become highly political."

"If you sensed something, as you suggest, between Lady Sarah and me, how can you think I'll be objective?"

"That's a chance I'll take, if you will."

"Great. You *are* in dire straits."

"We have another lead: Vasiliev's daughter, Nicola. We think she was contacted by her father before his death. Petrov's people are following her."

"I have to think about this."

"I understand. Oh, while you were looking through the newspaper articles on Lady Sarah, you probably missed this one." Dulac handed her a copy of an old clipping of the *Mirror*, page seven. It read:

Marchioness's illegitimate son drowns mysteriously off her yacht. Autopsy report: no foul play.

CHAPTER 25

Nicola couldn't control herself any longer. She flung the plate at the kitchen wall, shattering it into cheap, tiny fragments. Even in death, Sergei was interfering with her life, the life she was so painfully trying to build for herself. Her eyes moistened at the recollection of the few happy memories of her early childhood years, and she dug out from her trunk the one and only picture of her father, embracing her in his bearlike hug.

She thought she could ignore the letter, but 50,000 dollars was an absolute fortune. She could quit work and devote herself full-time to her last two years of medical school; it could even carry her into postgrad programs, perhaps a doctorate. Never in her most utopian dreams had she contemplated the possibility. It was now at her doorstep.

But she knew the FSB would be tailing her. She had to find a way to get at the safety deposit box without being followed.

"Think, Nicola, think," she said aloud.

Suddenly, Dulac's warning cast a dark shadow over the gleeful anticipation of becoming rich. *What if he's right? What if the mafia somehow knows of Sergei's letter? Can I trust someone to get the money? Anton?* The mafia wouldn't tolerate her knowledge, or anybody else's, of her father's killer. They might think she knew his identity already. *Damn you, Sergei! How could you put me in this predicament?* She cried until, dead tired, she fell asleep.

* * *

Dulac summoned Petrov to meet him in Paris, the following Monday. Surely, he thought, even the necessary *complaisance* between the FSB and the mafia had been breached by the boldness of the killings. This was Petrov's territory, and they had violated it.

"We must exchange all information," said Dulac. "It's the only way we can get them." His motive, he realized, was now a little more self-serving.

"Yes," said Petrov. "I will meet you in Paris."

Dulac showed the same professional courtesy toward Petrov and picked him up at Charles de Gaulle airport, in the chauffeured Peugeot limo. For Petrov, the Paris smog brought an unwelcome change from Moscow's crisp air.

"Let's go over what we have," said Dulac, once in his office. He pulled out a pack of Gitanes and offered one to Petrov. "Our lead witness, presumably one of the assassins, has been killed. We think it's the mafia."

"We are sure," interjected Petrov. "In Russia, only the mafia has the means and people to do this."

"We have evidence, or someone wants us to believe, that Pistis Sofia is linked to the murders. The Vatican has received an extortion letter from the sect, or from someone who wants us to believe they sent it."

"You have suspect?" said Petrov.

"The Marchioness of Dorset."

The right corner of Petrov's mouth twitched slightly.

"The letter is asking for the sale of four of the Vatican's paintings, with the proceeds going to the poor in Africa. It can be inferred that if the Vatican refuses, other archbishops will die. It comes directly from the Marchioness's private stationery. We are trying to trace the illuminator. And you, any leads on Kurganski?"

"Disappeared," said Petrov. "He set up his AK-47 before leaving his apartment, to kill the contract killer sent by the mafia. He ended up wounding the landlord's son."

"How long can he hide?"

"Months, if he has money and makes no mistakes. Also, he may be dead."

"What about Nicola?"

"She has her routine: Classes at the University, waitress at night, study at her apartment, movies with her boyfriend Anton. Are you questioning the Marchioness?"

"Not yet. If I try to bring her in, my boss will have me crucified — sorry, fired. Besides, there are jurisdiction problems."

"*Da*," said Petrov. "But tell me, Dulac, why would the Marchioness have the archbishops killed?"

"That's my problem: Motive. She's reprimanded the Church in the past for being stingy, but murder? Doubtful, unless the sect is using her. I asked for transcripts of the recent synod meetings in which Salvador and Conti participated. They may reveal something. Karen Dawson has a theory linking the names of the four Evangelists to the names of the dead bishops. The pattern has obviously been concocted on an *A posteriori* basis, as Immanuel Kant would say, but it may be followed out completely by the killers."

"What do you mean?" said Petrov, visibly out of his depth.

"Two of the Evangelists' names happen to fit the names of these dead archbishops, who share some life-threatening secret. There may be other archbishops involved, whose names match the other two Evangelists. Read this." Dulac thrust Salvador's letter to Conti into Petrov's hand.

Petrov read the letter and frowned: "Doesn't say much."

"On the contrary, it says a lot. Any idea who hired Vasiliev and Kurganski?"

"We are putting pressure on our contacts inside. These names come up: Casimir Dobkin. He deals in porno movies and prostitution; we try to crack a nationwide ring. Victor Oleyev, some oil money; we don't know where he gets the rest. Peter Nigensko is in real estate. His enemies disappear. Victor Olekseivitch is an oligarch. He has big amounts of shares in Russian businesses. He threatens poor citizens, and they give him their shares. These hoodlums play the big game. Only they have the 'ball', how you say, to break into Lubyanka."

Dulac was gaining trust in Petrov. He felt he had to tell him.

"Petrov, my time is running short. Find out who hired those two assassins. Working up the ladder is easier than down."

"You have problem?"

"The Vatican is putting pressure on the French Minister of the Interior. Unless I have a name by next week, you'll be talking to someone else from Interpol."

"A week? That's not much time in Russia, my friend." Petrov looked at his watch and rose to leave. "I will see what I can do."

CHAPTER 26

Karen mused over Dulac's request that she return to Isola Rossa. Did he know something about her that she didn't? Why didn't he think her 'fling,' which she now realized was quite apparent, would hinder her investigative skills? Or was he so desperate that he was willing to take that chance?

That seemed more likely. *I'll be taking all the risks.* Yet the challenge taunted her. Deliberate of him, she thought, to let her find out about her emotions *vis-à-vis* the Marchioness. Why had she felt so guilty the following morning? She realized her work had masked her need for sexual gratification and emotional fulfillment for too long. Now she needed to find out where those energies would flourish.

Later, Karen decided to call Lady Sarah.

"Hello, this is Karen Dawson."

"Well, hello, how are you?" The voice was intimate, inviting.

"Fine, thank you. I was wondering if I might impose on you: I've been doing some research on animal mythology in Gnostic traditions and couldn't think of a better source than your library. I would like to spend some time there. Would that be possible?"

"Of course, my dear, I happen to be leaving Tuesday for Isola. You can join me."

Karen cringed at the 'my dear,' but persevered: "Actually, I was thinking of going down next Thursday. The timing would be better for me."

"Wonderful. Will you attend the session?"

"Perhaps."

"Splendid. I can make the travel arrangements for you. It's easier . . ."

"No, no, please don't bother. I've already contacted my agent. She's made the reservations." As she spoke, Karen realized the transparency of the lie: Before phoning, she couldn't have known if the Marchioness would accept her request.

"Look forward to seeing you, then."

"Yes, goodbye."

Karen congratulated herself on how matter of fact she had been: Meeting the Marchioness in person, of course, would be quite different. She laughed at herself: *Is this some kind of test, self-exam of my sexual orientation?* Karen surprised herself with the elated feeling of her transformation: Where was the subdued, peaceful life of academia? The comfortable shelter of the classroom? She felt mixed feelings of fear and liberation, as if breaking out of a cocoon and discovering the world wasn't made of soft silk. *Why not call the whole thing off? She owed Dulac, or anybody else for that matter, nothing.*

Yet, deep down, she knew she had to continue: To stop now meant losing the opportunity of finding out, not who she was, but perhaps who she would become.

* * *

Dulac's thoughts raced throughout the night, and kept him in a superficial sleep: What was the nature of Conti's and Salvador's secret? What was so important that it had cost them their lives? Had they 'defended their faith with their very blood,' as Cardinals were summoned to do by the Pope upon their nomination? Surely a bit archaic, as a notion, he thought. Saints were a rare commodity, these days.

The coincidence of the names was disturbing. Then another idea occurred: Could the Marchioness be using this demonic opportunity to further some hidden philanthropic aims? If so, she was on the closest side of extortion he had ever witnessed. She was playing with fire.

Yet there was something more sinister, spectacular in the way these archbishops had been murdered. The assassins had not gone through the trouble of organizing crucifixions unless they proclaimed a message, either to the victims, who had, as the postmortems showed, witnessed their own horrific deaths, or to a greater audience. The plaques suggested a hidden warning. If he didn't decipher them soon, other bishops could die.

Not unimportantly, he'd also be out of a job.

Was Petrov faking his humiliation by the mafia? Was he corrupt? He showed no outward signs of corruption, but Dulac would never fully understand the Russian mind.

Amid his confused thoughts, Karen entered his semi-consciousness. The strong attraction he felt was sublimated by his professional requirements of her. Could he reasonably expect her to go to Isola Rossa? Even with an Interpol agent by her side, the danger wasn't negligible. The consequences of things going wrong were unthinkable.

* * *

That morning, Karen phoned Dulac: "I've decided to go to Isola Rossa."

"Actually, I was hoping you wouldn't accept. Are you sure you can handle this?"

"Yes, quite sure. Besides, I'm genuinely interested in knowing more about Pistis Sofia."

"When would you leave?"

"Thursday morning, on the Bahamas Air 7.30 a.m. flight to Mustique. After that, it's a twenty-minute boat ride to Isola."

"Karen, I'm having second thoughts about sending you. If the Marchioness is somehow connected to this, I don't think you should be there, even with our agent. Whoever is behind this plays for keeps."

"I realize that. I thought you said I could help."

"I'm sure you will. I'm worried about the price."

"I'll take that chance. Besides, I think you're wrong concerning the Marchioness."

"A distinct possibility. Before you go, drop over to my office, and I'll introduce you to our agent."

CHAPTER 27

Nicola kept her father's power of attorney on her at all times, thinking the FSB would probably search her apartment. She was right. Petrov's men had found nothing.

She decided that if the mafia knew of the existence of the letters, they would have dispensed with the niceties of waiting for her to open the safety deposit box, and that she would already be dead. At least Sergei had correctly judged the loyalty of his messenger.

The thermometer outside her kitchen window read two degrees Centigrade, as she donned her well-cut burgundy overcoat, the only luxury she possessed. She locked the front door, and again she noticed the new car parked at the end of the street, out of place amongst the older, beat-up sedans of her fellow students: *FSB*.

Waiting for the bus, she tried to hide her nervousness by opening one of her textbooks and reading her morning's lecture out loud. As she got on the bus, the car pulled out slowly and followed at an indiscreet distance.

Nicola alighted from the bus and walked nonchalantly toward the Kazerowsky Bank's large, columned entrance. Through the glass doors she could see the early-hour clients, already fighting for position in the rapidly forming queues. Nicola strolled past and went directly to the business counter.

"Yes?" inquired a young clerk with cropped, red hair.

"I want to open an account and a safety deposit box."

"Do you have an appointment?"

"Yes, my name is Nicola Vasilieva."

The clerk went behind to his desk and spoke with his colleague, a dour-faced matron.

As he returned, he took out a file holder and pen, and pushed them toward her.

"Fill in this questionnaire. Do you have identification papers?"

"Yes, here."

Twenty minutes later, Nicola entered the vault area and unlocked the safety deposit box, into which she inserted an envelope.

Alone in the bank vault, she took out her old brown overcoat from her student satchel, along with a gray hat and a pair of dark-rimmed glasses. She stuffed her red overcoat into the bag and left the bank vault, catching sight of the FSB man questioning the clerk. She walked hurriedly down the stairs, trying not to run, and hailed a taxi.

The FSB man was pressing the clerk: "I want access to that girl's safety deposit box."

"We cannot give you access without written authority."

The FSB man called Petrov.

"Nicola opened a safety deposit box. The bank people won't give us access."

"Where is she?"

"In the vault. We're waiting for her to leave."

"Get me the manager."

"Saminsky here."

"This is Petrov, FSB. Let my men into the vault. *Now*."

The manager hesitated, as the second FSB man accosted him. Then: "All right, but you must sign an inquiry form."

"Yes, yes. Later."

Petrov slammed down the receiver.

* * *

"To the Vinogourov Bank," said Nicola to the taxi driver, forcing herself not to look back in the rearview window. *Step one complete, two more to go.* As she approached the bank, fear again struck at her heart. *What if Petrov has had all banks searched for Sergei's accounts? What if this bank has violated its code of secrecy, under pressure from the FSB? Calm down, Nicola. Russia's bureaucracy is on your side; it will take weeks for the FSB to gain access to Vasiliev's accounts.*

Determined, she walked to the desk and showed her key and identification papers to the clerk.

"Yes?"

"Please give me access to box 3805. Here is my father's authorization, and here are my papers. Here is the key."

Again, after what was seemingly an eternity, the clerk came back and said, "Come this way, please."

Nicola could hardly contain herself. If Sergei hadn't lied, she was about to become very, very rich.

* * *

Petrov's men found the vault empty, a blank envelope in Nicola's safety deposit box adding insult to injury. They had just violated a recently enacted bank secrecy decree Putin had put in place, as a reaction to the Doumas's outcry toward his endlessly growing administrative powers. *To top it off, they'd lost the girl.*

Petrov was furious. The screw up would cost them a month's salary. He was back where he started, a step behind an infuriatingly smart young woman who had inherited the wrong father.

* * *

Nicola opened the deposit box, her palms sweating, her knees trembling, like a child opening a huge Christmas gift. Sergei hadn't lied. It was there, in small packets of hundred-dollar bills. She counted furiously, her heart racing, stuffing the money into her satchel. She opened the letter, handwritten in a tense scrawl:

Kurganski and I contracted to kill Salvador and Conti.
Victor Oleyev, five Negerov St. Rublyovka district, gave me
the instructions and paid me.
Sergei Vasiliev.

She froze, her heart sinking: *It was blood money.*

She tried to rationalize: Maybe this money wasn't related to the crimes. Maybe a leftover of Sergei's army salary, or pension — ha! A Russian general didn't save 50,000 dollars in a lifetime, let alone a simple soldier, she thought. She remembered her father's admonition: *Get out of Moscow.* She was sure Petrov and his men had found the empty envelope by now, and were all over her apartment again, waiting.

Stuffing the remainder of the money and the letter in her satchel, she locked the box and walked out, burdened by a heavy, coveted treasure, and a heavy, unwanted secret.

CHAPTER 28

Volpe had mixed feelings about Fiore. He admired his boundless energy and quick mind, but had started to notice that Fiore would try to avoid committing himself, unless he was assured of recognition and praise from his colleagues. He rarely took a position on controversial issues. Volpe caught himself wondering if Fiore, in fact, had deep convictions at all. Certainly, he hadn't acquired such a high office so quickly without having shown convictions to those who had appointed him. Or was Volpe envious, seeing in this young man political skill it had taken him so long to develop? If Fiore was untrustworthy, Volpe had a problem. His mentorship toward Fiore came with a price tag.

He would eventually want to collect. The next Synod was an opportunity to cement the allegiances he needed to support his own highest aspiration. He counted on Fiore to gather undecided votes. There would be a cardinalship for Fiore if he succeeded. The Pope's failing health reminded Volpe that time was not on his side. He was barely seven years younger than the Holy Father, and his own health showed signs of fatigue. He sought comfort in the inviolable precept that only those who had paid their dues through time and suffering were considered *Papabile*.

Momentarily putting his aspirations aside, he thought: *Could the Church continue electing septuagenarians, if it wanted to keep the younger flock within its bosom?* Deep down, he feared the pressure of the younger priests clamoring for access to positions still now reserved for the 'administratively mature.' Fiore was an example emeritus of this new breed. Yet Volpe wasn't ready to accept defeat and turn to a support role: The young lions would wait their turn. As long as elderly cardinals formed the electorate, he was still the odds-on favorite.

CHAPTER 29

André Dessault had studied painting at *Les Beaux Arts* in Paris for six years. His efforts at making a living with his art had met with limited success, and, like most of his colleagues, he had been forced to seek other means of subsistence. Impatient and wanting to enjoy the good life, he had slipped into copying works of famous artists, selling his meticulous, uninspired work as reproductions. He suspected that some copies were being sold as originals, but he'd convinced himself it was not necessarily in his best interest to police the morals of the art dealers' world.

Introduced to the skill of calligraphy and illumination through a friend, he quickly developed a lucrative niche. A well-to-do clientele enjoyed his fine, detailed work and requested ornate, distinctive letterheads. More than he could produce. Each letterhead was slightly different from its predecessor, and would become a sought-after original.

The Marchioness of Dorset was such a client, ordering a hundred of these exquisite miniatures every year.

Dulac's men had staked out his apartment and small shop for a week, without success. Inquiries with neighbors had proven futile: Dessault had vanished.

* * *

Three days later, a *Mandat de Perquisition* in hand, Dulac's men descended onto Dessault's apartment. A musty smell pervaded the small, dark rooms. Dessault was a meticulous man, as all had been tidily put away. Having gone through his belongings and having found nothing, they moved on to his small shop at 348b, Avenue de Rouen.

Behind the glass counter, Dessault had set up three easels to exhibit his miniatures, allowing him to work on letterheads simultaneously. Dulac's men found two works in progress, unrelated to the Pistis Sophia letterhead. Dessault kept files on each of his clients, and Dulac's men rifled through the wood cabinets, looking for clues. Drafts and completed letterheads were in every client's file, except one: The Marchioness's file was empty. Taking samples of Dessault's work, Dulac's men sent them to the Lyon lab.

Even if the letters matched the Pistis Sofia letter, they had to find Dessault, preferably alive.

CHAPTER 30

Like eighty per cent of the male population of Russia, Kurganski loved to play chess. His schizophrenic father had nurtured the Russian dream of training and producing another Alekin, Spassky or Kasparov. He had committed suicide three days after Kurganski's tenth birthday.

Emotionally unstable since that fateful day, Kurganski suffered from a mild form of attention deficit disorder. His small talent had leveled off in his teens, and his inability to see more than five moves ahead had dashed any hopes of ever making a decent living at the game. Still, he had hustled many a classmate and fellow soldier into believing his opponent could easily be beaten, only to find out that after a few bets, Kurganski had a good chunk of the poor fellow's allowance or paycheck.

He thought of resuming his hustling within the streets of Moscow, which was redolent with impromptu chess games at many a street corner, but a close call — recognizing one of Oleyev's chess-playing men — had sent him running into the crowds of Saturday-shopping Muscovites. The mafia knew his weakness, and wouldn't hesitate to checkmate him on the spot. He would forego his plan of listless wandering in the flophouses of the city. With a contract on his life and

Oleyev's men on the hunt, he had to get out. He had to escape to the country and become untraceable through anonymity. He was playing the ultimate hustle, the chess game of his life, for his life.

* * *

Others were luckier in their search for anonymity. Nicola had found refuge with Petra, a girlfriend from her days at preparatory school. The small two-room apartment in the gray, dismal Sokol suburb of Moscow, assured bleak insignificance to everyone there. Nicola promised to leave within a week, as the meager household furnishings could hardly bear yet another occupant. She slept on the short couch, and didn't leave her satchel out of sight, except to quickly shower and use the bathroom. She hatched a plan: Petrov had left his calling card. That morning, she waited for Petra and her husband to leave for work and dialed the FSB number.

"Hello, can I speak to Inspector Petrov?"

"Who is calling?" inquired the dispirited, mechanical voice.

"Tell him it's Nicola Vasilieva. I'll call back in five minutes."

"One moment. I'll—"

You'll trace the call, shithead. She hung up.

* * *

"Petrov here."

"Nicola Vasilieva."

"Da?" He put his hand on the mouthpiece and signaled to the assistant.

"I know who killed Vasiliev."

She knew Petrov was tracing the call. She had to talk fast.

"Where are you?"

"It's not important. I'll call you back in thirty minutes." She hung up.

"Damn," exclaimed Petrov. *Nowhere near enough time.*

126

Nicola bundled up, grabbed her satchel and left the apartment. Hailing a taxi, she ordered: "Nevsky Restaurant, near the University."

In the phone booth, she dialed Petrov's number. She got through directly.

"Petrov."

"I have proof of my father's killer."

"How is that?"

"I have a handwritten letter from my father."

"Why don't you come in? You are in big danger. You are a smart woman. The mafia will kill you for this."

"I'll take my chances. I need a Canadian visa, new passport, and acceptance to a Canadian medical school. You can get my records at Moscow University. I have 50,000 US dollars I will give you, and the letter. You will deposit 75,000 Canadian dollars in my aunt's bank account in Calgary: Reward money for giving you my father's killer. I want a new life, Petrov."

As the silence thickened, she pressed the receiver so hard to her ear that it hurt.

"Petrov, are you there?"

"Yes, yes. I'm listening."

"Good. I will call you back Thursday at 11 a.m."

"Will you testify in court?"

"Nyet. I won't commit suicide. The letter names my father's partner. He's your witness."

"Not much evidence, with only the letter."

"That's your problem, not mine."

"This is a lot of trouble for us, just to find out who killed your father."

"Oh, didn't I mention it? The man who hired Sergei to kill the archbishops?"

"Yes?"

"His name is right here."

Nicola hung up.

CHAPTER 31

Karen and Anna, the olive-skinned Brazilian-born Interpol agent, spoke briefly on the Bahamas Air flight to Mustique. Anna would be Karen's 'friend,' the Pistis Sophia recruit.

As the plane landed, Karen's mixed emotions resurfaced: *Can I control the situation? Too cool, and the Marchioness will be hostile. Too friendly, she'll be suspicious.* She had to strike a delicate balance, a tough act. Her 'friend' Anna was the buffer.

After a perfunctory stop at immigration, they boarded the water taxi to Isola Rossa, enjoying the sea breeze's caress and relief from the hot shore. Under the scant protection of the canvas top, Karen still felt the intense sun beating down on her bare arms and neck. The smell of half-burned diesel fuel mixed with the throaty thump-thump of the old motor, and a milky froth stirred behind the transom of the gray steel hull. Like embarrassed riders in an elevator, the passengers looked at each other, unable to speak over the din.

Twenty minutes later, the unmistakable silhouette of Château d'Or captured the simmering horizon, slowly defining itself against the luxuriant green foliage.

As the water taxi approached the large concrete dock, Karen recognized the pert silhouette of the hostess, wearing a flowing blue dress and an elegant straw hat: *A personal welcome wasn't required.* Sarah waved enthusiastically, forgoing nobility's usual restraint.

"Hello," said Karen, as she alighted. "Meet Anna Delgado. She's come to take the introduction course."

"Delighted," replied Sarah, as she instructed the chauffeur to load their suitcases into the Bentley. "Come, come."

She ushered Karen and Anna into the comfortable leather seats of the blue convertible. The short ride to the majestic splendor of Château d'Or reawakened Karen's appreciation of the architectural *chef d'oeuvre,* mixed with her growing discomfort with Sarah's already insistent gaze.

Karen noticed several large yachts docked on the far side of the concrete jetty. Evidently, some of the Marchioness' guests favored their own means of transport and lodging. One yacht drew her particular attention and sparked her curiosity: It was incongruous amongst the sleek, immaculately maintained white hulls of the mega-rich. Its high, roughly blue-painted steel topsides belonged on a working trawler. She read the large name in white on both sides of the bow: *Eastland.* Two huge, funnel-like tubes hung over the stern, like the forelegs of a gargantuan praying mantis. As Lady Sarah, Anna and she settled on the veranda chairs for cocktails, Karen couldn't contain her curiosity:

"What is that strange-looking vessel on your dock with the tubes on the back?"

"You mean the *Eastland?*" said Sarah.

"That's the one."

"It's a pet project of mine. I'm funding underwater research with the Maritime Museum of Rome. The *Eastland* is a hydrographic-archaeological vessel. Those tubes are giant water hoses that get rid of mud and sand around wrecks and their artifacts. It's working on two possible sites right now. It's all quite exciting."

"Have you found anything yet?" replied Karen.

"Nothing significant, but it looks promising. I'm told these digs take time," said Sarah.

"I'd love to see how it works," said Karen enthusiastically.

"Perhaps we can arrange it," replied Sarah mechanically. "It's not that interesting, unless you are into archaeological research. It's really just a big underwater water hose."

"I see," said Karen, feeling Sarah was trying to shut the door on the opportunity, contrary to her earlier enthusiasm.

Sarah turned to Anna. "How did you become interested in Pistis Sophia?"

"I'm dissatisfied with the teachings of the Catholic Church. I feel I've outgrown it. Actually, I'm trying to find a new meaning to religion. I've been reading Gnostic texts and find them fascinating. From what I've read, Pistis Sophia could be very fulfilling. That's what I'm here to find out."

Karen thought, *At least she's done her homework. Hopefully, the Marchioness won't probe.*

"Aren't we all? Dissatisfied, I mean," said Sarah, seemingly content with the reply and throwing an inquisitive glance at Karen.

* * *

The *portier* and Sarah escorted Karen and Anna to their adjoining rooms, as Karen marveled at the paintings adorning walls of the entrance hall and the main staircase. A Peter Brueghel the Elder winter scene caught her attention. Turning to Sarah, she asked:

"New acquisition?"

"Yes, as a matter of fact, I had my people pick it up at Sotheby's last week. Do you like it?"

Karen blushed slightly. "I love his winter scenes. They remind me of Vermont. I grew up near small lakes and rolling countryside."

"Dinner will be at seven in the main dining room," said Sarah. "I have some people I want you to meet."

* * *

Karen unpacked her two small suitcases and showered quickly. Wrapped in a soft blue dressing gown, she reclined in the plush sofa, careful not to wet the gilded silk brocade cover. She had noticed that the adjoining bedrooms were diagonally across the hall from a large room with ornate, massive wood doors. As they walked past, she caught a glimpse of two small sofas, lost in the vast décor. More ancestral portraits gave life to the high, dull walls. She had just finished dressing when the *portier* knocked apologetically and announced dinner. She walked down the staircase and turned toward the dining room and saw the already-assembled guests engaged in muted conversation.

The variety of ages surprised her. Women outnumbered men about two to one. Sarah introduced Karen and seated her between herself and a gaunt, bespectacled man, who introduced himself as Domenico, ex-Catholic priest.

"How did you hear about Pistis Sophia?" he queried.

"I'm a mythologist. I'll be studying in the library for a few days."

"Oh?" replied Domenico. "Then you are interested in the rites of the Tradition?"

"Mainly, yes."

"Are you Catholic?" Domenico pried, wasting no time getting to the mark.

Karen felt surprised at the intrusion. "Sometimes."

She looked away. *The subject was closed.*

After dinner, Lady Sarah welcomed all and introduced the next morning's speaker, a tall blonde woman in her mid-forties, who, apart from her Irish-setter-pointed head, looked Germanic.

"Mary Koeller will go over with you the historical origins of Pistis Sophia. After that, please feel free to enjoy the grounds and activities at Château d'Or. Monsieur L'Espérance will direct you to the appropriate instructors. Oh, yes, remember the service is at 5:30 p.m., at the amphitheater." Sarah started to leave. "Will you join me for a *digestif?*" she said, looking at Karen and Anna.

"Sure," answered Anna, and Karen felt obliged to follow.

The night breeze slowly cooled the terrace as the women settled into the lounge chairs, overlooking the moon's reflection on an ocean of silver.

After ordering her drink, Anna broke the growing silence: "Can you recommend some reading material for me tonight, for my course?" she asked Sarah.

"I think I have a copy of 'Pistis Sophia, Early Beginnings.' Let me ask the butler to fetch it."

"I'd like a copy also, if you have another," chimed in Karen.

"I'll see what I can do," answered Lady Sarah.

They sipped their drinks and the discomfort grew, the small talk clearly masking deeper issues, inappropriate to bring up. The butler brought one copy of the book and handed it to Lady Sarah. Seizing the occasion, Karen said:

"Actually, I'm feeling a bit tired. I think I'll turn in."

Anna took the book, and the threesome retired to their rooms.

Karen entered her bedroom and thought: *Do I lock the door? Clear message to anyone that I don't want to be disturbed. Maybe too clear. If I leave it unlocked, is it an invitation to enter?*

She locked the door. She felt her pulse quicken, her body adapting to its new surroundings, and she turned off the light. Later, she thought she could hear — *yes, definitely* — the sound of muffled footsteps and the rustling of silk approaching. Then, nothing. She tensed, sat upright, motionless: the door handle, almost imperceptibly, turned clockwise. She could almost feel the pressure on the reluctant door. She waited, breathless, as the pressure ebbed, and the door handle turned slowly back. The footsteps and rustling resumed, then faded.

She crumpled up her duvet pillow, turned onto her side and fell asleep.

CHAPTER 32

After breakfast, Karen walked briskly to the library, and started poring over the voluminous indexes of the world-renowned collection, cross-referenced and computerized.

At the side, a dust-free room, vaulted and with humidity control, protected the priceless manuscripts from the ravages of time: Nag Hammadi originals of the Gospel of Thomas, sheltered under bulletproof glass. Crisscrossing lasers warned any would-be intruders of the futility of any theft attempt. She marveled at the documents' state of preservation, which continued to endure through centuries due to the dryness of the desert and the monks' initial sealing of the Coptic jars.

She focused her research on the role of animals in Gnostic traditions: specifically, what was the meaning of the bull, lion, eagle and serpent in the Pistis Sophia tradition, and how had they become inscribed in its motif? Was there a link between the early developing Orthodox Catholic Church and its choice of these animals to symbolize the Evangelists, and the Pistis Sophia motif? Which had preceded the other?

As the bell rang for lunch, Karen saw the Marchioness about to sit down with the ex-priest again and joined them.

"Would it be possible for Anna and me to see the *Eastland*?" she asked.

"Yes, of course," said Lady Sarah. "Why don't we go down to the dock after lunch? I'm sure we can pry the captain away from his duties for a few moments."

* * *

"Welcome aboard," said Captain Kostas Stephanopoulos, a stout, mustachioed man with a sweaty complexion. He extended his grizzly hair-covered hand to each of the women, as they stepped off the gangplank onto the afterdeck of the *Eastland*.

"We start below," he said, as he led them across the afterdeck, through a watertight door down a steep ladder into the bowels of the rusted vessel, musty with the smell of diesel.

"Watch your step," he said, spotting the unseamanlike shoes of his visitors. "Don't catch heels in the grating."

The engine room was vast, impressive and complicated to the uneducated eyes of the women. Two huge 970 hp MAN diesels stood ominously silent, side-by-side, like hunched metal mammoths, ready to be unleashed at the captain's command.

"What's its top speed?" asked Karen, vying for safety in her questions.

"Thirty-five knots with the hydrofoils," answered the captain, as he pointed to large, boxlike indentures in each side of the hull.

Why does an archaeological vessel need so much speed?

"Motors and pumps for the hoses on the deck," said the captain, pointing to two cone-shaped pumps.

"How does it work?" asked Karen.

"Pumps mix air and water here and send into the hoses," answered Kostas, as if all this was self-evident. "We control hose ends with electric motors. Now, we go up to the bridge. Come, I show you," Kostas' voice becoming increasingly patronizing.

On the bridge, Karen was surprised at the simplicity of the controls. She had expected to see a vast array of screens, wheels, levers, similar to what she had witnessed as a child, on the bridge of her father's sports-fisherman yacht in Florida. Under the angled windows, only two screens, two long, curved levers, and two small stubby levers, occupied the otherwise-bare console.

"Where is the wheel?" risked Karen, feeling the question to be stupid but necessary.

"No more wheel," replied the captain triumphantly, as he fondled the rubber top of one of the small levers. "Joystick controls all moves. No more rudders. *Eastland* can turn itself," he said, as he described an unscrewing circular motion with his right hand.

"What are the other two levers?" asked Karen, reassured that her previous question had allowed the captain to explain the mysteries of his ship.

"For the pumps."

Karen noticed under one of the levers, the two small black labels: 'Pressure-Suction.'

"Why 'Suction'?" asked Karen.

The captain turned away, noticeably irritated: "To help flush the hoses," as he pointed out the second screen and the other lever. "These control hoses and underwater cameras."

"Come, ladies, let's let Captain Stephanopoulos get on with his work," said the Marchioness, getting restless and heading toward the lower deck staircase.

"Where are you looking next?" Karen asked the captain.

"Confidential," replied Stephanopoulos, a dry smile beaming across to the Marchioness under his graying mustache, showing spaced teeth yellowed by years of neglect and tobacco.

"I'll join you later, ladies," said Sarah, "I have to speak with the captain for a moment."

Karen and Anna glanced once more at the strange-looking funnels on the stern of the *Eastland* and made their way back up the road to the Château. As they walked, Anna turned to Karen: "We saw what they wanted us to see. I'd like to take a closer look."

"What do you mean?"

"What about late tonight?"

"You mean go aboard again?" asked Karen, incredulous.

"He didn't show us any of the storage areas."

"How would we get aboard?"

"By the stern platform, once the crew has left. What do you think?"

"I think it's called trespassing."

* * *

Later, at supper, Lady Sarah was absent. Rarely did she not chair, at the massive oak table, the four-course suppers in the company of her guests. The setting at the head of the table was still there, indicating this had been a last-minute change.

"How are the introductory courses going?" asked Karen of her neighbor.

A fair-haired young man, his face still unshaven, answered: "It's the most liberating experience I've ever had. Pistis Sophia is going to attract the Catholic youth of today. How can we Catholics go on droning and repeating that unbelievable Credo, drafted some 1700 years ago by a bunch of cowering bishops under the orders of a scheming tyrant? It's totally irrelevant. I just came back from the Pistis ceremony: Their Credo focuses on hope. I'm into hope, not dogma."

"What if you think of the Catholic Credo allegorically, instead of literally?" asked Karen.

"I guess that would help," replied the young man, "but we've been taught to take every word of the New Testament as historical fact. It would take a long, long time to rethink in allegorical terms. What about you?"

"I'm a mythologist," replied Karen, "so it's easier for me. But I agree that the Church has a credibility problem. Besides, even allegories — or myths, as we call them — need some connection with reality. Myths that don't have outlived their purpose. The Greeks developed new myths and discarded old ones. The Catholic Church doesn't want to understand that."

"I often wonder: Where will the Church recruit its faithful, in the future, I mean?" replied the young man.

"I guess from Africa and Latin America: The religious divide follows the economic divide, between North and South."

"Have you attended any sessions?"

"No, I've been busy working in the library."

At supper's end, Karen saw Anna rising to leave, eyeing her, then the hallway entrance. Karen got up.

"Maybe we can continue this conversation later?" asked the young man.

"Yes, some other time."

* * *

"We'll go down to the dock at eleven tonight," said Anna. "By that time, the crew should've left, and we can take a quiet look. I'll bring a flashlight. Don't forget to lock your door."

"I didn't think I had agreed to this insanity," said Karen. "Besides, even if I had, how would we get from our rooms to outside the Château without being seen?"

"The fire escape stairs in the back, next to the salon. Do you have soft soled shoes?"

"My tennis shoes."

"Wear them."

Karen thought, *If we get caught, all I have to do is outrun her.*

CHAPTER 33

"Dmitri, get Dulac on the phone, *now.*"

"*Da,* Inspector Petrov, right away."

"Dulac," answered the familiar French voice.

"Petrov here. I talked to Nicola Vasilieva: She says she has Vasiliev's confession. It names the contractor who ordered the job. She's carrying 50,000 dollars of Vasiliev's money."

"She's running around Moscow with 50,000 dollars in cash? Is she insane?"

"She probably doesn't trust the banks. She wants to make exchange: this for 75,000 Canadian dollars with a visa and acceptance to a Canadian medical school."

"Why the exchange for Canadian money?" said Dulac, thinking she was right not to trust the banks.

"She says it's dirty money."

"I see," replied Dulac. "Well, if it's any help, we've made such deals before."

"She wants an answer in three days."

"As they say in America: Go for it."

"You know the Canadian Ambassador in France, yes?"

Dulac was taken aback. *How could Petrov know this?* Through his father, Dulac had contacts in the diplomatic corps. Obviously, the FSB knew more than he thought.

"I'll contact him. Petrov, you must get that letter. If the mafia hears of this, she's as good as—"

"Don't worry, we won't make the mistake again," promised a solemn Petrov.

Dulac believed him: If he screwed up, Petrov would be lucky to be arresting drunks off the permafrosted streets of Irkutsk.

"We'll take care of the visa. You take care of the rest," said Dulac.

"What if she is lying?" said Petrov.

"You'll know before she gets on the plane."

"*Da*, you are right. Plenty of time to abort if she doesn't have the letter. I will tell Nicola we agree."

CHAPTER 34

At 10:45 p.m. Karen heard a soft rap on her door.

"Anna?"

"Yes. Ready?"

"Coming." Reluctantly, Karen put on her windbreaker. She left her nightgown on the chair and rolled back the cover on the bed. If anyone were to come in the room, her story was that she couldn't sleep, and went for an evening walk. She locked the door.

The two approached the sparsely lit cement dock, and Karen saw that only the small courtesy lights shone from the deck of the *Eastland*. They were in luck: The gangplank had been left in place, ready for boarding. The women crouched in silence behind a row of rhododendrons, on the other side of the road parallel to the jetty. Karen looked for any signs of activity on the *Eastland*.

"Here goes," whispered Anna, as she crossed the road and approached the gangplank, while Karen waited in the darkness.

Anna boarded, and a small lizard scampered by, touching Karen's leg. *"Oh!"* exclaimed Karen uncontrollably.

Anna froze. She waited for a reaction on the *Eastland*. Nothing.

Anna signaled Karen to board.

They crept cautiously across the aft deck, and Karen saw bundles of ropes, neatly coiled and pegged along the bulwark, their loops draped loosely onto the deck. She stepped carefully, to avoid tripping on the threatening snares. A strong scent of industry-grade soap arose from the freshly scrubbed deck, moist from the evening dew.

"Let's go below," said Anna.

"No way," replied Karen, feeling more and more uncomfortable.

"Something's definitely wrong here."

"What *are* you looking for?"

"I don't know, but there's only one way to find out."

Anna opened the watertight door and started down the metal staircase to the engine room below. She turned to Karen: "Coming?"

"I can't let you go in there alone."

The women felt their way down in the semi-darkness, when suddenly Karen heard the sound of faraway voices. "Shit, someone's coming! Let's get out of here." They scrambled up the staircase back onto the deck.

Too late: Three men were walking down the jetty, talking as they approached the gangplank. The women ran to the opposite side of the deck, away from the lights of the jetty, and hid behind the port side of the aft cabin.

The men boarded the ship, their voices getting menacingly louder. Karen recognized Stephanopoulos, as he blasted one of the crew for having left the gangplank on deck. Her already jangled nerves tightened a notch.

Karen looked around and saw a small staircase leading from the main deck up to the bridge. Halfway up, off a small platform, a lifeboat hung suspended from davits, its top covered with a canvas cloth. Karen thought that if the men stayed on the starboard side for a moment longer, she and Anna could get to it unseen. *It was now or never.* She signaled to Anna, and they tiptoed silently up the staircase.

"Get in," Karen whispered, unhooking part of the cover. They tumbled into the lifeboat, which creaked upon receiving its clandestine cargo. Karen heard a man's footsteps starting up the staircase.

I must hook that cover.

The man neared the small platform, and Karen recognized Stephanopoulos' voice: "I start the motor. Check the oil pressure," he shouted to the crew below.

She fumbled with the cover. *Too late to rehook*: She couldn't risk keeping her arm out of the lifeboat any longer. She heard the captain's breathing, louder with each step. The steps stopped. He hissed heavily. *Shit, he sees it.*

After an eternity, the captain's footsteps resumed, slowly receding onto the bridge.

"Just goddamn great," she whispered to Anna. "You got me into this. Now what?"

"Looks like they're doing some kind of tests."

The big MAN diesel exploded into life, and the captain grabbed the microphone. "Bringing up to 2000 rpm." He moved the throttle forward and the engine's purr became a throaty roar.

"Oil pressure OK, Captain," yelled a strident voice over the intercom, barely audible over the din of the diesel.

As the captain throttled back the motor, Karen felt relief: *Anna's right. Just a test. They're through now.*

Then, the second motor started and idled. Kostas shouted: "Prepare to cast off."

"Jesus, we're leaving," exclaimed Karen, her heart sinking into her tennis shoes.

Anna, finding her flashlight: "Shield the light. I've got to see the time." *11:56 p.m.* read her bulky watch.

The dull roar of the motors increased, deepening Karen's fear. Now she could feel the waves hitting the sides of the *Eastland*, as it started to roll and pitch, heading out to sea.

"*What are you doing?*" hissed Karen, irritated at Anna's tinkering and seeming lack of concern.

"Timing and position. We'll see where we're going. Remember the numbers I tell you." Anna turned on the GPS function of her watch and whispered repeatedly the latitude and longitude of the *Eastland*, and its direction. "We're traveling southeast, away from Mustique," said Anna.

Karen felt a surge of panic rise, flood her brain, as she fought off the urge to get out, out into the fresh revivifying air. "We can't last long in here," she said, distress in her voice. She hadn't told Anna about her claustrophobia.

"We'll stay put for a while," replied Anna. "If they're doing sea trials, they should go back to Isola Rossa. We'll track their course with the GPS."

"And if not?"

"We'll have to blow the cover and call Interpol; they also have our track. They see I'm no longer on land."

* * *

On the bridge, Kostas Stephanopoulos lit a cigar, put the *Eastland* on automatic pilot, and reclined in the comfort of the plush leather seat. He watched the ship progressing like an ant across the colored screen of the chart plotter, toward the 'X' on the upper left-hand corner. A while later, the chart plotter let out an intermittent beeping sound, as the ant closed in on the 'X,' the screen indicating *waypoint arrival*. Kostas slowed the *Eastland* and brought her to an idling stop. He punched the command *auto-position* on the autopilot. The motors and thrusters would keep the ship in that spot, automatically.

"Connect the hoses," Kostas shouted to the men, who were already pulling out long serpentine brown hoses from a large box on the afterdeck.

Karen peered from underneath the cover and saw the men lower the other end of the hoses overboard.

"Lower the funnels," directed Kostas, to the whining, high-pitched sound of hydraulic rams. The funnels were lowered into the sea, like giant elephants about to quench their immeasurable thirst.

Strange time to go artifact hunting, thought Karen, her curiosity briefly tempering her fear.

Kostas turned on the underwater cameras and remote control with the other joystick, and steered the hoses along the ocean floor, searching, probing, sifting silently underneath the surface layer of the sandy brown carpet.

Suddenly, he stopped the joystick, a broad smile baring the discolored teeth. He chewed the soggy end off the cigar, spit it onto the floor and brought the lit match to his face. "Maximum suction," he shouted to the man below.

After a few seconds, Karen heard the whirring of pumps, electric motors, and then a strange soft, irregular thumping noise coming from the angled funnels, as if the elephants were having trouble ingurgitating their drink.

"What the hell is that?" asked Karen.

"Sounds like they're sucking up something from the ocean floor."

"In the middle of the night?" Immediately, Karen wished she hadn't asked.

"The captain said 'Suction' was to flush the hoses. They can do that at the dock. It doesn't make sense," said Anna.

The soft thumping of objects on the inside of the funnels continued.

"They're not retrieving artifacts," said Karen. "They would break. They must be retrieving some kind of packages."

"Drugs," exclaimed Anna.

The two looked at each other in disbelief, the full realization of their predicament slowly sinking in.

"If you're right and they find us, we're dead," said Karen.

"Not quite," said Anna, patting a small object on her hip. "It's a Kevlar pistol."

"That's just great. Forgive me if I sound sexist, but there are *three big apes down there.*"

Anna didn't reply.

* * *

After half an hour, the thumping noise stopped and Kostas ordered, "Get the hoses in."

The hydraulic rams retrieved the funnels, the men raised and disconnected the hoses, and Kostas pressed 'off' on the automatic pilot. He still marveled at how his massive ship could be steered at the finger touch of the small joystick. He thrust forward the throttle of the diesels.

Anna looked at her GPS and breathed a sigh of relief.

"We're returning to Isola Rossa."

As she tried to control her shaking body, Karen couldn't help letting out muffled sobs.

Forty minutes later, the *Eastland* slowed, and the women felt a slight jar, as Kostas expertly brought the ship alongside the worn tires of the concrete dock. Anna looked at her watch: 2:10 a.m.

Karen heard the crew as they secured the lines of the *Eastland*. Moments later, the sound of their voices slowly receded into the night. She flung open the canvas cover, rose, stretched, and breathed in the moist morning air.

As they clambered out of the lifeboat and down onto the afterdeck, Anna said: "Damn, they've removed the gangplank. Can you swim?"

"Yes, but what about our clothes?"

"We can dry them on the balcony tomorrow."

The two started up the road to the Château, wet, cold and tired, when Anna felt a faint buzzing on her arm. "It's Interpol," she said, as she put her watch to her ear.

"We tracked you on open water. What gives?" said a voice, crackling with interference.

"I couldn't talk; I'll call Dulac tomorrow. Right now, I'm getting some sleep."

CHAPTER 35

Karen finally awoke. She felt like she'd been trampled by a pregnant elephant. *10:30 a.m. Half the day is gone.* She ambled downstairs for a well-needed coffee and impromptu croissant, when Lady Sarah, in tight jeans and a red, open blouse, met her halfway up the staircase.

"Good afternoon," she chided. "Sleep well?"

"Actually, not great. I couldn't get to sleep." She tried to discern if Sarah knew anything.

"I passed by last night and your door was locked. There is no need here, you know."

"It's a childhood phobia. I went for a walk; it usually works."

"Will you join us for lunch?"

"Yes, I'll probably skip the library this morning."

"Good, see you at lunch."

Karen wondered if Anna had contacted Dulac, and what her plan was. She went to the main lecture hall and spotted Anna studiously taking notes amid a group of students, while the lecturer, a small woman with caterpillar eyebrows, droned on about the offerings of the Pistis Sofia cells in North America. Karen drew Anna's attention and she joined her in the hallway entrance.

"I spoke to Dulac," said Anna. "He's having the *Eastland* followed. They won't board her until she reaches port."

"What about us?"

"He says we should stay a couple more days to see what else we can learn."

"I think the Marchioness is getting suspicious."

"All the more reason to stay and do everything we're supposed to: You in the library and me at my courses."

"It's not quite that simple."

Karen didn't want to share with Anna the underlying complexity of the situation, but thought Dulac might have already briefed her. At lunch, Karen could hardly stay awake, and had trouble keeping up with the conversation. After a short, invigorating walk, she sought refuge in the library and tried to focus by reading: "Pistis Sofia, Early Rites."

The afternoon wore on, as Karen read about sacrifices of animals in the third to sixth century A.D. Suddenly, she felt a hand touching the nape of her neck, first softly, then squeezing more firmly. She sprang up, only to meet Sarah's soft gaze, and incoming breasts. She was completely naked.

"Hope I haven't startled you, dear?" said Sarah coyly, her voice husky.

Karen recoiled, her back against the bookcase, as she clutched the book and took in the moment in utter disbelief.

"Well, I wasn't expecting—"

"I love the unexpected, gives piquancy to the experience, don't you think?"

"But someone might come in . . ."

"Don't worry, the doors are locked," said Sarah, dangling the chain around her neck, the small key visible between her breasts.

"You'll have to take it from me," she said teasingly, removing the book from Karen's hands, breaching her last defenses.

"I don't think we should," as Sarah's naked body was now pressing against Karen and her left hand started to gently stroke Karen's right breast. Karen gasped in surprise, as

Sarah's left hand reached down and stroked her, still pinned against the bookcase.

"Come, let's take these off," said Sarah, already unbuttoning Karen's blouse, as Karen closed her eyes and felt desire surge from deep within.

"Really, I . . ."

At that moment, a knock on the door startled them.

"Who is it?" asked Karen.

"It's Anna. I just . . ."

"I wanted some privacy. I'll be out in a minute," said Karen.

Karen let go of Sarah's arms, and Sarah slowly backed away. "Well, I guess that's that," she said curtly.

Karen was about to reply, but then thought, *Shut up, Karen. There's nothing, absolutely nothing to say.*

Sarah turned away from Karen to get dressed, as Karen picked up the book from the floor and gathered her things. Sarah unlocked the door and walked out.

CHAPTER 36

Nicola slept fitfully on the worn-out couch, her back aching, the lumps of the thin cushions poking at her every bone. She tried to comfort herself: *Thursday is tomorrow; only one more day. Petrov has to accept. What has he got to lose? But even for him, it's a tall order. Does he have the contacts? How badly do they want this information? Maybe they know already, and don't need the letter?* She had to get out of her friend's apartment. Her attachment to the satchel was becoming increasingly suspicious.

The following morning, Nicola was at the Nevsky at 10:15 a.m. She didn't want to risk being late. She nervously read the morning newspaper, dipped her croissant in the black java coffee and waited.

11 a.m. at last: She paid the bill, went to the phone booth and dialed the FSB number. Her mind was a dull blank, and the pit in her stomach was moving up to her chest, the same feeling she had before seeing her exam results, posted on the university's notice board.

"Petrov."

"Nicola Vasilieva."

"We agree."

"Da?"

"It will take some time."

Nicola felt electric pulsations run from her ankles to the top of her brain.

"You will get conditional acceptance from a Canadian university."

"What do you mean?"

"You must pass their exams."

"In Canada?"

"Yes."

"And the money?"

"As soon as we have the letters."

"No, you first."

Petrov hesitated, but was willing to concede the point. She was smart enough not to lie to the FSB, he thought. "OK," he said, "but you must deposit Vasiliev's money in your account the same day."

"I'll phone my aunt tomorrow. You'll have your money the same day. What about the Canadian visa?"

"You will get it: They promised me."

Nicola knew she was taking a huge chance: If Petrov was lying, she would be stuck, helpless, in Russia, with no way of getting to Canada, and no money.

"Give me Dulac's number."

"No problem. It's 33 21 30 42, but you won't get through. Let me connect you."

"Thanks. I'll try myself."

Nicola phoned Dulac, and recognized the nasal, clipped French accent.

"They have agreed in Canada," he said. "The visa is on its way."

"You are sure?"

"You have my word. We have done this before."

After a moment, she said: "I'll wait for it."

"As you wish."

Nicola phoned Petrov: "I'll wait for the visa."

"Why? It's coming."

"Because I don't trust you."

Petrov cursed under his breath. *Damn, I would have done the same.*

CHAPTER 37

The Holy Father had instructed Legnano to review the activities of the Vatican Financial Committee. The Vatican's finances were wavering, and the Pontiff wanted to know why.

Legnano applied his talents to learning the intricacies of the financial world and dove into the ledgers and balance sheets of the Vatican Treasury with the concentration of an Amsterdam jeweler. He inspected the activities of the Investment Subcommittee of the Financial Committee, responsible for the structure, assets diversity and targeted yield of the Vatican's portfolio.

He hadn't liked what he had seen: During the last three years, doubtful counseling had led to risky investments, most of which had tanked. This had forced even riskier investment, with capital losses, if crystallized, of some 300 million US dollars. His discreet inquiries had confirmed his apprehension: There was no recovery plan. The timing was disastrous: Catholics' contributions to the Vatican's Treasury, 'Peter's Pence,' were at their lowest in the past decade..

Fiore, as head of the Financial Committee, had direct responsibility for the Investment Subcommittee's activities. He reported to the Secretary of State, Cardinal Volpe.

* * *

On the morning of May 26, 2006, Cardinal Legnano received a phone call that would shake his faith.

"Monsignor Legnano, my name is Umberto Tondino. I don't believe we've met. I work with Casparelli, Vickers and Smith—"

"Yes, yes, the auditing firm."

"Exactly, Monsignor Legnano. I know this is unusual, but I would like to meet you privately, as soon as possible."

"What is this about?"

"I can't tell this over the phone. Could we meet soon, today even? It's very important."

"I'm busy, but I suppose I could free myself briefly, say at 11 a.m."

"Yes, but not at your office. Can we meet at the restaurant *L'Eau Vive*?"

L'Eau Vive is always crowded with members of the Curia, thought Legnano. *I will certainly be recognized there.*

"*Cantabile's* is more private, if that's what you want. This sounds quite mysterious. Why the secrecy?"

"You'll understand when we meet."

"How will I know you?"

"Don't worry, I will recognize you. Oh, I ask that you keep this confidential."

Legnano hung up slowly, perplexed by the mysterious caller. He asked his secretary to phone Casparelli, Vickers and Smith.

"Yes, Monsignor, Tondino is a junior accountant at the firm," replied his secretary.

Very strange, thought Legnano. He phoned Tondino, to verify the authenticity of the call: "Signor Tondino?"

"Yes?"

"Cardinal Legnano: Just checking."

"I understand."

* * *

"*Cantabile's*," Legnano ordered his chauffeur.

As he walked into the already crowded restaurant, the maître d' showed him to the reserved table.

"This way, Monsignor, a Mr. Tondino is waiting for you."

Embarrassed, Legnano made his way to the small table where a young man — he guessed him to be in his early thirties — rose, blushing from ear to ear, and introduced himself.

"Thank you for coming, your Eminence."

"Yes, yes. This had better be important, young man," said an impatient Legnano, looking around to see if he'd been recognized.

"Cardinal Legnano, if I'm wrong, what I'm about to tell you will finish my career."

"Really? You're still quite young. You have time," as he sat back, smiling.

"Monsignor, I haven't told this to anyone. I don't think I can trust the members of my own firm," he said nervously, his skinny hand fidgeting with the corner of his napkin.

Now Legnano was becoming really interested in this bookish young man with the stubby nose.

"I, I don't know where to start," said the accountant, his voice faltering.

"Calm down; try at the beginning," said Legnano, turning on his warm, comforting, father confessor's tone.

"A year ago, when I was working under Mr. Casparelli on the Vatican's books, I came across some large sums of money that had been transferred to the Vatican's Treasury."

"Go on."

"I wasn't satisfied, so I started investigating the many transfers of US dollars into the Treasury. What would come up, always, was: 'Anonymous Donor.' I went to see Mr. Casparelli, and he said he had knowledge of this and he knew the donor. Everything was perfectly all right. I wasn't to be concerned. That was fine, as there are many anonymous donations to the Vatican, so I went on with my audit."

"What amounts are you talking about?"

"From January last year, about 50 million US dollars."

"Mannaggia la Miseria," exclaimed Legnano. "That's quite a lot."

"Yes, when I took up my audit last month, I noticed that the donations in US dollars had increased, were always transferred on the same date of the month. I had never seen this before. When I went to see Mr. Casparelli again last week, he nearly threw me out of his office. He said he had dealt with the question before with me, and that the subject was closed. I thought he would fire me."

"I see, and why did you contact me?"

"I noticed through my audit papers that you had joined the Investment Review Committee recently. This kind of nomination has to receive papal approval, so I thought you would be the best person to talk to. I couldn't keep silent any longer."

"You are well informed on Vatican procedure."

The young man drew closer across the table.

"Monsignor, now I must tell you something else. I think this is only a coincidence. I had asked about these donations during one of our meetings with the Finance Committee, with Monsignor Fiore."

"Yes?"

"During the meeting, Monsignors Salvador, Conti and Durivage told me to investigate these donations and report back."

Legnano frowned.

"I see what you mean," said Legnano.

"But surely this is a just coincidence," said Tondino, looking a little pale, slight desperation in his voice. "Even so, I had to tell someone."

"Of course," said Legnano, trying to be reassuring, as if to give absolution to his penitent.

"What should I do?" asked the accountant, his shaking hands incapable of bringing the cup of coffee to his lips.

"For the moment, absolutely nothing, young man," said Legnano. "As you said, this is only a coincidence."

The accountant understood that Legnano was trying to convince himself, as much as the accountant. Nevertheless, Tondino was buying into this temporary refuge, a safe haven for his conscience. He felt immensely relieved, the weight finally off the shoulders of his soul.

"I'll see what I can find out," said Legnano reassuringly. "Can I give you a lift?"

"No, it's all right, I prefer to walk."

CHAPTER 38

Karen endured one of the most uncomfortable dinners she could remember. She sat at the middle of the table, trying to avoid eye contact with Sarah, and suffering the Marchioness' cold, reproachful gaze. Throughout the meal, Karen had made small talk with her immediate neighbors, left early and gone to her room where exhausted, she had fallen asleep. At around midnight, she awoke. Unable to get back to sleep again, she turned on the light of her bedroom table and started to read. Fifteen minutes later, she turned off the light. She tossed and turned, tried to breathe deeply. She lay in bed, wide awake, tense, staring into the darkness. *This is ridiculous. I need some exercise, some fresh air.*

She slipped on her sweater over her night robe, laced her tennis shoes and stepped out into the corridor. A courtesy light shone dimly at the end.

She made her way quietly down the corridor toward the granite staircase leading to the entrance hall. As she walked quietly down the staircase, she could hear the faint sound of voices coming from somewhere below. As she reached the bottom, she looked to the right and recognized the entrance of the room from where the voices were coming from. It was the small room, the one with the velvet drapes and the Brueghel, to which the Marchioness had invited Dulac, Lescop and her for that first meeting.

A small ray of light emanated from the room, as the door had been left slightly ajar.

The voices grew louder.

Her curiosity aroused, Karen approached quietly. She was next to the door when she recognized Sarah's angry voice.

". . . never. You changed the letter. I never agreed to that last sentence. It changes the whole picture," said Sarah. "That letter is a murderous threat."

"My dear Marchioness, you are naïve," said a man's voice. "I remind you that when we first discussed this, you agreed to be used as a decoy. As a matter of fact, you didn't have much choice: When we became aware of your little scheme, to be euphemistic, you either went along or faced the law. You wisely chose to cooperate with us."

Karen thought she recognized the man's voice, but couldn't place it. She tried to get a better angle with the ray of light, but the light was indirect, and she couldn't see inside the room. She didn't dare press on the door, lest it squeak.

"I didn't think you would go this far," said Sarah.

"In for a penny, in for a pound, as the English say," replied the man.

"Dulac is getting close. I'm having trouble fending him off. It's only a question of time until he finds the source of the Pistis Sophia letter."

"Highly unlikely," replied the man. "Besides, Dulac can't prove a thing: He has a few bits of circumstantial evidence, some mythological speculations. We have him exactly where we want him. But I'm quite surprised at how quickly that woman found the Evangelists' connection. I thought she would have taken more time. That's always the risk with *A Posteriori* thinking."

Karen felt a flow forming under her armpits and running down to her hands. She could hear the quick thump of her heart, hammering the bell of her chest.

"What if Dulac realizes the Pistis Sophia letter is a decoy?" said Sarah.

"Yes, you see, he has one major problem: Motive. Or more precisely, the lack of motive. He can't see why Pistis Sophia would have two archbishops killed. Blackmail? Revenge? Possibly, but historically, it doesn't make sense. So that's all he has: a dead end. Besides, Dulac won't last long in that job."

"What do you mean?"

"Never mind. In any case, soon all traces of this will have been erased."

"You mean . . ."

"Yes, every link, except the highest, will be removed."

Then a deathly silence. Karen thought: *They must hear my breathing.* She held her breath. She suddenly felt ill, her legs shaking uncontrollably, giving way: *God, not now, please! I have to get back to my room. Don't panic, don't run. One step at a time. They don't know. Don't change that.*

Resisting with all her might her urge to run, she walked back up the staircase, along the interminable corridor, entered her bedroom and locked the door. She undressed, crept into the large bed and shut off the reading light. She sat upright, her arms and hands soaked in sweat, grabbing her still-shaking knees. Staring at the empty darkness, she tried to fathom and digest the enormity of what she had just heard.

Her head buzzed with random thoughts: *Sarah is involved in the murders, or learned about them. She has some scheme going: It must be the* Eastland. *This man has an inside track on the investigation, the murders. He may have planned them. I must call Dulac. No, it's four o'clock in the morning. I have to talk to Anna. Sweet Jesus, how did I get into this mess?*

Finally, she lay down, feeling very alone and very, very scared.

* * *

The day before, Dulac had been stunned and elated by Anna's call: If the women were right, the Marchioness would have a lot of explaining to do. He immediately contacted US Interpol to have the US Coast Guard shadow the *Eastland*. It left port the next morning, bound directly for Naples. On hydrofoils at thirty knots, if the weather was good, it would take the *Eastland* five, maybe six days to reach port. The Coast Guard search and rescue helicopters would follow it until it reached the Azores. The French would shadow it through Gibraltar. Italian police had been advised and were preparing seizure documents in Naples.

He thought of scheduling a meeting with the French Minister of Justice and Minister of the Interior, to request extradition and arrest of the Marchioness. He realized, in his elation, that he was getting way ahead of himself: What if the cargo on the *Eastland* proved to be innocuous packages of wrapped artifacts? Or worse, what if the *Eastland* had been only cleaning its tubes? He knew he needed rock-solid evidence before facing the Ministers.

* * *

The following morning, Dulac's phone rang. He saw the notation of an encrypted call on the screen.

"It's Karen." Her voice was agitated.

"Hello, how are you? Is everything all right?" He sounded genuinely concerned.

"I've got to leave here. You won't believe what I've just found out."

"More about the *Eastland*?"

"No, last night, I overheard a conversation between Sarah and some man. It sounded as — as if she's being blackmailed into using Pistis Sophia as a decoy. The letter comes from the murderers, and this man is in on it."

"Which man?"

"I don't know, I couldn't see who was talking, I could only hear through the door. But his voice, that voice, I've heard it before."

"Go on."

"This man knows the whole thing. He said Sarah didn't have any choice, after he found out her 'little scheme.' He said you don't have a case against Pistis Sophia, for lack of motive. He knows I'm involved, and he shared that with Sarah. Now she knows. Thierry, I'm really scared. I've got to get out of here."

This was the first time she had ever called him by his first name.

"Don't worry," said Dulac. "We'll get you out."

"There's more: He mentioned that all traces of this business were going to be removed. They're going to kill others, others who know, *like me*."

"Karen, don't panic. They don't know that you know. Try to remember where you heard his voice before. What does Anna think of this?"

"I didn't tell her yet. I called you first; it's 6 a.m. here."

"Stay calm, find a reason to get off the island: Your classes, your studies are over at the library, whatever. When do Anna's courses finish?"

"Saturday."

"By then we'll know what's on the *Eastland*."

CHAPTER 39

Cardinal Legnano felt unwell. He relived the pain he had suffered at the news of Salvador's death, then Conti's. He realized during his meeting with Tondino, that this could explain Salvador's letter to Conti: Salvador could be measuring the pros and cons of exposing a scandal.

His anguished mind raced: *What do I do with this? Who do I speak to? Who is not suspect? The members of the Investment Committee, are they part of this? Why not go directly to Dulac? No, we must avoid another scandal. Besides, the Omerta, the Code of Silence. I am bound.*

He remembered Tondino mentioning Durivage had also questions concerning the provenance of the donations. He called Durivage.

Durivage was terminally ill. The anxiety and sadness of a man condemned by prostate cancer had finally overcome his usual joviality.

"*Buon giorno*, Monsignor," said Cardinal Legnano, "I've come to see you concerning the late Archbishop Salvador's letter to Monsignor Conti."

"I still think of them every day; I have nightmares," replied Durivage.

"I know, so do I. I understand how difficult this is for you. I won't take much of your time, but I'm concerned about what happened after the three of you inquired about these anonymous donations. Salvador wrote that letter shortly after. Didn't you think Salvador's letter was connected to the donations?"

"It was so nebulous. I didn't think there was any connection with the Investment Committee."

"Do you have any other thoughts on the matter?"

"I'm waiting for the auditor's report. I assumed Salvador and Conti were also."

Durivage wouldn't live to see the auditor's report.

Legnano's meeting with Monsignor Fiore had found the younger man haughty.

"Why are you asking me these questions? We simply must accept the report from the Audit Committee. The donor has requested anonymity, and as you realize, Monsignor, we cannot risk losing valuable donations."

Especially with your terrible investments, thought Legnano, but he bit his tongue. "At any price?"

"No, but Casparelli has assured us of the integrity of this donor. Are we not to trust him?"

"I have no reason not to."

"Fine, then let's wait for the report."

"You don't think Salvador's and Conti's death had anything to do with this?"

"These murderers are misguided religious fanatics, not corporate philanthropists."

"Possibly, or someone wants us to believe that."

"My dear Legnano," said Fiore, with a hint of impatience, "let Dulac make the suppositions: We have enough work to do."

"Perhaps you're right."

Legnano realized he wouldn't be getting any further. He returned to his Venetian-style office, where looking through the high vaulted windows at the walkway below, he paced back and forth uneasily. There was something too smug about this, which jarred his earthy, Tuscan common sense. He had endured through the Banco Ambrosiano scandal. He didn't want to suffer through another. He had to see Cardinal Volpe, the Secretary of State.

CHAPTER 40

The *Eastland* docked in Naples three days late, since the weather in mid-Atlantic had been rough: thirty-five knot headwinds and significant seas had forced it to slow to ten knots. The night before docking at port, the *Eastland* sat at a mooring, quarantine flag hoisted, awaiting customs clearance. The following morning, the Italian customs officers searched it and found nothing. The captain and crew were detained, but let go after the police's failure to find any incriminating evidence. Afterwards, the captain brought the vessel to the local shipyard, for routine maintenance.

* * *

"Nothing?" said an incredulous Dulac.

"Only a few artifacts off a sunken ship," replied the Italian policeman.

"What? Are you sure?"

"Of course."

Dulac couldn't believe it. Karen and Anna's vivid description didn't amount to a 'nothing' finding. He didn't trust the Naples Port Authority. He had to go to Naples, see for himself.

He phoned Karen. "Can you fly down to Naples with me tomorrow? I need you to identify those sounds you heard on the *Eastland*."

After an uncomfortable parting with the Marchioness, Karen had taken an early flight from Mustique to Paris.

"I've only just returned a day ago, I'm wiped out."

"The Italian police found nothing on the *Eastland* and—"

"Nothing?"

"A few artifacts."

"That's impossible. Anna and I both heard something being sucked in. The thumping noise went on for over half an hour."

"That's why I want to take a look. I want the captain to work those pumps."

"Can't Anna go? She heard them also."

"She's sick. Gastro . . . something."

"Can't it wait?" replied Karen.

"No, I'm leaving at eight tomorrow morning."

"I guess I could make it," she said wearily.

"Fine. See you at the Alitalia counter at 7 a.m."

* * *

"Napoli Beverello," Dulac instructed the taxi driver at the Naples Airport.

Karen sat uncomfortably in the old Lancia, reveling in the special, schoolgirl memories of her first trip abroad. How simple life was, back then. She had fallen in love with Naples and Ischia, where her clean young American good looks had attracted the ready hormones of the smooth-talking tour guide, Aldo.

He had been her first lover, whom she had never seen again after that week-long awakening of her womanhood. The letters had been sporadic, and after two months, had ceased. She wondered what became of Aldo. He was studying law at the time. Had he become a prominent Neapolitan lawyer, judge, or — as he'd predicted — an under-employed, permanent student of the human condition?

"Everyone in Naples is a lawyer. I know three waiters and many taxi drivers with law degrees," Aldo had said.

She had sensed Aldo was more ambitious.

* * *

As the taxi drove down toward the old port, Mount Vesuvius surged menacingly into view, warming its slopes with a thick coat of pollution. Dulac opened the door, and two policemen walked up and introduced themselves.

"I'm 'Spector Basso. My colleague Sergeant Cotini," said a short overweight man with bluish-tinted hair, probably close to his pension.

"Dulac, of Interpol, and my assistant, Ms. Dawson."

As they approached the *Eastland*, Dulac noticed the crew were busy preparing the vessel to be hauled out of the water, next to the shipyard's lift.

"We are coming aboard," said Basso to Captain Stephanopoulos, in a tone devoid of doubt.

The captain acquiesced, looking annoyed. But then, recognizing Karen: "We met before. What are *you* doing here?"

Before she could answer, Dulac intervened:

"I'm with Interpol, Captain. I want your crew to connect your search hoses and start those pumps."

"What for?" said Stephanopoulos, hunching his shoulders and opening his palms outwards, looking at Basso.

Basso nodded.

"Just do it, captain," said Dulac.

"If you want," said an incredulous Stephanopoulos.

The crew started pulling out the hoses, and Dulac noticed a bit of brown mud, still stuck on the end of one of the hoses.

"What are we looking for? Artifacts in the Port of Naples?" laughed the captain, as the hoses were being lowered into the water.

"Stop, stop right there," Dulac shouted to the crew. "Bring back those hoses."

"Now what?" said Stephanopoulos, exasperated.

The captain sweated in the Neapolitan sun, and mopped his face and neck with his wrinkled, green handkerchief.

Dulac didn't speak, but walked briskly to the aft deck and turning to Basso, asked: "Do you have a bag?"

"Yes." Basso snapped his fingers at Cotini.

Dulac grabbed the small plastic evidence bag, and carefully removed cakes of the still-moist mud from the hoses. Dulac looked at Stephanopoulos, standing aside one of his men, on the bridge:

"There is no mud at Isola Rossa, Captain. The bottom is sand. Where does the mud come from?"

At that moment, the crew member looked at Stephanopoulos, sweating, not answering, and panicked. He ran to the gangplank and crossed it.

"Stop," yelled Cotini from the side of the *Eastland*, "or I shoot."

The man continued running down the dock, zigzagging.

A shot rang out. The man fell, clutching his leg.

"Arrest them," ordered Dulac, and Basso's man handcuffed Stephanopoulos, swearing in Greek at the wounded man.

"What's *that* all about?" asked Karen, looking dumbfounded.

"They've pumped the packages back into the bay," said Dulac.

"Holy shit," said Karen.

"We're going to the Port Authority, *right now*," said Dulac.

Basso summoned help, as Kostas and his crew were carried off, handcuffed, to the Naples Port Prefetura.

"Don't let them contact anyone. No, especially not their lawyer. No one until I return, is that clear?" said Dulac to Cotini.

* * *

Karen, Basso and Dulac entered the harbor master's office. Dulac looked at the weary-looking man behind the large counter.

"Dulac, Interpol. Get me the navigation reports. I want to see where the *Eastland* was anchored last night, before clearing customs."

Furrowing through his records, the harbor master pointed to a mooring buoy, about three-quarter mile offshore.

Dulac turned to Basso: "Get a diving team here. We may be too late."

"What you mean?" said Basso, perplexed.

"If I'm right, you're in for a big surprise," replied Dulac.

Basso made a few phone calls. Ten minutes later, an emergency dive team arrived.

"You can borrow one of our patrol boats," said the harbor master to Dulac.

While Karen waited at the harbor master's office, Dulac, Basso and the two frogmen headed out to the mooring buoy.

The men dove, and Dulac leaned over the boat's side, looking anxiously at the bubbles rising, breaking the surface and marking the slow route of the divers as they progressed methodically over the ocean floor. They stopped, and after a moment, the bubbles increased in frequency and size, until one of the divers broke the surface. He held a small white package in his outstretched hand, and swam clumsily over to the boat.

Dulac took the mud-covered packet nervously, almost dropping it back into the water.

"Give me a knife," he said to Basso.

Dulac cut the wrapping twine and noticed the letter M printed on the material underneath the transparent, waterproof envelope. As he unwrapped the last remaining folds, he exclaimed, jubilant: *"Banco!"*

A small lead weight fell onto the floorboard. Atop, four wads of hundred-dollar bills, neatly stacked. Dulac counted fifty in each wad. Basso stared silently in amazement, as the other diver surfaced with two packets.

"How many more?" Dulac yelled to the diver.

"Molto, molto."

Dulac signaled the divers to come in, and the men, looking perplexed, climbed over the stern of the patrol boat.

"We must get a net," said Basso.

"No, not now," replied Dulac. "We're after bigger fish; the bait stays here," he said, pointing at the water.

Dulac instructed the boat's driver to head toward shore, while he carefully put the muddy packets in a plastic bag.

* * *

Dulac ordered Basso to have the *Eastland* lifted out of the water, under strict surveillance.

"Everything should look as if the maintenance work is proceeding as planned," he said.

"Get me Inspector Belli, of Interpol, Italy, " said Dulac. He waited until the familiar voice answered. "I'll need four armed patrol boats and a helicopter on standby."

"No problem," said Belli.

"Get down here as quickly as you can and wait for me at the harbormaster's office."

CHAPTER 41

"But you can't interrogate him, that's our job," said Basso to Dulac, as Dulac walked into the cell area were Stephanopoulos was kept.

"You're wrong: The Interpol–Italian police agreement allows me to interrogate a suspect I'm chasing cross-border. What do you think *this* is?"

Basso complied and opened the cell gate, in complete ignorance of what Dulac was talking about.

"Where did you get them?" Dulac showed Stephanopoulos the two white plastic bags.

"Get what?" replied the captain, defiant.

"These." Dulac took a packet out of the plastic bag.

"Don't know what you're talking about. I want to see a lawyer."

"Later. You're facing fifteen to twenty years in an Italian prison, *Captain*. I'm told they rate with the best." He smiled sarcastically. "You're no longer a young man, *Captain*. They like old men in prison: They can't defend themselves as easily."

"Prison for what?"

"Try money laundering, smuggling, obstruction of justice, for a start."

"You have no proof."

"*Captain*, as we speak, the other packets are being sent to Lyon. We're raising the *Eastland* tomorrow. Your crew tell me they have done this many times with you before."

Dulac stepped closer, smiling smugly, looking directly into his eyes, which were now sullen and scared.

"For the last time, where did you get these? Who is in on this? Did you get orders from the Marchioness? Where are the packets going?"

Stephanopoulos was sweating again, trying desperately to avoid Dulac's eyes: They seemed to be bolted onto his as Dulac came closer, inches from his face.

"I, I know nothing,"

"As you wish." Dulac slowly released his icy stare and lit a cigarette.

"Smoke?"

"No."

"You're on your own, Captain. This ship is sinking, fast: It's every man for himself. I'm your only lifeboat. Cooperate and I'll help. Don't, and I'll see you get twenty years. Think about it." Dulac opened the cell gate and left.

Stephanopoulos knew it was over.

Tomorrow, they'd find the double bottom he'd had installed on the *Eastland*. They would find the bypass valve that linked the pumps. He also knew that his only hope of survival was to show *them* he would not flinch. Omerta: He must take the rap on his own. He knew the rules: *They* warned him that if he was ever caught and he betrayed *them*, he, his family, were dead.

These weren't threats. Simply the rules. No exceptions.

He thought of his wife Aspasia and their two children, Theo and Paul, and his eyes welled with tears. How could he have done this to them? How could he have been so stupid as to forget washing the hoses? He had to warn them, but how? Basso wasn't about to let him make any calls, at least not now. Besides, with a good lawyer, he could still beat this. They had bought judges in Naples before, many a time. But

Dulac. What did he have up his sleeve? Could he have him extradited? To where?

The ship was going down, but he had to shut up and stick to his guns. He steeled himself for the imminent suffering he knew he would face.

CHAPTER 42

Dulac returned from the precinct and went to the harbor master's office to meet Belli.

There, poring over a map of the bay, they conferred with the harbor master on the size of his boats, their speed, and their armament. Once the money was on board the pickup boat, the three patrol boats would intercept it. The helicopter would assist on request.

"It has to be tonight," intoned Dulac. "They can't leave these packages in the water much longer."

"Hope you're right," said Belli.

A half hour later, Belli confirmed the arrival of the patrol boats, and synchronized the VHF radio channel. As dusk fell, Belli and Dulac stared at the large radar screen covering the bay.

"Now, the waiting game," said Dulac.

Dulac and Belli settled into their chairs, trying to rest, like generals on the night before the battle. The harbor master continued fielding calls from the boats at anchor in the bay, giving customs clearance instructions and allocating berthing schedules.

Midnight, and still no sign of anyone approaching the mooring. Maybe it's not the night, Dulac thought. He felt tired and his eyes watered, straining to see the dots on the radar screen, ships quietly at anchor in the bay.

"Maybe they called it off," said the harbor master.

Dulac arose to stretch and lit a Gitane.

He looked at Belli, for any reaction to the harbor master's comment. He didn't trust the Italians as far as he could heave them. *Had someone from the police tipped off the crooks? Belli or Basso could have easily made a phone call. If so, they could all go home.*

Belli got up to pour another coffee, and, returning, shouted: "Look, something is moving on the screen."

Dulac got up and peered at the radar. A small white dot was creeping inwards from the outside edge of the radar screen, but not in the direction of the mooring.

"Probably a night fisherman," said the harbor master.

The three men watched intently, and the dot started to turn slowly.

"They may be checking for boats," said Belli.

After making a slow, complete circle, the boat turned suddenly toward the mooring ball.

"That's them," exclaimed Dulac. "Get on the radio."

"We have suspects on radar. Can you see them?" said Belli to the patrol boats.

"No, we don't see any navigation lights," replied one of the drivers.

The boat reached the mooring ball and stopped.

"Let them get the packages on board," said Dulac.

"Patrol boats on standby," whispered Belli over his radio.

The three stood breathless, captivated by the radar screen, knowing the timing had to be perfect: Too early, or too late, and the crooks would escape. Belli couldn't get the patrol boats moving early; the crooks might also have radar.

Minutes dragged by slowly. Dulac coughed nervously and looked at the large wood-framed clock: *twenty-five minutes gone.* The pickup boat was still at the mooring ball. The harbor master looked at Dulac, expectantly, the ticking of the large clock beating away like an old metronome.

What is he waiting for? thought Belli, sweat dripping from his eyebrows.

"*Now!*" exclaimed Dulac.

"*Go!*" shouted Belli on the VHF.

The three patrol boats' drivers each gunned their twin 300 hp Yamaha outboards and aimed their boats straight at the mooring ball. The onboard policemen ratcheted their machine guns, crouching, shielding their eyes from the incoming phosphorescent spray.

Suddenly, one of the patrol boats turned on its spotlight and shone it in the direction of the mooring ball.

"Not yet, idiot," exclaimed Dulac in disbelief.

Belli yelled: "*Stupido!*"

The four men in the white, shark-shaped, modified Donzi 35 ZR speedboat looked up, dazed for a moment by the glare of the rapidly approaching spotlight. The crane operator on the stern of the Donzi, busy hauling the large net, froze. At that moment, a second spotlight, coming from the opposite direction, flooded the other side of the Donzi. The driver reacted instantly: No time to haul the net or cut the line.

The twin 525 HP Mercury V-8 straight-piped inboards exploded into a deafening roar, their propellers digging furiously into the warm Mediterranean, spitting a wave of white foam behind the Donzi.

Let the cable run, the driver signaled the crane operator. The speedboat still accelerated, the wheel of the crane spinning furiously. Suddenly, a sickening crack: The boat lurched slightly and the crane broke clean off the stern into the water. He had rid himself of the most expensive anchor in the Bay of Naples.

The third patrol boat now converged at forty-five degrees onto the speedboat's bow, and one of the men yelled over the megaphone: "Stop or we shoot."

The Donzi answered with a hail of bullets from its Uzis, shattering the patrol boat's spotlight. The first and second patrol boats, directly behind, opened fire. The speedboat zigged and zagged, then veered and aimed straight for a large tanker at anchor. The patrol boats stopped firing. At the last possible second, the Donzi swerved to avoid the tanker, swerved again and aimed for a freighter, a few hundred yards away. The patrol boats followed helplessly, quickly losing ground.

"We're losing him," yelled one of the patrol boat drivers to Belli.

"Get the helicopter up," called Belli on the VHF.

The Donzi veered again, missing the freighter by inches. The patrol boats opened fire as the Donzi made a tight left turn. Then it straightened, aimed at a fishing trawler. The patrol boats, oblivious to safety, opened fire again. As the Donzi closed at full throttle onto the fishing trawler, the driver suddenly fell forward, inert on the controls.

"*Get him off!*" yelled one of the crew to the man nearest the limp driver. The man reached under the driver, frantically trying to turn the steering wheel.

Too late. The Donzi slammed into the trawler, exploding into a fireball of fiberglass, human flesh and gasoline. Seconds later, the fiery debris bombarded the trawler, igniting its wooden decks. Soon the small trawler sat engulfed in flames, lighting the bay with its eerie yellow and orange tinge.

Dulac, Belli and the harbormaster stood for a moment, frozen in stupefaction.

Finally, grabbing the VHF radio from a thunderstruck Belli, the harbor master yelled: "Look for survivors, check that trawler, assist in any way!"

Switching his radio to the emergency channel, the harbor master ordered: "Get the firefighter boat out there."

A few moments later, the flames began to abate. Then a second explosion rocked the harbor. The trawler, tilting heavily to starboard, disappeared slowly in a wall of fire.

"*Quelle catastrophe,*" said Dulac under his breath, peering through the binoculars at the sinking inferno.

* * *

The next morning, the *Corriere della Sera's* bold headline read:

High-speed chase in the Bay of Naples: Speedboat and trawler sink; four dead, three wounded. Police suspect drug connection.

Having put his newspaper aside, and after ordering breakfast at the Hotel's dining room, Dulac phoned Belli.

"Get the net up, find out who owned the Donzi," exclaimed Dulac. "Send me the autopsy reports. Let me know if Stephanopoulos cracks."

Dulac's plan had failed miserably: The four men in the Donzi were dead. The three badly burned fishermen on the trawler were barely alive. He felt unwell. In the afternoon, an exhausted Dulac flew back to Paris, recounting the night's events to an amazed yet compassionate Karen.

"What now?" she asked.

"They're working on Stephanopoulos. The Marchioness must be in on it, but unless I have direct evidence, I can't press charges."

"What about my testimony?"

"It's circumstantial — no, actually, hearsay. We're getting court orders for wiretaps. I have to find out about the *Eastland*. I'll know more when they haul it out."

* * *

Stephanopoulos always called Lady Sarah after the ship docked in Naples. "They did the usual search and found nothing," reported Stephanopoulos the day before Dulac boarded. "I will bring the *Eastland* to the shipyard tomorrow for maintenance."

That was the last communication she had with the captain.

The following day, Lady Sarah received a call.

"They've arrested Stephanopoulos," said a man's voice.

"That's impossible. I spoke to him yesterday and everything was fine," replied the Marchioness.

"Didn't you read today's Italian newspapers?"

"We get them two days late here."

"Go to the Internet: Interpol has intercepted the shipment. The men who were on the Donzi are dead."

The man hung up.

God, Dulac will be down here at any moment. I must call my lawyers. No, if Kostas had cracked, Dulac would be here already. Kostas won't crack. He was tortured by the Greek government before the overthrow in 1967 and didn't reveal any names of the resistance members. That's why we chose him, she reminded herself, trying to remain calm. *He'll take the punishment: After a few years, he'll come out a wealthy man. He'll do it for his family; family is everything for Greeks. But Dulac will call soon.*

CHAPTER 43

Nicola was getting impatient. She had overstayed her welcome at her friend's house, and she wanted desperately to get the exchange over and done with. She tried to imagine how a new life, a normal life outside of Russia, would be: No more intrigues, no more hiding from the FSB, no more policemen breaking into apartments, violating what little privacy she had. Every aspect of Russian life seemed darker, more oppressive than ever before.

From her aunt's letters, Canada could give her all of the normalcy she could hope for.

Sometimes, she felt herself almost forgiving Sergei. Without the sacrifice of his life, this couldn't have happened. *What is taking Petrov so long?* She phoned the FSB.

"Petrov," answered the familiar, gruff voice.

"Vasilieva. What is happening?"

"I'm waiting for Dulac. All passport papers are ready."

"Good, when is the visa coming?"

"Don't worry. Soon."

"I'll call you tomorrow."

* * *

Petrov hadn't heard from Dulac in three days. *Was this French cooperation?* He asked for FSB reports on his whereabouts and got his answer.

Interpol: Dulac in Naples. Italian police seized Eastland, *a Caribbean flag vessel. Police arrested Kostas Stephanopoulos and crew for attempted money smuggling. Drug connection suspected.* Eastland *owned jointly by Marchioness of Dorset and Maritime Museum of Rome.*

Petrov phoned Dulac.

"The Canadian visa came yesterday, while I was in Naples," said Dulac.

"Naples?" said Petrov, feigning surprise

"You didn't know?"

"Nyet."

"We have arrested the captain and crew. They're smuggling and laundering drug money. We retrieved 5.2 million US dollars."

Petrov whistled. "Who else is involved?"

"We don't know yet. The sting operation went badly."

"What about the Marchioness?"

"How do you know about her?"

Petrov knew he'd blown it. Before he could answer and try and dig himself out, Dulac let him off the hook: "Anyway, let's talk about Nicola. What's your plan?"

"Send the visa: We will put with passport and acceptance in her bank. She will put money and Vasiliev's letter in the safety deposit box."

CHAPTER 44

As the Marchioness sat sipping her G and T, the Caribbean southerly breeze was just starting to fill in over the bay and its first gusts were beginning to cool the air of the hot terrace. The phone rang. Nervous, she answered and immediately, her fears were confirmed.

"Lady Sarah, Thierry Dulac of Interpol."

"How are you, Inspector? I was expecting your call." She cleared her throat. "I've heard about the *Eastland*. I'm absolutely shocked." She waited, fearing she'd sounded a bit too forceful.

"We'd like to meet you at your London apartment, Thursday, 10 a.m."

She knew that any suggestion to meet on her turf at Isola Rossa was now out of the question. "That's a bit inconvenient. I'd planned to say here until the end of the week."

"Lady Sarah, let's cut to the chase. Your ship is involved in a crime. As owner of that vessel, you have urgent legal responsibilities. Meet us in London on Thursday," said Dulac.

It was impossible to put him off. "In the afternoon, then?"

"We want to see your ship's documents and logbooks."

"I believe I have some old ones here. The current ones are on board. You probably have those."

"Correct."

"See you Thursday afternoon then," said Lady Sarah, gradually regaining her composure.

The line went dead. *This is serious*, she thought. Sarah hung up and phoned her London barristers.

Alder, Hawkins and Emory, had been the family lawyers since Sir Thomas' time. They had helped build his empire, every step of the way.

"Lord Hawkins, please. This is the Marchioness of Dorset," said Sarah to the receptionist.

"My dear Marchioness, how are you?" said a mellifluous voice, a brief moment later.

"Well, thank you, Lord Hawkins, but I have a slight complication. Could you pop by for tea this coming Wednesday morning? Say ten-ish?"

When a triple 'A' client like the Marchioness phoned, the golden rule at the firm was: *Drop whatever you're doing; yes, you are available.*

"But of course."

"Splendid."

"Anything in particular?"

"I'll tell you when we meet."

By her tone, Hawkins guessed the complication to be serious.

* * *

"Good morning, Lord Hawkins, good of you to come," said Sarah, as the butler took the barrister's bowler and coat and showed him into the vast, high-ceilinged parlor.

"Please sit down," said Lady Sarah. "Tea?"

"Please. Now, Marchioness, what is this about?"

"You've heard of this *Eastland* business in Naples?"

"Yes, briefly."

"I partially own and fund the *Eastland* in its archaeological digs, along with the Maritime Museum of Rome."

"I see."

"As you might have read, the crew are being detained and charged with smuggling money into Italy."

"Yes, I read that."

"Inspector Dulac of Interpol is coming to see me tomorrow morning."

"I think we should be there also."

"Won't that imply guilt?"

"Not at all. You and your lawyers simply want to know what is happening to your crew, to the *Eastland*, to see if all appropriate measures are being taken. We will ask the questions."

Sarah felt relieved, congratulating herself on her decision to call Hawkins. There was a moment of uneasy silence.

"Aren't you going to ask me if I'm involved in this?"

Hawkins had faced that one many, many times before.

"No, I'm not. I'm sure you would tell me if you were."

"Yes, of course," said Sarah, her lower lip curling slightly. "There is something else: Dulac has previously visited me on Isola Rossa, concerning the murders of Archbishops Conti and Salvador."

"Why on earth would he do that?" said Hawkins, twisting a little in his seat.

"Because he thought I might know something about a letter sent to the Vatican by Pistis Sophia."

"This is the, ah, sect you are involved with?"

"It's not a *sect*, as you call it. It's a legitimate Christian Church. Older than your Protestant Church, I might add."

"Please, I meant no offense, Marchioness. I didn't mean to be disparaging. I don't know what other term to use."

"Quite. I'm used to it by now."

"You don't know anything about this letter?"

"No, as I mentioned to Dulac, all members have access to the Pistis Sophia stationery."

"Then there's nothing to worry about, is there?"

"No, but I thought I'd mention my previous meeting with Dulac."

"Anything else?"

"No, not that I can think of."

"*À demain,* then."

"Excellent; I feel better having spoken to you."

Hawkins felt better also: A new, juicy file with his open-check-book client. What better way to start the morning? Trials of the ultra-rich attracted free publicity. He couldn't wait to get back to tell his partners. His instinct, honed by years of questioning witnesses, clients, and police officers, told him that Lady Sarah wasn't being entirely truthful. No matter; that could wait.

CHAPTER 45

Volpe didn't like Legnano. It wasn't personal, he told himself, but apart from his vows, he had little, if anything, in common with the man. Legnano's modest country upbringing and lack of sophistication erected a permanent barrier to any deep philosophical conversations and exchanges. Legnano's earthy, sometimes vulgar humor always brought down the few talks he had with him to a lower common denominator. Volpe caught himself sometimes smiling at Legnano's rustic jokes, only to regret having stooped to his level.

Legnano had left a message requesting a meeting, and Volpe had returned the message, stating he was overly busy. After receiving a third call, he couldn't put him off any longer.

"Does this concern the Pistis Sophia letter?" inquired Volpe.

"No, it has to do with the Investment Review Committee," said Legnano.

"Shall we say tomorrow morning after Mass, at my office?"

"Fine."

Legnano admired, but didn't trust, Volpe. He envied him his brilliant intellect, his encyclopedic knowledge of Canon Law, History and Philosophy. But he had also witnessed his scathing arrogance. And his machinations, intrigues and alliances, directed toward getting himself elected to the Papacy, were hardly secret. Serious *Papabile*, eventual candidates for the papacy, canvassed their electorate support early.

Legnano knew he had to be cautious. Yet not to meet with him on the matter would appear suspect: The Secretary of State was the Pope's right-hand man.

"Do you know of this anonymous donor, who enriches the Vatican's Treasury every month?" asked Legnano.

"Which one? I hope we have many," said Volpe, his tone light.

"The one that Conti, Salvador and Durivage inquired about during the Financial Committee Meeting last month," said Legnano sternly.

"I, yes . . . I believe the audit firm is looking into this," said Volpe, detached.

"Exactly. Do you think that . . ."

"It has to do with the murders? No," he said rhetorically. "Besides, if their request for information were cause for foul play, wouldn't Durivage have been affected?"

"Possibly."

"No, I think Salvador was alluding to whoever is behind the Pistis Sophia letter. Any news from Fiore on the subject?"

Legnano paused, surprised. Why had Volpe suddenly mentioned Salvador's letter, out of context?

They were silent for a moment: Legnano knew they both suddenly recognized the curious leap of logic. *Volpe knows that to try and correct it will only worsen the situation*, thought Legnano.

"I wasn't referring to Salvador's letter," said Legnano, "but no, I haven't received word from Fiore. I'm more interested in why you think the murders aren't related to the donations."

"It's not impossible," replied Volpe, "but I must tell you, I've had word from Casparelli. His findings, so far, are positive. Let's wait for his complete, official report."

"That's what everyone keeps telling me."

"We'll meet once we have it," said Volpe, rising from his chair, and accompanying Legnano toward the door. "We can discuss it more intelligently then."

Legnano, his face flushed red at the near insult, left in a huff.

CHAPTER 46

The day after the Naples incident, Harris had summoned Dulac to his office in Lyon. Looking at the small, balding bureaucrat's back, Dulac waited patiently as Harris finished his phone call. Finally, Harris hung up, and swiveled in his chair away from the window and faced Dulac. "I have the Minister of the Interior and the Minister of Justice asking me why I haven't replaced you in the archbishops' murder case, and now *this*?" said Harris.

"We did get the money. And the *Eastland*'s crew."

"But you don't know where the money was going, four men are dead, we're facing lawsuits from the fishermen for grossly negligent police procedure, maybe a claim for abuse of police powers from the Italian government, and a revision of the Interpol Cooperation Agreement with Italy. Do you have anything to add?"

"I wasn't driving the boat."

"I don't need your sarcasm, Dulac. What else?"

"The smuggling is probably linked to a money-laundering scheme. The Marchioness of Dorset could be involved. Stephanopoulos won't talk, for the moment."

"I don't have to remind you we need a bulletproof case before we can even think of arresting the Marchioness."

"I'm perfectly aware of that."

Dulac knew the General Secretary was referring to the Dangel case, where Interpol's circumstantial evidence had been blown to bits by the billionaire's defense lawyers.

"I have circumstantial evidence linking the *Eastland* and the Pistis Sophia letter," said Dulac.

"That's not good enough. What about the murders?"

"We're making progress. We'll soon find out who hired Vasiliev and Kurganski."

"By the way, I got a call from Berne yesterday. They said you have an attitude problem."

"Now it comes out: You mean because I roughed up their 'peon' from Sion?"

"Not funny, Dulac. Of all people, you as a lawyer should know that we at Interpol are 'support only' to the local police force."

"Yes, yes, I keep forgetting. I'm just filling the voids. I use my cross-border authority. Anything wrong with that?"

"You know damn well that technically, no, but politically . . ."

"That's why they hired *you*." Dulac gave him his best Cheshire cat grin.

"Dulac, someday you'll go too far, and I won't extend that safety net."

"Then I'd better train harder," said Dulac, rising, knowing it was time to leave.

"To do what, exactly?"

"To land on my own two feet."

Dulac smiled, bowed slightly and left.

CHAPTER 47

Karen listened distractedly to the evening news on France 2 television, as she hastily finished preparing her supper. At 7 p.m., she was running late, as the opera started at 8 p.m., and it was a twenty-minute subway ride from her apartment to l'Opéra. Tonight was the third presentation of Mozart's *The Magic Flute*, her favorite opera.

She disliked the Italians: Too shrill. And the Germans: Too dramatic. The lightheartedness of Mozart filled her with immense, childlike joy every time.

As she took the steak off the stove, she suddenly stopped, almost dropped the pan and rushed to the living room. *That voice.*

A reporter had finished interviewing the President of Miranda Group on another large real estate development project in the La Défense Paris suburb. She phoned Dulac.

"Hello, Thierry, it's Karen."

"How are you?"

"Fine, I'm on my way to the opera. Can you meet me there later?"

"Surely, what's happening?"

"I'll tell you after the concert. Meet me at the central staircase."

Dulac was elated. Not only was he glad to see Karen, but he'd discovered she shared his passion for classical music. She had just salvaged his day, a welcome change from the somberness of his meeting with the General Secretary. He finished his drink and continued poring over the reports. If he left at 10:30 p.m., he would be in time to meet Karen at the end of the concert.

Karen felt mixed emotions: She anticipated the joy of relaxing in the plush lounge seat she had reserved for the last two seasons and being lulled into the diffuse escape of the music. But now, she could hardly wait until the opera finished, to share the news with Dulac.

"How was the performance?" queried Dulac.

"Excellent, Fischer-Dieskau was fabulous as Papageno."

"He's the greatest baritone ever. Shall we have a drink?"

"Wonderful. Where to?"

"Around the corner: Dumont's usually has a table."

"Thierry, I've just heard the voice of the man I heard on Isola Rossa. The man with Lady Sarah," she said excitedly.

"Calm down. Where?"

"A few hours ago, during the evening news. The interviewer was talking to the President of Mirana Corporation, or Group. I didn't get his name."

"You mean Miranda?"

"Yes, that's it. I'm sure that's the voice I heard at Isola Rossa."

"That's Hughes de Ségur, one of the richest, most powerful men in France."

"Whatever. It's the same voice, same tonality, same inflections."

Dulac could relate to that. A musical person could better distinguish and remember a voice. Listening to the radio, he would distinguish and identify a pianist, solely by the sound of his playing and technique.

"It's been a week since you've left Isola Rossa. Are you absolutely certain?"

"Absolutely."

Dulac probed into those almond eyes: They didn't waver.

"Before I start investigating de Ségur, we'd have to go to France 2 and hear the recording of that interview. De Ségur is an influential man. He's connected everywhere."

"No problem," assured Karen.

CHAPTER 48

Her every neuron danced with excitement. The new passport, the visa, the conditional acceptance letter from the University of British Columbia's medical school, a copy of the deposit into her aunt's bank in Calgary, plane ticket to Vancouver: Everything was there.

The day before, Nicola had received confirmation from Petrov to go to the bank. She brought her father's letters and the money and deposited them in the safety deposit box.

"No FSB. If I suspect anything, you'll never get the letters," she warned.

"Okay, okay," said Petrov, obvious reluctance in his voice.

Petrov had kept his word. She put away the documents carefully in her satchel and felt a breath of fresh air envelop her.

As she walked out and stood a moment at the doors, she thought: *Nicola, you've done it.*

She hailed a taxi. *Finally, back to my apartment and start packing. The flight leaves in two days. Barely enough time to say goodbye to Anton, to my friends, to Russia.*

While the taxi crept along in heavy traffic, Nicola allowed herself to wonder what life would be like in the land she had heard her aunt rave about.

"Only one problem: The weather is much like Russia," she'd said.

Nicola knew her English was good by Russian standards, *but would her level be sufficient for her studies*? She would take courses. She deposited the documents in the other safety box and directed the taxi to her apartment. As the car approached, she was reminded of the shabbiness of student living. It was grayer than Sokol, if that were possible.

She paid the taxi and started up the staircase, when suddenly she felt the presence of someone behind her, and as she half turned, two men grabbed her arms, turned her around and lifted her. They dragged her, writhing helplessly, into the waiting car.

"What the hell?" She tried to free her right arm.

"Don't resist, and you won't get hurt," said the lantern-jawed bulldog face, as he pushed her head down past the open car door.

"What do you want?" pleaded Nicola.

"We protect you: FSB," said the bulldog, as all three piled into the backseat, and the driver roared off.

"Petrov gave me his word," said Nicola angrily.

No response, as the other man looked behind, to see if they were being followed.

These aren't FSB, thought Nicola.

The car drove out to the suburbs of Moscow, and Nicola realized her short-lived dream was being fractured, shattered by the cold steel hammer of Russian reality.

CHAPTER 49

"Lady Sarah," said Dulac, bowing slightly as he and Lescop entered the parlor.

"Good morning," replied Sarah, extending her down-turned hand. "Please meet my lawyer, Lord Hawkins."

"Hello Inspector, Mr. Lescop," said Hawkins, his tone upbeat. "Terrible, this *Eastland* business. Where are the crew being held?"

"In Naples, at the Port precinct," replied Dulac.

"I trust you've advised the other owner?"

"Yes, we have. I'll ask the questions, if you don't mind."

"Ah, yes, of course. I presume you have interrogation authority?"

"Yes, under the Interpol–Britain police agreement."

"But only if the person is a 'suspect'. Surely Lady Sarah isn't a 'suspect', Inspector, or we wouldn't be here."

Dulac was cornered. If he said she was a suspect, there would be no further questions.

"Your client has agreed to this meeting," replied Dulac, knowing he was walking a fine line. "For the moment, let's keep it informal."

"Of course," intoned Hawkins, smiling at Lady Sarah.

"Marchioness, what do you know about this *Eastland* business?" asked Dulac.

"Sorry," interjected Hawkins, "but could you be more specific?"

"Very well," replied Dulac, looking at Lady Sarah, "When did you become aware of the smuggling activities of the *Eastland*?"

"Two days ago in the news," replied the Marchioness firmly. "I was as shocked as you were to learn of this."

"Really? How shocked am I?"

"Well, it's just a figure of—"

"So Captain Stephanopoulos gave you no hints, signs, or clues that he might be smuggling?"

"As far as I'm concerned, Mr. Stephanopoulos has always been a conscientious and competent captain. Ask the archaeologist who works with him."

"Marchioness," said Dulac, "the logbooks show the *Eastland* has taken regular trips from Isola Rossa to Naples, on about the same day every month since last year. Doesn't that strike you as odd, for a boat supposedly doing archaeological research? One doesn't find artifacts on a regular, predetermined monthly basis, would you think?"

"Frankly, I don't keep a diary of the *Eastland*'s whereabouts. Captain Stephanopoulos has entire discretion concerning his schedule."

"Did he report all finds of artifacts to you?"

"No, only those judged significant by the archaeologist."

"How many so far?"

"About eight."

"Isn't that very little, for all the money and effort?"

"We're just at the beginning, I'm told."

"Do you get a tax benefit from this?"

"I must object, Mr. Dulac," said Hawkins. "This has nothing to do with the Marchioness's business ventures."

"Has any crew member of the *Eastland*, or the archaeologist, ever come to you concerning the captain's behavior?" said Lescop, eyeing the Marchioness.

"No, they haven't."

"Are you aware that the *Eastland* has a double bottom?" asked Dulac.

"What do you mean?" replied Sarah.

"It can carry cargo in a hidden compartment."

"No, I wasn't aware of that."

Dulac hastened the tempo: "Why did you have hydrofoils fitted to the boat last year? At major expense, I might add,"

"Stephanopoulos told me it would be a good idea, and it would save time and fuel."

"I see. Didn't it strike you as odd that an archaeological vessel would require such equipment, as opposed to say, a ferry?"

"No, it didn't. Again, this is Stephanopoulos' domain. I just pay the bills," replied Sarah, desperately trying to add levity to the exchange.

Dulac stared at her and noticed an almost imperceptible curl of her lower lip.

There was a long pause, while Lescop finished taking notes.

Dulac rose and signaled to Lescop.

"If you don't have any further questions, Mr. Lescop, I think we are through, Lady Sarah . . . for today."

"If I can be of help, please don't hesitate to call," replied the Marchioness, getting up.

The *portier* escorted Dulac and Lescop out of the room and into the hallway toward the door. As Dulac crossed the doorway, he turned to Lady Sarah and Hawkins, standing behind her: "Oh, by the way, have you met with Hughes de Ségur lately?"

Lady Sarah, visibly shaken, fumbled for words. "Ah, oh, I don't think so . . . no, I don't recall."

"Really? Then I bid you good day Marchioness, Lord Hawkins." Dulac turned, smiled at Lescop, and started walking toward the waiting car.

"She's lying," said Lescop, getting into the car with Dulac.

"Obviously. Are the wiretaps installed?"

"Yes. I wonder what she's told Hawkins?"

"Very little. She'll use his office to call de Ségur — or, better, have Hawkins call him."

* * *

At Heathrow, Dulac and Lescop's plane was late. Dulac's phone rang. It was Petrov.

"I have big news: We have Vasiliev's letters. It's Victor Oleyev. He hired them to kill Salvador and Conti."

"Good job, Petrov. Does it say why?"

"No. Vasiliev said Oleyev would kill him. We have problem: We can't find Nicola. We sent men to her apartment. Her plane for Canada leaves tomorrow."

"Perhaps she's staying with friends."

"Her boyfriend Anton has not heard from her."

"Not good. Did you verify the authenticity of the letters?"

"Yes. We'll move on Oleyev."

"With only the letters?"

"*Da.* Oleyev will talk."

"Won't he fight back?"

"First, we must get support from the government. He has many contacts inside."

Dulac didn't want to think of what Oleyev was facing at the hands of Petrov's men. A mafioso who had violated their territory and killed a prison guard and an innocent victim wasn't going to buy himself a cushy, quiet cell. *I should go to Moscow,* thought Dulac. *We need Oleyev alive. He's just an intermediary.*

"Petrov, wait until you have better, solid evidence," said Dulac. "If you arrest him now, with only the letters, we lose the surprise element against whoever hired him. They'll destroy any remaining evidence linking him to the crimes, and to them. We risk never knowing who hired him."

"You think you are the only one with pressure? I can't wait long."

"Tighten your surveillance on him. We must be patient: If we time this right, we catch more game with a bigger trap." Dulac hoped the analogy would appeal to Petrov's interest as a hunter, if not as a policeman. "Without your help, we risk losing it all."

"When I clear the government contacts, I move," said Petrov.

"You must find Nicola. We need her testimony. Any news on Kurganski?"

"He was seen outside Moscow. Don't worry, we find him."

Dulac knew that Petrov was under tremendous pressure to tackle and bring in Oleyev. A murky high roller like Victor Oleyev was an eyesore to the policies of the reformed Russian government, eager to shake off its reputation for gangsterism and corruption, eager to prove the credibility of its emerging, Western-inspired legal system. Petrov was becoming a dinosaur in this Russia, still using antiquated methods. Dulac worried that if the courts went by the new rules of strict evidence and a fair trial, Oleyev could get away. He knew Petrov's career was on the line, as was his.

CHAPTER 50

"Good afternoon, your Eminence." Tondino proffered a meek, soft hand and sat down timidly before the Cardinal, Legnano. Tondino had called earlier that day to report that he had news, and Legnano had suggested this meeting at the Cardinal's office.

"How are you, young man?"

"Scared. If my firm finds out I have leaked this, I'll be fired. Worse, I'll probably be barred from the order of auditors."

"You are doing what's best," said Legnano, trying to be reassuring. "Besides, you're giving an early version of the facts to your client. There's nothing wrong with that. What have you there?"

Tondino opened a brown envelope and pulled out a document. "It's Casparelli's report."

"Good. What does it say about this anonymous donor?"

"It's legalese to me, but it says Casparelli and the firm undertake to maintain the secrecy of the donor, except to divulge his or her name to the Financial Committee members. They must first sign a secrecy agreement. It also gives a copy of the financial statements of the donor, prepared by . . . you guessed it, our firm."

"Who's the donor, young man?" said Legnano, growing impatient.

"Miranda Group."

"The French real estate group?"

"Yes. It has assets in the billions of euros."

"Good. They can keep up their donations, maybe increase them," said Legnano, looking relieved.

"But look at the report on shareholders at page six: The main shareholder that controls the group and owns fifty-three per cent of the stock, is a numbered Swiss company, 06584 — 9 Capital. Also look at page two, the Board of Directors."

Legnano's eyes widened.

Hugues de Ségur: President and CEO
Enrique Gonzales, Businessman
Felipe Montoya, Businessman
Archbishop Paolo Fiore, Legate, Vatican
Lady Sarah Litman, Marchioness of Dorset
Howard Atkins, Felman Group
Andrea Bellini, Fiat Group.

Legnano carefully replaced the report in the envelope and rose.

"Young man, you have been of great help. May I keep this?"

"Sure, of course."

They shook hands, and Tondino left.

Cardinal Legnano felt partially relieved by the news: Miranda Group enjoyed an international reputation as a major real estate developer, property owner, and urban manager. It managed some of the Vatican's prime real estate in Rome. *But why request anonymity? Surely the publicity of a 5 million-dollar monthly donation would enhance the reputation of the group*, he thought. Also, why didn't Fiore, as board director, inform him about Miranda during their meeting? He must have known that Legnano would eventually learn the identity of the mysterious donor. Did Volpe also know?

And there was the matter of the Swiss numbered company shareholder. Not uncommon in European business, thought Legnano. But there was something unusual, paradoxical about the composition of the board. *Why was the Marchioness of Dorset, acknowledged Pistis Sofia member, involved with a donor to the Catholic Church?*

He had to confide in and discuss this with the one person beyond the intrigues and politics of the Vatican, beyond the human frailties, ambitions, of his fellow cardinals: the Holy Father.

* * *

"His Holiness will see you now," announced the Papal Secretary, as Legnano rose from his chair.

He had requested a private meeting, and the Pontiff preferred hosting one-on-one meetings in his private library, a simply decorated, austere room adjacent to the Apartment of Audiences. As Monsignor Legnano knelt and kissed the papal ring, the Pontiff said a short prayer: "Divine Holy Spirit, guide our thoughts and minds during our exchange today. May our talks be to the benefit of our Church, amen."

"My dear Legnano, what brings you here today?" The Pope smiled broadly and invited the Cardinal to sit beside him under the painting by Perugino, *The Resurrection of Christ*.

The Pontiff always enjoyed his conversations with Legnano. He welcomed his simplicity, his openness of heart.

"Thank you for receiving me, Your Holiness. My visit concerns the Financial Review Committee."

"That's Volpe's responsibility."

"If you recall, you asked me to review activities of the Financial Investment Committee, headed by Archbishop Fiore."

"Forgive me, yes, of course I remember."

"Frankly, I'm worried about certain donations and the shroud of secrecy around them. The secrecy seems to be encouraged by some of our prelates."

The Pontiff's face grew serious. He reclined slightly in the chair behind the walnut desk.

"The Miranda Group's donations are what I'm referring to."

In an instant, the Pontiff's smile dissolved. He rose, turned away from Legnano, and walked to one of the bookcases lining the library's walls. He took out an older Bible and opened it at random.

"Do you know that Hugues de Ségur is a Cathar?"

"No, I didn't," said Legnano in astonishment.

Cathars were an early Christian sect, which, along with Pistis Sofia, had been persecuted by the Roman Catholic Church. The gathering and burning of 220 faithful at Montségur by 10,000 Roman Catholic troops in 1244 A.D. had marked the darkest hours in the history of the Church, and had brought the Cathars to near extinction. A right-wing group of the sect had vowed revenge. For a Cathar to make donations to the Church was unthinkable, inexplicable.

"Your Holiness, then you know about the donations?"

"Yes, I know," said the Pope, his voice breaking slightly.

"Then these donations could be related to the Pistis Sofia letter you received recently? I don't think I understand," said Legnano in disbelief, slowly rising from his chair.

The Pope, whose back had been facing Legnano, turned toward him, his eyes moist. He suddenly looked frail.

Legnano approached the Holy Father and extended a hand to steady him.

He motioned Legnano to sit down.

"My dear Legnano, what I'm about to tell you must not, cannot leave this room, is that clear?" said the Pontiff, wiping his eyes with a small handkerchief.

"Yes, your Holiness."

"As you are aware, since my predecessor Pope John XXIII started it, it has become customary for popes to hear confessions during Holy Week before Easter."

"Yes, of course."

"I need not remind you that any penitent's identity and what he confesses, even to a pope, must remain secret. The penalty for the breach of this obligation is automatic excommunication of the confessor."

"Yes," Legnano replied, feeling more and more apprehensive.

"I have received confessions for the assassinations of Archbishops Salvador and Conti."

"*Mio Di*o," Legnano gasped and put a hand to his mouth, then crossed himself.

The Pontiff cleared his throat.

"Never, never did I think I would have to bear such a burden. You realize that I cannot continue this conversation."

"I understand."

"I ask you not to jump to conclusions."

"May I inquire if these persons received absolution?"

"No, you may not: This is solely between the penitent and the priest."

"Your Holiness, I cannot help noticing that you brought up this subject after I mentioned the donations. Are the deaths related to—?"

"Legnano, I've spoken enough, maybe even too much. *You* must see this through. Have you seen this Interpol inspector lately?"

"No, I was hoping not to have to disclose my findings, to avoid scandal."

"Please, see him about these donations as soon as possible," said the Pontiff, escorting Legnano to the doorway, his hand suddenly heavy on Legnano's left shoulder. "We must let the law take its course. My dear Legnano, this is a very difficult time for me. Pray the Lord to give me courage. Let's ask for His forgiveness. You must promise me now, Legnano: *This will never leave this room.*"

"Yes, Your Holiness."

He embraced Legnano and retired to his chambers, accompanied by his secretary. He canceled his appointments for the day.

CHAPTER 51

The car drove down the dusty road, and Nicola recognized the trappings of the rich Moscow suburb: Rubliovka. It confirmed her mounting fear that these men were mafia, and that she was going to meet her father's executioner. Her eyes welled with tears. The huge mansions appeared, one after the other behind high walls of concrete and steel, protecting its mega-rich occupants from intruders. *Like me.* Ironic, she thought, that in her wildest dreams, she saw herself as a plastic surgeon, beautifying the faces of the wealthy. *I could have been making a house call. Now I'm the one who'll need surgery.*

The car stopped in front of a large wrought-iron gate and guardhouse, and the driver spoke to the guard. He opened the gate. As the car drove up the sinuous road, tall maple trees drooped, their heavy, low-lying branches welcoming her. *The calm before the storm.*

The extravagant, neoclassical pink mansion surged into view. The car stopped between the large granite veranda in front of the entrance and a fountain, over which stood a statue of a man in a business suit, looking authoritatively into the distance, one hand on his breast, Napoleonlike.

Nicola smiled, but the view of the men standing with machine guns on the veranda quickly sobered her mood.

Oleyev's place. The thugs escorted her past the guards and into the entrance. The décor was the epitome of Russian kitsch, a mixture of cheap Greek statues, abstract paintings and fake gold-lined Louis XVI furniture. On the ceiling, late Renaissance-style frescoes depicted what must have been members of the owner's family, in half-naked, cherub-like poses. To add to the garishness, over the center of the hallway hung an immense pastel-multicolored chandelier, in Murano frosty glass.

If the owner wants to induce acute artistic indigestion, he's achieved his goal, thought Nicola.

The thugs guided Nicola into a huge adjoining salon, where the ridiculous turned to the sublime. To her disbelieving eyes, at the center stood a man dressed in the rich red velour padded shoulder coat and cap of Henry VIII. He was striking a royal head-on pose. Facing him, with his back to Nicola, a portrait painter was busy immortalizing the imbecility and vanity of his client on a life-sized canvas. At the King's feet, a footstool had been placed, on which one of his tights-clad legs rested, slightly bent. Around the footstool, two Slouhgi dogs were resting, both of which immediately got up and barked at Nicola.

"Hello," said Henry VIII, looking embarrassed as he waved away the portraitist and the dogs. "Please excuse this; I wasn't expecting you." He took off his hat.

"Obviously not," retorted Nicola, desperately trying to control her convulsions.

"I am Victor Oleyev." His imperious voice momentarily giving credence to the costume. "You must be Nicola Vasilieva, yes?"

"Why have you brought me here?"

"Not so fast. There is no rush. How do you like my house?"

"It's different. I'm sure you didn't get me here to talk about your house."

"Very well then, let's get down to business: I'm told you have a letter concerning me, is that correct?"

"What letter?" She searched for what to say next.

"Please," he said, extending his right hand. "Your father's letter."

"I have no such letter," replied Nicola, shaking.

"In that case, we have a problem, you see. If that letter falls into the wrong hands, I'm told it could prove, shall we say, upsetting. I really, really hate being upset. High blood pressure, you know. At my age, my doctor says I must be careful."

A large smile had overtaken the earlier embarrassment and spread all over his oval, wide face.

She could guess how this almost charming character had risen to where he was. There was something vaguely attractive in the stocky figure, the slightly graying temples, and the expertly cut hair.

Oleyev was handed Nicola's satchel. He opened and rummaged through the satchel.

"Now, where is this letter?" Oleyev drew closer, his face now threatening.

Nicola hunched her shoulders.

"Wrong answer," he yelled, as he struck her across the face with the back of his right hand.

"You bastard! You killed Sergei."

He hit her again twice, as she recoiled. "Trash, nothing but trash, a hired assassin! I have dozens like him."

She had to cool down and think her way out of this, she thought. She had to buy time. "And I suppose you're not?"

He was about to strike her again, but stopped in mid-swing.

"We won't get anywhere like this, will we?"

She didn't reply.

"Does the FSB have this letter?"

"Honestly, I don't know," replied Nicola.

"Yes, you do. They have it. You're smart enough to have given it to them if you had it."

Nicola had a brain wave: "If the FSB have it, then why aren't they here already?"

Oleyev was taken aback. The FSB was not known to be slow on the trigger.

"Good point," said Oleyev, pacing near the footstool in his leotard white tights and effeminate deerskin shoes. His face changed again, back to the broad smile: "Then you have seen it."

She was caught. She felt her face flush, and as blood rushed to her head, she had another idea: "It's in my safety deposit box, at the Vinogourov Bank."

"Ah, that's better," said Oleyev, the smile increasing even more. "*Now* we are getting somewhere."

Nicola thought: *Why isn't the FSB here, arresting this thug?*

"We'll have to get it, won't we? And it better be there, Nicola Va-si-lie-va." He pounded every syllable of her name.

"Now, let's have some tea, shall we?" he said, suddenly as docile as a cocker spaniel.

At least I'm buying time from this psychopath, she thought. *The FSB will surely realize something is wrong if I don't show up at the airport tomorrow.*

CHAPTER 52

Legnano left the library and walked briskly to the gardens. He needed fresh air. He felt depressed, overwhelmed by what he had heard. He had sought guidance in his dilemma and had come out of the meeting with more questions than answers.

How to interpret the Pope's reaction? Was he upset by the memory of Salvador and Conti? By the fact he couldn't name the assassins? Why did he react at the mention of Miranda? De Ségur must be one of the penitents. Or was he troubled by the inevitable, looming scandal? He certainly knew about Miranda. How much did he know about the donations?

Legnano couldn't help but think the unthinkable.

Yet His message had been clear: Let the law take its course.

At all costs? Legnano chastised himself for even thinking of the Pope being involved. The Church was still reeling from the Banco Ambrosiano scandal. Another was rearing its ugly head, he thought.

* * *

Dulac's flight to Paris had been delayed. He'd phoned Karen to postpone the meeting with the France 2 interviewers, and then his phone rang.

"Mr. Dulac, this is Cardinal Legnano's office. I will pass you his Eminence, please hold," said the Cardinal's secretary.

"Mr. Dulac, this is Cardinal Legnano. I have some matters I'd like to discuss with you. When could we meet?"

"I am available tomorrow afternoon," said a pleasantly surprised Dulac. He hadn't counted on any of the Vatican's representatives being so forthcoming. Was one about to breach Omerta, the Vatican's Code of Silence?

"Let's say, 1 p.m. at my office?"

"With pleasure, your Eminence."

Dulac arrived in Paris late, after having canceled his meeting with Karen and the interviewers. He poured a Pernod, threw himself into the reclining chair and lit a cigarette: *I must stop soon*, he thought; his doctor had recently noticed the shortening of his breath, the first sign of emphysema. Finishing his refilled drink, he reserved his ticket to Rome, repacked his suitcase, set the alarm for 9:30 a.m. and dozed off into a heavy sleep.

* * *

"Good afternoon, Mr. Dulac," said Legnano, grasping Dulac's hand with both of his. "How was your flight?"

"Restfully uneventful," replied Dulac.

"Please sit down." Legnano invited him to a worn leather L-shaped sofa.

Legnano's secretary offered them coffee.

"I have been reviewing some donations the Vatican receives, and I'm quite worried."

"How is that?"

"For the last year, a donor has been giving five million US dollars per month directly to the Vatican Treasury. This is an unusually high amount to be given on such a regular basis."

"I see."

"We had our audit firm produce a report on the provenance of such gift. The Holy See is particularly sensitive about such donations since the bank scandal."

"Yes, of course. Do you have the identity of this donor?"

"The Miranda Group."

Dulac stared dumbfounded at Legnano. Finally, regaining his composure: "You're saying that Miranda Group, headed by de Ségur, has been giving five million dollars a month to the Vatican for the past year?"

"Yes. Here is a report on the Group prepared by Casparelli, from our auditing firm."

Dulac leafed through the pages, his nicotine-stained right hand trembling slightly.

"Interesting: The Marchioness of Dorset sits on the board, as does Archbishop Fiore. Quite extraordinary."

"That was my reaction. Also, de Ségur is a Cathar. It doesn't make sense."

"Your Eminence, you must know that we are investigating the Marchioness in relation to the *Eastland* vessel scandal. We've caught the captain of her vessel trying to smuggle 5.2 million dollars into Italy from Isola Rossa. We have evidence it happened monthly for the past year."

"*Mannaggia la Miseria!*" exclaimed Legnano.

"There's more. Someone overheard a conversation between de Ségur and the Marchioness about the murders, and about the Pistis Sophia letter."

"Who?" exclaimed Legnano.

"It's not important at this time." Dulac thought there was no need to involve Karen.

"Anything else, Your Eminence?"

"We tried in vain to find out about the numbered Swiss company, majority shareholder of Miranda."

No wonder, thought Dulac. *Only the Swiss are more secretive than the Vatican.*

"Do you have any news on the provenance of the Pistis Sophia letter?" asked Legnano.

"We are sure it was painted by the illuminator who does the Marchioness's private letterhead, but he's disappeared. Monsignor, how does Archbishop Fiore fit into all of this?"

Legnano squirmed. His brief exchanges with Archbishop Fiore in the investigation of the Finance Committee, and in the murder investigation, had left him uneasy. He was still unsure as to Archbishop Fiore's trustworthiness. But the Vatican always put on a unified, secretive front before outsiders.

"He represents the Vatican for some of its investments," replied Legnano.

"Your Eminence, I presume he's under a lot of pressure to maximize the Vatican's financial performance?"

Dulac's probing was wandering into the sacrosanct territory of Vatican finances.

"I'm not at liberty to say," Legnano answered.

"I understand," replied Dulac. "In any case, your Eminence, all this is most interesting, perhaps helpful, even."

"Yes . . . I thought . . ."

Dulac's cell phone rang.

"Excuse me, your Eminence."

"It's Petrov."

"Yes?"

"We can't wait. We arrest Oleyev."

"If you must," said Dulac, resignation in his voice.

"We think he has Nicola. She didn't pick up her ticket for Canada, and she didn't show up at her apartment."

"Not good. Remember, Petrov, we need Oleyev and Nicola alive."

CHAPTER 53

Nicola had spent a nervous, sleepless night in one of the gaudy guest rooms, wondering what would become of her when Oleyev found out there was no letter in the safety deposit box. He had to have either a power of attorney, or escort her to the bank, to open the box. *I've got to delay that.* Ironic, she thought, that now she hoped the FSB would pick up her trail, and quickly. *With the FSB on his back, could Oleyev afford another disappearance, another murder? Ha! This man stops at nothing: One more, one less, what's the difference?*

As she looked out the window facing the wooded area underneath, the hope of escape crossed her mind briefly, only to be quashed by the presence of two patrolling armed guards.

Nicola got dressed, descended the long spiraling staircase and entered the breakfast room.

Seated at the breakfast table, a bespectacled Oleyev, still in his dressing gown, was already busy, telephone in hand, giving orders to one of his sidekicks. Another was busy sorting out the voluminous stack of morning newspapers for his boss. It seemed Oleyev was a voracious reader.

"Bring me the power of attorney," he barked at the taller sidekick.

"Yes, Mr. Oleyev."

"Hallo, Vasilieva, sleep well?"

She didn't like being called by her last name. It reminded her of the impersonality of her professors at grade school, where she had been treated as an inconvenient encumbrance, to be dealt with as mechanically and expeditiously as possible. *Was this how he distanced himself from the human being he was about to destroy?*

"As well as possible," she answered curtly.

"Let's get down to business. Sign this," as he thrust the power of attorney across the table, and the shorter sidekick offered a pen.

Gathering all of her courage, she blurted:

"No, thanks."

"Well, now really, Vasilieva," said Oleyev, smiling at the taller goon. "I know you're a lot smarter than that. How long do you think you can last?"

"You need me to open that box. If I sign it, I'm dead."

"You're right," said an obviously amused Oleyev, putting down his newspaper, crossing his hands behind his head and reclining in the swivel chair. "Do you have another suggestion, Vasilieva?"

"Yes, I go down to the bank with your ape here and get the letter for you. Once you have it, you don't need me anymore."

"I have a better idea," replied Oleyev. "Why don't I hand you over to *my ape*, as you call him, and let him do what he wants with you? I'm sure he and his friends are very imaginative."

Nicola's fear deepened, as the threat of torture and rape became alarmingly real. She had a last, desperate card to play.

"Listen, if my boyfriend doesn't see me at the airport tomorrow, I've told him to contact the FSB and open that box. They'll be onto you in an instant."

"If what you say is true, Nicola, then we must keep you in one piece," Oleyev said, laughing. "Get me her satchel," he barked at the shorter sidekick.

He opened it again and dumped its contents onto the breakfast table. A small key, separate from her keychain, fell out.

"Is this the key to the box?"

"Yes," replied Nicola.

At that moment, a guard erupted into the room, went straight to Oleyev's side, and whispered into his ear. Oleyev's face turned crimson.

"Bastards, fucking bastards." He rose and pounded the wall with his right fist. "I'll piss on your graves." He turned and punched Nicola in the face, hard: "Lying bitch! You'll pay for this."

Nicola fell backward on the floor. She felt her upper lip swell, and tasted the blood.

"Get her out of here," he yelled to his goons.

Nicola realized the FSB were on their way. *I've got to survive until then.*

CHAPTER 54

Upon his return to Paris, Dulac picked up Karen to go to the offices of France 2 TV.

"Someone at Miranda Group is behind the murders, not Pistis Sophia," said Dulac.

"Then that confirms what I heard at Isola Rossa," said Karen.

"The Marchioness is laundering money for them, and they are reinvesting it in real estate."

"Where does the money come from?"

"We don't know yet; probably South America. I'm having Miranda investigated."

Dulac had unofficial contacts in Switzerland. They had pierced the usually impenetrable corporate veil of secrecy and found information that, if made public, would cost him his and his contacts their jobs.

"But how is this related to the murderers?"

"Hopefully, we will find out when I get the information from Switzerland."

They approached the France 2 headquarters. Dulac sensed a growing uneasiness in Karen, as she swept her hair repeatedly from her face.

"Are you all right?"

"Fine, fine," she replied nervously.

Dulac was sure she knew the consequences of identifying de Ségur. His cell phone rang, and he snatched it from his pocket: "Dulac."

"They found Dessault's body — the Marchioness's illuminator? — in the Seine, about three hours ago," said a policeman's voice.

"How did it happen?"

"Not sure, but there is a mark on the right side of his neck. We're having the autopsy done now."

"Let me know the results."

Dulac turned to Karen: "The Marchioness's illuminator, Dessault, was murdered."

"God, the poor man," said Karen, as she felt the assassins' coils growing tighter.

They entered the viewing room, and Karen could feel her pulse quickening, the events of that chilling night tumbling uncontrollably into her consciousness. *Perhaps I've forgotten the voice by now.* The technician turned on the television screen, the interviewer came into focus, and as he introduced his guests, the camera turned onto de Ségur.

"Good evening, Mr. de Ségur."

"Good evening."

Karen knew, at that instant, that she couldn't escape, couldn't go back, and that she had no control, no idea what awaited her.

She listened distractedly, and Dulac finally turned to her: "Well?"

"It's him."

"Sure?"

"Absolutely."

Karen and Dulac got into the waiting limo. Dulac spoke: "Karen, I didn't tell you this before, because I wanted you to be sure, but we had de Ségur's recent travels investigated. He flew to Isola Rossa and back last week, in his private jet."

CHAPTER 55

Stephanopoulos had had better days than this. Inspector Basso had applied his usually effective technique on him for the obtaining of information. Basso had put the captain in a cell with three other suspects, about to appear for their bail hearing on a variety of charges. *Just soften him up a little,* were their instructions. *No permanent injuries.* In exchange, Basso had agreed to drop two of the charges against them. That way, the police wouldn't be held responsible for the brutality.

Stephanopoulos, his face swollen beyond recognition, had not cracked. He would protect his family to the grave. Outraged, his lawyer had obtained a postponement of the bail hearing.

* * *

"Good morning, Marchioness. It's good of you to come," said Lord Hawkins. She was at his offices to discuss matters that couldn't be aired over the phone, for fear of a wiretap.

"Lord Hawkins," she extended her downturned right hand.

"Please sit down." He invited her to sit across the large mahogany table in the oak-paneled board room. "What can we do for you this morning?"

"I'm afraid I should have given you more information during our last meeting, you know, about this Pistis Sophia letter business."

"I see."

"My personal letterhead is prepared by the same illuminator who did the Pistis Sophia letter: André Dessault was his name."

"Was?"

"The police found his body in the Seine yesterday. It was in the newspapers this morning."

"Awful," replied Hawkins.

"Dulac might think I had something to do with it; he's inferring that I had that letter drafted."

"Well, surely this is an unfortunate coincidence."

"Exactly, but you see, someone is doing this deliberately, to try and frame me in this whole sordid affair."

"Who do you think that could be?"

"I don't know. Perhaps another Pistis Sophia member?"

"Who would have access to Monsieur Dessault."

"Yes."

"Interesting. Anything else?"

"No, not really." Lady Sarah's lower lip curled.

Hawkins knew she was withholding information. He rose and asked for coffee from one of the girls outside the conference room. "Would you prefer tea?"

"No, coffee is fine."

Hawkins was a master at making witnesses talk. It was all a matter of rhythm, like music. *Vary the tempo of your questions, vary the theme, break into a sub-theme, finish with a staccato finale, and the witness will sing your tune, every time.* The coffee arrived, and Hawkins poured it personally into the Marchioness' cup. He waited for her to sip it.

"Lady Sarah, I must tell you, as your barrister, that I have certain reservations concerning our last meeting."

"Really? I thought it went rather well."

"Not exactly. You see, a witness' credibility, like a pregnancy, is usually an all-or-nothing matter. In our business, one is not half-credible, or half-pregnant: Either one is or isn't."

"And how does that apply to me?"

"I don't think Dulac believed you when you said you hadn't seen de Ségur."

"Obviously you didn't either."

"I'm just telling you what I perceived. As your lawyer, what I believe or don't believe is unimportant. It's evidence, circumstantial or direct, that I'm concerned about."

"And if I follow your analogy, Lord Hawkins, that puts my whole testimony into doubt, correct?"

"I'm not saying Dulac is going to appear tomorrow on your doorstep, but time is on his side. If he were to find out—"

"Let's be clear, Lord Hawkins," interrupted the Marchioness. "I'm not about to confess to something I didn't do."

"I'm not asking you to confess to anything."

"I answered, I thought truthfully, when he asked if I had seen de Ségur lately. I answered no. Of course, I see de Ségur: We sit on some charities and corporate boards together. We are bound to meet occasionally — socially also, for that matter. In any case, I don't think it's a crime to meet a fellow aristocrat, or member of . . ." She hesitated for a second.

"Member of what?"

"Never mind, it's not relevant."

"Frankly, Lady Sarah, you should let me be the judge of that."

"He's also a member of Pistis Sophia. At his request, for obvious reasons, his membership is kept confidential."

"Could he have had the Pistis Sophia letter drafted?"

"I, I really don't know."

Hawkins had his information.

"I see. I wouldn't worry about this Dessault matter. Your being a customer doesn't involve you in his death, surely."

"It's an immense relief to hear you say that, Lord Hawkins."

"I'm glad we've had this discussion."

"Oh, by the way, I'd like to use your phone. I have some personal calls to make," said Lady Sarah.

"Of course, I have work to do. Let me know when you're finished," said Hawkins, bringing the phone to the conference table and leaving.

She stood, walked to the door and closed it. She returned to the table and picked up the phone. "I'd like to speak to Mr. de Ségur, please. It's the Marchioness of Dorset."

CHAPTER 56

Oleyev's options were shrinking rapidly. He could make a run for it: The helicopter was in the back, always on the ready. Surely the FSB knew this and wouldn't hesitate to take him down; a suspect trying to escape had no rights, especially in Russia. Besides, he thought, where could he run to? He was too far from the nearest border. He hadn't built his empire during all these years of hard work and determination to have it taken away from him by some FSB bureaucrat. No, he would do as always, he would fight, but on his terms. He had connections. He phoned the Ministry of Defense.

"Minister Abramov' s office," said a secretary.

"I'd like to speak to the Minister. Tell him it's Victor Oleyev."

There was a pause.

"I'm afraid he's not here. Is there a message?"

Bastard. Like fuck he's not there. Oleyev slammed down the receiver, picked it up again and phoned the assistant to the Minister of the Interior, his hunting friend. Same result. *The FSB have short-circuited my connections. They will pay dearly.*

Suddenly, one of his guards erupted into the study: "FSB are all over the perimeter. They have a couple of personnel carriers at the front gate."

"How many men?"

"At least forty."

Oleyev was outnumbered three to one.

At that moment, another guard burst in: "The FSB. They want the gate opened now, or they'll break it down with the armed carriers."

"Get me the man in charge on the intercom," said Oleyev.

"This is Petrov."

"Are you in charge?"

"Yes. Who is this?"

"Victor Oleyev. What's all this about?"

"We have a warrant to arrest you for the murders of Sergei Vasiliev, Olga Fedova, and Dmitri Antonov."

"You have no evidence."

"We have Vasiliev's written confession."

"Is that it? Someone planted that; it's a fake. Besides, I have Nicola Vasilieva. Without her, you have no case. It would be unfortunate if she died from a stray bullet."

At that moment, Oleyev heard the sound of helicopters hovering overhead: The FSB wasn't taking any chances.

"Don't be a fool, Oleyev: It's over, there's no way out. You have three minutes to open the gate."

Oleyev wasn't surprised that Petrov wouldn't back down to a hostage threat, especially with only one hostage. He knew he couldn't win. Besides, this was the new Russia; one didn't go into a shoot-out with the police. *Better lose this battle and win the war.* He had done so many times before. But this time, the charges were serious. He knew he had upset the FSB with the boldness of his move on Lubyanka. This was their retaliation. The FSB had to save face. *In Russia, one always has to save face. Probably why my connections have gone sour.*

A bloodbath would only worsen his case. He had access to Moscow's best lawyers. *No, give them what they want. Plenty of time to call in favors.* In the meantime, he called his friend at the *Pravda* editorial desk: At least his notoriety would provide protection against physical abuse by the FSB.

"Open the gate," shouted Oleyev to his guard on the intercom. "Tell the men not to resist."

The gate opened, and the armed personnel carriers roared up the road in a cloud of fumes and dust, their helmeted occupants crouching behind the bulletproof glass windows. Other members of the FSB Special Task Force clambered over the walls and entered the perimeter.

"Get Vasilieva down here," Oleyev barked.

As she came down the staircase, he said:

"Vasilieva, if you talk . . ." Oleyev mimicked cutting her throat.

At that moment, Petrov burst into the room with three men. They seized Oleyev.

Petrov signaled the men to bring Oleyev to the hallway. "Upstairs!" ordered Petrov.

The men looked puzzled.

"You heard me. Up."

They dragged a resisting, vociferous Oleyev, his face white, up the long staircase, past the Murano chandelier and onto the wooden top floor landing.

"You can't do this. You won't get away with this. I phoned them, I phoned *Pravda*."

"I'm giving you a better chance than you gave my people at Lubyanka," said Petrov.

He signaled his men to throw him down the staircase. One grabbed Oleyev's feet, and the other two grabbed his torso. Together, the three tossed Oleyev, gesticulating, headfirst down the staircase. He catapulted head over heels, hitting the middle steps with his head and shoulder, then tumbling all the way down in a crunching of breaking bones.

"You bastard," moaned a bloodied and battered Oleyev, looking up at a smiling Petrov.

Petrov ordered the premises searched: All documents were to be brought to FSB headquarters. As one of the personnel carriers took Oleyev, Nicola, and Petrov through the gate, a group of cameramen and journalists waited, blocking the entrance. Oleyev's *Pravda* friend had complied, but too late.

Petrov stopped the carrier and spoke briefly: "Yes, we have arrested Victor Oleyev, on charges of murder. He tried to escape. You will have a formal press release later."

"Who is the woman?" asked a reporter.

"No comment," said Petrov, blocking the camera.

The rest of the FSB men were busy rounding up Oleyev's men in the perimeter. In the mansion, a young recruit saw the almost-finished painting of Oleyev as Henry VIII.

"This guy's a megalomaniac. This'll make a great piece of evidence."

"You don't know the Rubliovka set," replied his supervisor. "Putin has one of these of himself as Francis I of France."

The recruit's face reddened, and he continued his search.

* * *

The morning edition of *Pravda* had a triple-bold headline:

> *FSB arrests Victor Oleyev for Lubyanka murders. Woman hostage freed. Oleyev claims innocence, says government is using him as scapegoat.*

> *An FSB task force yesterday arrested well-known businessman Victor Oleyev at his home in Rubliovka, for the murders at the Lubyanka prison. Said it has documents evidencing Oleyev is behind the murders. Oleyev asserted documents are fakes. FSB's Sergei Petrov, investigating officer, mentioned he has evidence of Oleyev's involvement in other murders. He would not elaborate further.*

The article went on to praise the task force members' courage and initiative. Their efficiency and the lack of bloodshed was obviously alluding to the massacre during the Moscow theater hostage crisis in 2002, where the FSB had been criticized for its ineptitude, resulting in the death of some 200 hostages.

Petrov advised Dulac of the operation's success.

Dulac knew that the clock was ticking, that Oleyev's customers were scrambling to erase any possible connection with him, if they hadn't done so already.

CHAPTER 57

Dulac had called for a meeting with the General Secretary, Harris, and the French Minister of the Interior. "Gentlemen," said Dulac, "you saw the news concerning Victor Oleyev. We have strong evidence that Oleyev is the contract man for the archbishops' murders. We have a written note from Vasiliev stating Oleyev hired him and Kurganski to kill Salvador and Conti. We have evidence that the Marchioness of Dorset is involved in money laundering. Her captain has been caught red-handed smuggling 5.2 US million into Naples, four days ago. Although she has denied knowledge, we have evidence that she not only knew of it, but that she profited from it."

"What sort of evidence?" interjected the Minister.

"I'll come to that later. At the same time, the Vatican has been receiving, shortly after each smuggling operation, an almost identical amount of money from the Miranda Group, through anonymous donations. The Marchioness, along with the Vatican's representative Archbishop Fiore, sit on the board of Miranda, with de Ségur. At first we thought, because of the demand letter to the Vatican, that someone at Pistis Sophia was behind the murders. Someone carefully crafted an elaborate scheme, leading us to believe they were after four archbishops, named after the Evangelists, as attested by Ms. Dawson.

Revenge was the possible motive, as Pistis Sophia had been persecuted through the centuries by the Catholic Church."

"But why would someone within Miranda have the archbishops killed?" asked Harris.

"The archbishops probably got wind of the money-smuggling scheme and were going to go public."

"Do you have proof of the money being deposited in the Miranda accounts?" asked the Minister.

"We're working on that now, Minister," replied Dulac.

"What makes you sure that Lady Sarah is involved?" said Harris.

"So far, two pieces of evidence. First, Ms. Dawson overheard a conversation at Isola Rossa, between the Marchioness and de Ségur, where he apparently said she had to go along with the Pistis Sofia ploy, lest he reveal her smuggling scheme to the authorities."

"That's circumstantial," said the Minister.

"Actually, it's hearsay. We checked her financial statements and those of her captain's, Kostas Stephanopoulos: Last year, Stephanopoulos ordered and paid for modifications to the hull of the *Eastland*, including the addition of a double bottom used to store the money. When asked, the Marchioness denied knowledge of this double bottom."

"Go on," said the Minister.

"The Marchioness reimbursed Stephanopoulos in the form of a bonus, at the end of the year, for exactly the same amount of the costs of the double bottom, to the last penny."

The Minister and the Harris exchanged concerned glances.

"I must add that Ms. Dawson overheard de Ségur mention to Lady Sarah, that 'all was being taken care of' and 'all traces of this business were going to be obliterated'."

"Where did this happen?" asked the Secretary.

"On Isola Rossa, the Marchioness' private island. We have proof of de Ségur traveling to the island at that time. We think de Ségur could be involved in the archbishops' murders," said Dulac. "However, there's a slight problem."

"Yes?" replied the Minister.

"Ms. Dawson didn't actually *see* de Ségur at Isola Rossa. She only heard him, as she was outside the room. She later identified and confirmed his voice."

"What are you requesting from us?" said the Minister.

"I want your support to have the British authorities arrest Lady Sarah for extortion, money laundering, smuggling and accessory to the murders of Archbishops Salvador and Conti. We'll require from the French Minister of Justice her extradition to France."

"And de Ségur?" asked the General Secretary.

"We're moving in on the Miranda Group. We don't have solid enough evidence to press charges. I've requested a search warrant for their premises."

"What is the Vatican's involvement in Miranda?" asked the Secretary.

"Apart from being a shareholder and a customer whose properties are managed by Miranda, we don't know."

Dulac waited for someone to dare to ask the next question. No one volunteered what was on everybody's mind:

In the Vatican, how high up did the knowledge go?

"Minister," asked Dulac, "will you contact your counterpart in London?"

"I will give this matter serious attention. It could be premature."

"Minister, the more we wait, the less chance we have of a conviction," said Dulac.

"I'm perfectly aware of that, thank you, Mr. Dulac," replied the Minister, as he rose and closed his attaché case. He made a calming gesture toward Dulac, and added, "I will let you know my decision. Keep me informed of any developments, gentlemen. Good day."

Dulac's plan had worked. He knew that the Minister and the General Secretary were so preoccupied with the politics involved in the arrest of Lady Sarah, that they hadn't dared object to the search and seizure warrant of the Miranda Group.

He knew he wouldn't get an answer from the Minister quickly. He had to force his hand.

CHAPTER 58

"What is the meaning of this?" Hugues de Ségur's outraged voice rang in the corridor, while Dulac and his men invaded the thirtieth floor of the Miranda Tower.

"We have a search and seizure warrant for Miranda's finance and corporate books," said Dulac.

"Why? What's all this about?"

"We believe Miranda personnel are involved in money laundering and improper donations to the Vatican."

"Preposterous."

"Is it?" said Dulac, looking at de Ségur coldly, his jaw set in confrontation. "Justice Pierre Bellet doesn't agree with you." He waved the warrant in de Ségur's face and strode past him toward his office.

"You can't barge in like this. I'll contact the Minister of the Interior. You'll be cleaning police cars, Dulac," yelled de Ségur, trying to keep up.

"Go right ahead. I'll enjoy the rest."

"Enough! I'm calling our lawyers," said de Ségur.

"I want to see your minute books, ledgers, financial statements, disbursement records, everything," said Dulac, as he approached the large corner office, presumably de Ségur's. "Particularly your donations records."

In his haste, Dulac almost walked right by the small room, with its door ajar. He stopped: A meeting had seemingly been interrupted and its four occupants sat passively, as if waiting for its resumption. Dulac couldn't help but smile. "Well, well, what have we here? Good afternoon, Lady Sarah, Archbishop Fiore," said Dulac. "Just passing by?"

Fiore stood, flustered for a moment, but regained his composure and extended a hand. "Inspector Dulac, this is quite a surprise. We're having an executive meeting," Fiore said, slightly defensive. "What brings *you* here?"

"Police business. We're investigating Miranda's books."

"We have nothing to hide," intoned de Ségur, standing behind Dulac. "The inspector thinks someone at Miranda has to do with supposedly phony donations to the Vatican."

"I can assure you all our donations are quite genuine, Mr. Dulac," said Fiore.

"But where does the money come from, Monsignor Fiore?" replied Dulac.

Fiore blushed, as Lady Sarah rose, finally, to extend her hand to Dulac.

"My dear Dulac, we seem to meet in the strangest of places."

Dulac noticed a slight curl in her lower lip again.

"Lady Sarah," acknowledged Dulac.

At that moment, one of Dulac's men signaled for him to come outside and handed him the phone.

"Excuse me." He turned and left the room.

"What the hell are you doing?" It was the Minister of the Interior.

"Minister, I mentioned to you during our meeting that I would be investigating Miranda's books," replied Dulac, surgically.

"You'd better be right, Dulac, or you're *out*. Do you understand?"

"Thanks for your support, Minister."

The line went dead.

* * *

It was late afternoon before Dulac's men finished carrying the Finance Department's ledgers and corporate books into the vans, as de Ségur watched impassive, his lawyer by his side. De Ségur's call to the Minister had been futile. He returned to the small meeting room, where Lady Sarah and Monsignor Fiore waited anxiously.

"Listen, Hughes," said Lady Sarah, resolve in her voice, "I'm not going to be the sacrificial lamb here. I won't go down alone. Stephanopoulos won't hold out much longer. They've arrested Oleyev. One of them is bound to talk."

"Not so," replied de Ségur. "Stephanopoulos won't talk: My men have assured him a pension. And Oleyev knows he's as good as dead if he reveals his contract. Lady Sarah, we're all in this together. Can't you see that the only way we win is to close ranks? Otherwise, Dulac will divide and conquer."

"He's right," said Fiore.

"Ha, you should talk. If it weren't for your ideas, I wouldn't be here," she replied, her eyes burning.

"Perhaps," said Fiore, smiling coolly, "but your scheme was well underway before we joined."

"Dulac has probably linked the monthly payments to Miranda's monthly donations," said the Marchioness.

"He can't prove it. One doesn't win cases with coincidences," said de Ségur.

"And it's just one step to tie the donations to the deaths. I didn't have anything to do with those deaths," replied Lady Sarah.

"Yes, but try and convince a jury of that," said de Ségur. "My dear Marchioness, when will you realize that *Fraus omnia corrumpit* as my Latin professor used to say: Fraud incriminates *everyone*."

"What do you suggest we do?" replied Sarah nervously.

"Nothing. Dulac doesn't realize what he's in for. Besides, we don't have much choice. If we panic, that's playing right into his hand."

"May I remind you that we all have to go along with this? Or risk the same fate as Salvador and Conti," said Fiore.

CHAPTER 59

The registration formalities of the arrest completed, Oleyev was whisked off under heavy guard to an unidentified Moscow apartment. Petrov wasn't risking another Lubyanka fiasco. Nicola had been freed, after depositing her passport and Canadian visa with Petrov at FSB headquarters. She had accepted the risks of testifying against Oleyev, in exchange for the FSB providing her with an identity change and was under heavy FSB protection.

Petrov had been informed that Kurganski had been identified by a suspicious travel agent in Vladivostok, where he had tried to change his US dollars to pay for a ticket to China.

Kurganski was being brought in an armored vehicle to Moscow. Petrov was jubilant; the cards of good old luck were finally falling his way.

"We have Kurganski," Petrov announced to Dulac.

"Excellent, where did you find him?"

"In Vladivostok."

"Does he know who hired Oleyev?"

"We will interrogate him tomorrow. What about the Marchioness?"

"I'm waiting for the extradition request; we want to arrest her in France. Have you charged Oleyev?"

"In Russia, bringing to trial is a slow process. Maybe two months, or three."

"Any chance of a confession?" said Dulac.

Petrov knew that Dulac was testing the waters, whether he would consider negotiating a lesser charge in exchange for a confession.

"Not now. Maybe later," replied Petrov."

"I want to talk to you about the charges for the murders of Salvador, Conti and Dessault. I will go to Moscow. Could we meet next Thursday?"

Dulac had to ensure that Petrov didn't take the lead in his murder case. He wanted to keep control of the file, especially in light of the Miranda developments. If Petrov decided to indict Oleyev on these counts, it would be disastrous. Oleyev was Dulac's key witness. He had to convince Petrov to let him testify against the Marchioness and de Ségur.

CHAPTER 60

Dulac's Swiss contact had come through.

"Yes, we have news, but you won't like this," said Gustav Thoeni.

"Try me," said Dulac.

"The numbered company belongs to two brothers, Henrique and Renaldo Gonzalez, Venezuelan citizens who deal through a Swiss agent, Soperca SA. Its corporate headquarters are in Zürich, thirty-one Banhoffstrasse, a one-room suite. The company is listed as a trading company. They bank with Bank Zulder. We did a check on them."

"Yes?"

"Our Bogota people have been trailing them for two years. The brothers are experts at corporate layering and camouflage. We think they're members of the Vega cartel."

Dulac paused, not surprised, taking in the consequences of the development. The Vega cartel was the most powerful drug organization in South America, having roots in the defunct Medellin and Cali cartels.

"Did you obtain any financial information?"

"No, but I will try to contact someone at the bank. My wife's cousin works there."

"Gustav, I'm in your debt."

"Good luck," said Thoeni.

CHAPTER 61

Dulac felt depressed. He needed distraction from his daily dose of the underworld's brutality. Concerts being a reliable cure, he'd asked Karen to join him for the first performance of the *Nozze de Figaro*, a black-tie affair, and dinner afterwards.

"Hello, Thierry, come in," said Karen warmly, as she opened the door, clad in a sleeveless black dress. The shoulder-length auburn hair framed her oval face and accentuated the sensuous, oblique eyes.

Dulac stood for a moment in rapturous contemplation. *God, she's beautiful*, he thought, but didn't have the courage to tell her.

"*Bonsoir*, we don't have much time," he said. "The performance starts at eight." He walked into the familiar warmth of the salon.

"What's new in the investigation?"

"A lot: I have an extradition request for Lady Sarah's arrest, sitting with the Minister of the Interior."

Karen blushed at the news that ignited thoughts of Isola Rossa.

"We have Miranda's books: The majority shareholder might be related to Vega, the drug cartel."

"Wow," she exclaimed.

"Let's go. I'll tell you the rest on the way."

As Dulac took Karen's coat and draped it over her naked shoulders, he caught a glimpse of the sensuous curve in her lower back, highlighted by the deep V of the dress.

* * *

The traffic to the Opera was heavy.

"Will we make it?" asked Karen, while Dulac weaved impatiently between lanes.

"Plenty of time," replied Dulac, looking at his watch. "I have to convince Petrov not to try Oleyev for the archbishops' murders: We want him here."

"That's a tall order," exclaimed Karen.

"Yes, especially since he now has Kurganski as a witness. We'll need a confession from Oleyev."

"I see, you want Petrov to agree to press lesser charges in exchange for a confession."

"Exactly."

"Where does de Ségur fit in?"

"Everywhere, nowhere: I have to prove that as a board member of Miranda, he knew of the transfers from Vega to Miranda."

"As did Fiore."

"We'll have to prove that also. Speaking of which, I met Lady Sarah and Fiore at Miranda's headquarters. The Vatican and Lady Sarah are also shareholders of Miranda. See how it all fits?"

"I'm beginning to."

"The money comes from offshore, probably Venezuela, is dropped off at Isola Rossa. The *Eastland* sucks it up, delivers it to Naples. Miranda's contractor picks it up and deposits it in Vega's bank in Zürich. Then, through their numbered company — a shareholder of Miranda — they transfer it to Miranda's account and in turn, it makes donations to the Vatican for almost the same amount."

"But what's Vega's interest to do this, if the money ends up in the Vatican?"

"It legitimizes Miranda, but that side of the equation, we're not sure of yet. I suspect some of the money goes back to Venezuela. But even if it stays in Miranda, the money is already laundered: As the majority shareholder, Vega gets yearly dividends on its investments, tax-free. I'm checking with Cardinal Legnano tomorrow. He's reviewing the activities of the Vatican's Finance Committee."

"So the Vatican is in on this also?" said Karen.

"Not necessarily. Don't forget Miranda has legitimate interests in real estate all over the world. The Vatican being a shareholder doesn't automatically incriminate it."

"With the use of drug money?"

"That's where things get tricky: Suppose Miranda receives, say 50 million dollars of laundered money per year. Small change compared to the Vatican's investment of 500 million dollars, as a shareholder. Can't the Vatican argue that its portion is untainted? Don't forget, Miranda has other, perfectly legitimate interests and investors."

"So if I understand, you're asking: How rotten does the apple have to get, before you throw it away?"

"Basically, yes. Do you remember the Roberto Calvi scandal?"

"You mean 'God's banker,' as they called him? Wasn't he found hanged off Blackfriars Bridge in London?"

"On June 17, 1982, to be exact. Why do you think Calvi died?"

"You're telling me it's not because he knew too much?"

"Yes, but we think he threatened to go public with the scheme and expose the Vatican."

"So Salvador and Conti were murdered for the same reasons."

Dulac nodded.

"But who would have planned such an elaborate and grisly scheme, and planted the Pistis Sophia letter?"

"Answer your own question, Karen: You have all the essentials, and the suspects."

As the car approached the Opera, Dulac said: "I'll drop you here and park the car."

"I'll wait at the top of the steps."

* * *

They walked hastily up the steps with the last stragglers, and Karen turned to Dulac: "Only a person with a good knowledge of mythology, and access to the Pistis Sophia letterhead could have planted that letter. Wouldn't that point to Fiore?"

"Did I forget to tell you? We found wooden plaques at Dessault's workshop: the wood is identical to the plaques found around the archbishops' necks. They were ready for other informers."

They took the escalator up to the mezzanine, where Dulac led Karen down to their seats. Karen's buzzing brain would soon be engulfed by the soft arias of Mozart's opera. *A welcome respite*, she thought.

At intermission, they walked down to the bar and Dulac ordered two glasses of white wine. As Karen waited, slightly aside, and looked around the assembled glitterati, clad in Dior, Versace and Gaultier, she caught sight of Hugues de Ségur, talking to a young woman, visibly enthralled. As Dulac was about to rejoin Karen, a man walked up to de Ségur and they shook hands. The woman smiled and left. Karen signaled with her head to Dulac, to look over her shoulder.

"Well, well, speak of the devil . . . and the Minister of the Interior. Misery seeks its own company," said Dulac.

"I thought you might be interested."

"I know they're friends. We'll soon find out how close."

At that moment, the lights flickered three times, announcing the resumption of the concert. As Dulac and Karen rejoined their seats, he had a persistent feeling of being watched.

"Let's go quickly," said Dulac, at the end of the concert. "I don't want them to know I've seen them."

"Understood," replied Karen.

They walked toward the exit doors, and someone approached from the side: "If it isn't the ubiquitous inspector," said de Ségur.

Dulac nodded, ignoring the offered handshake.

"I didn't know you had time for such frivolity. Shouldn't you be knee-deep in my ledgers? After all, that's what the taxpayer pays you for, isn't it?"

Dulac kept walking, taking Karen by the arm.

"By the way, I'm suing you personally for abuse of police authority and business interruption. My lawyers are preparing the lawsuit right now. You should be looking at, say one million euros per day."

"Good luck," replied Dulac smiling. "Maybe you know of some assets that I don't know about."

"Make no mistake, Dulac: I *always* get my pound of flesh."

"That sounds like a threat."

"Wouldn't cross my mind." Then, smiling at Karen: "I must admit you have good taste . . . for a policeman."

As they made their way down the steps into the parking, Dulac tested his apprehension, and looked back discreetly.

"We're being followed," said Dulac, annoyed.

"De Ségur?"

"Someone else."

"Great. Aren't I supposed to feel safe with an Interpol senior officer?"

"Not funny. I'll call headquarters." He took out his phone. "Yes, it's Dulac. I'm at the Opera parking. We're being followed. Get a patrol car here, *now*."

Dulac and Karen waited in the car. He took the 9 mm Benelli 80s pistol out of the glove compartment and placed it on the console, between Karen and himself.

"You can't be serious," exclaimed Karen.

"Just a precaution."

Suddenly, the tall tuxedoed man who had been following them jumped into the parked car, started it and roared toward them.

"Get down," yelled Dulac. Karen ducked onto the seat and Dulac covered her.

Sharp cracks shattered the windshield and the side rear window, and the car sped past, disappearing into the night.

"Jesus," said Karen, while Dulac got up and tried to read the license plates.

"Are you all right?"

"I think so," said Karen, whiter than Dulac's shirt.

"Maybe I took his parking spot," he quipped.

At that moment, a patrol car screeched to a stop. Two officers got out, looking first at the shattered glass, then at Karen and Dulac.

"We're fine," said Dulac. "White car, recent Peugeot, but I couldn't get the plate number."

"We'll send a dispatch," replied one of the officers.

"There probably aren't enough officers in all of Paris to search for the underground parking they're hiding in, by now," replied Dulac.

Dulac hailed a taxi.

"I need a drink," said Karen.

"So do I."

Dulac climbed into the taxi after her, and Karen gave the driver the address of her apartment.

Dulac sat down, put his hand distractedly on her thigh, and patted it to comfort her.

She turned to him and placed her hand on top of his and pressed his hand upwards. She kissed him passionately, as she lifted the hem of her dress. With her other hand, she gently pressed his now-aroused maleness. He set his free hand around her soft shoulder and freed her breast from its nearly non-existent support. She gasped as his other hand found its mark.

The taxi arrived at the apartment. While Karen rearranged her coat, Dulac whispered to her: "I can't go out like this. Lend me your purse."

She laughed, Dulac paid the cabbie and they walked quickly up the stairs, Dulac holding Karen's too-small purse in front of him. While she fumbled with the key, he dropped the purse and grabbed her breasts from behind and pressed his hungry penis against the split of her buttocks. The door opened, and they nearly tripped onto the carpet, as he relentlessly pressed himself against the taut lobes of her bottom. She dropped her dress to the floor and turned, naked, to undo his shirt. As he tossed off his jacket, she grabbed the suspenders of his pants and ripped them downwards, grabbing his shorts in the motion. He ran his hands — *those refined, deft hands* — she thought, in her full hair, as she stroked his sex. He closed his eyes in abandon. She rose and mounted him and entwined her legs around his waist, leaning her back against the door. She lowered herself onto him slowly, and gasped as he entered her.

They fell onto the lush carpet, her legs still entwining him, as they pulsed to the rhythm of pure, unfettered joy.

They both lay on the bed, exhausted and replete, and Karen turned to him: "You really didn't have to plan all that, just to have sex with me."

"Who says music and violence don't make a great aphrodisiac?" he replied.

She laughed. "Were they after you, or me?"

"Me, I'm the threat now. They know that I know Pistis Sophia is a false flag. They have no interest in you any longer."

"Do you?"

"That's totally unfair."

"Who did this?"

"I'd put my money on de Ségur. That was probably a warning shot."

"What do you mean?"

"If they'd wanted to kill us, they would've fired through the doors."

* * *

Karen awoke first, got up and drowsily prepared breakfast. Strange, she thought, even with the chaos and scare of the previous night, she somehow felt content.

"What a night," exclaimed Dulac, as he stretched in the comfortable, thick-mattressed bed.

"Ham and eggs, or croissants?"

"American, please."

"You know, when you told me to 'answer my own question' last night, I thought, maybe the Marchioness has the knowledge. She certainly has the library for it."

"Yes, Miss Marple."

"Do you want your juice in the glass, or on you?" She aimed the orange juice glass at the bed.

Dulac turned onto his side, and looked at the woman's back, as Karen bent over to search for the frying pan. He caught himself enjoying the domesticity of the scene.

"It's my fault for getting you into this. But sometimes I feel you like the challenge, right?"

"The pay is poor, but the fringe benefits aren't bad." She winked at him. "But seriously, isn't Fiore your best suspect?"

"How is that?"

"When I first met him, I remember him saying that he'd studied mythology as part of Greek history."

"So does every student taking a classical course."

"Perhaps, but couldn't you find out if he's got any special interest in the subject?"

"Yes, Miss . . . Sorry."

After Dulac had showered and dressed, he noticed how ridiculous he looked in his black tie, shirt and tuxedo at seven o'clock in the morning. Once out of the apartment, he would be telling the whole world of his sexual escapade. *I might as well be naked.*

The taxi arrived and he prepared to leave. He kissed Karen. "One last favor: Not your purse, but can I borrow a coat?"

Karen laughed. "Here, this should do it, but I want it back."

CHAPTER 62

The TGV to Lyon fast-forwarded the pastoral green coun-tryside into a soft blur. Looking out the window of the high-speed train, Dulac would catch himself now and then trying to decipher a town's sign, as the speeding projectile swished past it, silent, blind.

The General Secretary's office was fully windowed, sparsely decorated and as austere looking as the man who inhabited it.

"I've been lied to, led down the garden path, shot at. My job has been threatened, and my work is totally unappreciated. What more can I ask for?" said Dulac as he paced vigorously to and fro in front of the General Secretary's desk, sucking his Gitane. "Plus, I have the distinct feeling I'm being set up."

"If you wanted a cushy job, you should have stuck to law," said Harris. "As far as your job security, *I* will decide who stays or is removed from this case, no one else."

Dulac bit his tongue: Somehow, he doubted it. "I'm sick and tired of politicians interfering with my work. It's hard enough to get the evidence. Now that we have it, we can't act on it."

"I think the Minister has probably contacted London and—"

"I have a better idea: I'm going to arrest the Marchioness in London," said Dulac.

"On what charges?"

"For starters, money smuggling and accessory to murder. I can think of a few others."

"That complicates the case against de Ségur. Besides, we'll have jurisdiction problems."

"Not if she agrees to testify against him."

"How is that?"

"We charge her with accessory to murder, money laundering and smuggling. In exchange for her testimony, we drop the first two and plea bargain on the third."

"She won't take the bait. Too risky."

"If I were her, I'd take it."

"A high-profile person like her can't afford the scandal. She risks being shunned by her peers, a fate worse than death. Plus, we haven't been very efficient in providing protection to our star witnesses."

"She's got enough money to hire all the protection she needs."

"Dulac, be patient. Give the Minister a chance: He'll have to make a decision."

"If he doesn't, I will."

CHAPTER 63

De Ségur had convened Fiore and Volpe to his villa. The limousine, its tinted windows hiding the two prelates, wove silently up the hill along the narrow driveway, halting before the entrance of the cantilevered house overlooking Portofino Bay.

"Come in, Monsignors," said de Ségur, answering the chauffeur's polite knock. "Welcome to my little hideaway."

"Yes, yes," said Volpe, "it's been a long drive, and we haven't much time. I must be back by seven this evening."

"I've asked you to come here because Miranda's offices have been raided and are probably wiretapped. Dulac seized the financial and corporate records and raided my home in Paris. They haven't searched here yet. I'm afraid there are serious developments: The French Minister of the Interior, Jean Gavroche, has agreed with the Minister of Justice to file an extradition request for Lady Sarah, for her to be tried in France."

"On what charges?" asked Volpe.

"Money smuggling and accessory to the murders of Salvador and Conti. The link is Salvador's French nationality. Gavroche hasn't advised Interpol yet, but will do so tomorrow."

"Go on," said Volpe, his face somber.

"I'm afraid Lady Sarah wasn't a model of calm and composure during our last meeting, as Monsignor Fiore will attest."

Fiore nodded meekly.

"She's worried me since our meeting at Isola Rossa," said de Ségur. "We can't trust her anymore. If she goes to trial, she'll crack and bring us down with her. She's even told us she wouldn't take the blame alone."

"What if we get rid of Dulac?" asked Volpe.

De Ségur knew Volpe couldn't have known, wasn't referring to, the failed assassination attempt. That was strictly personal business.

"You mean have the General Secretary take him off the case?"

"Yes."

"We've tried: The Secretary won't move. He doesn't want to be seen as obstructing justice. Besides, it's too late."

"Then, where does that leave us?" said Volpe.

"We must get rid of her."

Volpe broke the silence.

"Do what you must." He rose, looking at Fiore, who hadn't uttered a word. "Anything to add, Monsignor?"

"No," whispered Fiore, timidly clearing his throat.

"Monsignor, this isn't easy for any of us," scolded Volpe, "but it's an affair of state. We all know what's at stake here."

As de Ségur walked them to the door, Volpe said: "If only Salvador and Conti hadn't threatened to disclose, we wouldn't be here."

After they left, de Ségur made a phone call, a deadly one.

CHAPTER 64

John, Lady Sarah's butler, had dutifully received the package from Harrods', as usual. She often had dresses and shoes delivered to her flat in London. But John hadn't noticed that the van wasn't from Harrods'.

The blast had severed the butler's head and blown it across the hallway into the salon, like a bloodied bowling ball.

The windowpanes of the first level covered the floor with a dangerous glittering carpet, and the chandelier lay in the middle of the hallway, like a large tilted silver Christmas tree.

The Marchioness had fared better. The French doors of the dining room had absorbed the impact, and she had been blown out of her chair onto the dining room wall, ten feet away. She was covered with minor lacerations from the glass and suffered a broken arm.

Marchioness of Dorset narrowly escapes death. Butler killed, read the headlines of the *Daily Telegraph*, a copy of which Lescop had brought Dulac early that morning.

> *A bomb blast rocked the Marchioness of Dorset's London flat yesterday afternoon, killing her butler. The Marchioness has suffered multiple injuries and is in a stable condition at*

a London hospital. Her injuries were classified as serious,
but not life-threatening. Police say they have no suspect. No
motive has been uncovered.

Dulac had been called by British Interpol the night before and had felt mixed emotions upon hearing the news. Gratuitous acts of barbarism repelled him, but he also knew that he now had an opportunity. He had to seize it.

"The minute she is discharged, call me," said Dulac to Harry Wade, the Interpol agent at the London office.

Wade phoned Dulac the morning of the third day after the bombing.

"She looks terrible, but she'll live."

"Thanks," replied Dulac. He called Lescop and told him to get tickets to London.

A copy of the French Minister of Justice's letter issuing the extradition request for Lady Sarah arrived in his office at noon.

* * *

The early flight from Paris to London was bumpy, and the Boeing 737 landed jerkily, buffeted by wind and rain squalls. Dulac spent the morning in the office of Chief Inspector James Innes of Scotland Yard, briefing him on the charges against the Marchioness. Innes had called the British Minister of Justice and the latter had confirmed receiving the extradition request from his French counterpart.

"We usually don't arrest someone who's just been the victim of a bomb blast," said Innes.

"I know," replied Dulac. "I don't want to seem insensitive, but she's a prime suspect in a murder case, and also in a money-smuggling and laundering scheme. Do you agree with my proposal?"

"Since you'll have her extradited if we don't, we haven't much choice," replied Innes.

"Fine. Let's go, gentlemen," said Dulac, donning his raincoat and stepping out into the deluge.

* * *

"I'm Inspector James Innes, of Scotland Yard. Is Lady Sarah Litman in?" asked Innes, as the three men and two constables stood dripping wet at the doorway.

"Why, yes," answered a startled young woman dressed in a maid's uniform. "Just a minute."

A moment later, Lady Sarah appeared, heavily bandaged, her left arm in a sling. Dulac could see the blackened eyes behind the lightly tinted sunglasses.

"Gentlemen?" she said, with an air of surprise and annoyance.

"Lady Sarah, may we come in?" said Dulac.

"You again. What are *you* doing here?"

Dulac thought her good manners and patience had been shaken a bit by the blast.

"I'm sorry," she amended "I'm a bit edgy these days. Gentlemen, do come in."

The policemen took off their wet overcoats and entered the hallway still full of broken glass.

"Please excuse the mess. As you can see, I'm in the middle of redecorating."

Dulac said calmly, "Lady Sarah, you might want to call your lawyer."

"This isn't about the bomb, is it?"

"Not really," replied Dulac.

Sarah's mind grew numb. She felt her interior world starting to crumble. She walked into the living room and dialed Hawkins' number. "It's Lady Sarah. Could you come over immediately? I think I'm about to be arrested."

She reluctantly returned to the hallway, and Inspector Innes spoke. "Lady Sarah, I'm arresting you on charges of conspiracy and accessory after the fact for the murders of

Archbishops Salvador and Conti, smuggling of 5.1 million US dollars, and money laundering of 5.1 million US dollars. We retain the right to press other charges at a later date. I must warn you that anything you say may be held against you as evidence in a court of law. You have the right to see a barrister."

Sarah sat down on the small seat and stunned, stared into space. The nightmare was continuing. It had to be real.

"I've called him. He won't be long."

"He can join us at the Yard," said Innes. "Please come with us."

* * *

The reporters were assembled around the flat, taking pictures of the damage.

"What's this about, Chief Inspector?"

"No comment."

"Who are you?" a journalist asked Dulac.

"Interpol."

"This is big," said a photographer.

The journalists took to their cars and followed the police to the Yard, hoping to get a shot of Lady Sarah as she was escorted into the Yard's offices.

After the registration formalities, Lady Sarah was led into a large interrogation room, while they waited for Hawkins.

"I say, gentlemen, you might at least have the decency of letting the woman recover from her injuries. This is most inhuman, most uncivilized," said Hawkins, throwing his raincoat and bowler on a nearby chair.

"Lord Hawkins, we've arrested your client as an accessory to crimes committed in France and Italy," said Dulac.

"Show me the charges," said Hawkins.

Innes handed him the warrant.

"Worthless. You have no right to arrest her: The main charges are unproven. And you're out of your jurisdiction, Inspector," said Hawkins turning to Dulac.

"Be advised that I've started extradition procedures in France," said Dulac.

"On what evidence?" replied Hawkins.

"Enough to satisfy the extradition requirements," said Dulac.

"I see," said Hawkins. "Inspector Innes, is this correct?"

"There's an extradition request from the French, sitting on the Minister of Justice's desk. I'm told it looks valid."

"Lord Hawkins," said Dulac, "I have a proposal that may be satisfactory to your client and us. But we must resolve the issue quickly. You'll see why."

"Let's hear it," replied Hawkins.

"We are willing to drop the charges of accessory to the murders of the two archbishops, in exchange for a guilty plea by Lady Sarah on the charge of money smuggling and laundering. She must undertake to appear in Paris as a witness for the prosecution in the trials of Hugues de Ségur and Monsignor Paolo Fiore. If your client agrees, we will accept that your client remains in house arrest, and we will make no divulgation to the press until the trial for money smuggling and laundering. We can agree on a late trial date."

"And if we don't accept?" said Hawkins.

"We will charge her on all counts, keep her here and oppose bail on the grounds of her high mobility," said Innes. "We won't withhold any information from the press."

"And we will continue the extradition proceedings," said Dulac.

"I'd like to confer with my client — alone, if you please, gentlemen," said Hawkins.

"Obviously," said Dulac, as he signaled the others to leave the room.

"Somewhere else," said Hawkins.

"Right," said Innes. "Follow me, please."

Hawkins took Lady Sarah by the arm and escorted the Marchioness, her mien diminished, into the corridor.

"Please sit down," he said, as they sat on the hardwood bench.

"Lady Sarah, if what Dulac says is true, I'm afraid he has us in a bit of a corner."

"He's quite smart, isn't he?" replied Sarah pitifully.

"Lady Sarah, you must tell me everything."

"But I have."

"No, you haven't. You knew about the smuggling."

"Well, yes."

"Did you participate in it?"

"Yes, I did," said Sarah, breaking into tears.

"But why?"

"You haven't seen my bank accounts."

"Quite. Did Stephanopoulos propose this scheme?"

"Yes, he said we'd split the surplus fifty-fifty."

Hawkins put his hand on the Marchioness' shaking shoulders. He bent over, close to the side of her face, paused for a moment. "And the murders?"

"No, no. I didn't think they would go that far. I agreed to the planting of the letter. Otherwise, they would go to the police. I knew nothing of the murders."

"They who?"

"De Ségur and Fiore."

"And why did you think they asked you to be the decoy?"

"To divert attention. To lead the police down the garden path. This way, they had control over the investigation. The letter was drafted before the murders. But they added the last sentence, the death threat, after the murders."

"So you gave them a blank check?"

"I had no choice."

"I see. Lady Sarah, as your lawyer, and friend, I must ask you: Are you willing and able to go through all of this, the rigors of a murder trial, the stress? The publicity? It won't be easy. Also, bear in mind the uncertainty of the result."

"Those bastards tried to kill me. They killed my John. Poor John, he didn't deserve to die so horribly."

"I understand how you feel, but that shouldn't be the reason for your decision. Vengeance is always a poor substitute for sound judgment."

"I know, I know. God, what a mess I've made." She clasped her face with her free hand and wept uncontrollably.

"Do you need more time?" asked Hawkins, feeling uneasy.

"No, I'm all right." She tried to control her heaving shoulders. "What do we do next?"

"I think we have little choice but to accept his offer. That being said, there is still considerable risk."

"I'm aware of that."

"I'm sure they'll provide complete protection."

"I'll rely on my own."

"Yes, well, whatever. We'll have it anyway."

As Lady Sarah and Hawkins walked back to the room, the journalists were waiting, cameras firing, microphones waving at the senior desk officer. They caught a glimpse of Lady Sarah in tears.

"What did she do?"

"I really don't know, gentlemen. You'll have to ask Inspector Innes."

Returning to Dulac and Innes, he spoke: "Gentlemen, my client will accept your offer under the following conditions. She gets full police protection, now, during and six months after the trials. The only charges my client will plead guilty to is attempting to smuggle five million dollars. All other charges will be dropped in all countries: England, France, Italy and Switzerland. We want an undertaking from the Italian prosecutor that he will ask for the minimum sentence, to be served here in London. In exchange, she will testify in the trials of de Ségur and Fiore. Of course, you will release my client today. No announcements: The official position is you've had her in for questioning in relation to the bombing: The matter is highly confidential. Your registration records will be changed accordingly."

Dulac conferred with the others for a moment in private, then turned to Hawkins.

"We accept, Lord Hawkins. Your word and Lady Sarah's that she will deposit her passport here."

"Agreed."

"It will take some time to get acceptance from the ministers, but I see no problem."

"Can we leave through a side entrance?" asked Hawkins.

"They'll be there also, though perhaps less of them," replied Innes.

* * *

Lady Sarah and Hawkins jostled their way through the microphones, cameras and antennas, and into the limousine. Sitting down in the darkness of the plush interior, she felt strangely relieved, renewed. The lie, the duplicity of her life was slowly dissolving, but she knew she had to find the courage to face its inevitable consequences.

Beginning to find her composure, she turned to Hawkins: "You know, this must be the second worst day of my life."

CHAPTER 65

On the plane to Paris with Lescop, Dulac felt exhilarated, celebrative: He shared a bottle of Bordeaux with Lescop. He had got what he came for, the wood wedge that when wetted, widens the crack and eventually breaks the block of granite. He phoned the General Secretary.

The next morning, Dulac met with Mrs. Gorma, in the small boardroom next to his office. Mrs. Gorma was head of the financial investigative section of Interpol.

"What do you have?" said Dulac.

"Miranda has been transferring significant amounts of money to various institutions in the following countries: Italy, Spain, Austria, Venezuela, France, and others," the petite, curly-haired woman answered. "This is done on a regular basis. There are donations to health clubs, Scout organizations, outdoor clubs, charities—"

"What amounts?" interrupted Dulac.

"Two to three million per year, per club."

"Total?"

"Thirty-three million dollars. That's on top of the donations to the Vatican."

"What about income?"

"The main source of income is its real estate interests: The Swiss transfers are minor in comparison. It'll be interesting to see if they stop, now that the *Eastland* is impounded."

"Don't bet on it," said Dulac. "They'll keep funding, somehow."

"We also came across this memo."

The memo's letterhead showed the crest of the Republic of France.

Strictly Confidential. September 20, 1999

Mr. Hugues de Ségur, CEO,
Miranda Group

Dear Hugues,

I'm pleased to inform you that the project is well underway, thanks to the splendid work of the Miranda Group. Your contribution is appreciated by all. I cannot overestimate the importance of its impact on the member countries.

Yours sincerely,

Pierre Bétancourt
Minister of State

Dulac's face sombered. "Have you a list of these institutions and their membership?"

"No, not yet."

"Get them. What do you have on de Ségur?"

"Nothing unusual. How are the searches going?"

"We haven't searched his yacht or the villa in Portofino. We're getting warrants for both. We'll start with the yacht," said Dulac.

* * *

The 105-foot, white Camper & Nicholson aluminum sloop *Mon Reve* lay sparkling against the trees lining the small Bay of Portofino, as it tugged lazily at its mooring. The two crew were busy washing her, removing the fine dust and sand brought in daily from the Sahara Desert by the warm Mediterranean breezes.

Lescop and his two policemen, accompanied by three *carabinieri*, had hired a small fisherman's boat to ensure surprise. While they motored toward the yacht, Lescop thought: *Ostentatious, but probably run-of-the-mill in de Ségur's world.*

"Captain, this is Interpol! Lower the gangplank. We have a search warrant for this yacht," yelled Lescop over the megaphone.

The captain was on his cell phone in an instant, trying to reach de Ségur. He instructed his crew to lower the gangplank.

"Your ship's papers, Captain," said Lescop. "Please open the safe."

After studying the search warrant, the captain handed the logbooks and registration papers to Lescop.

The men went below and the intimate luxury of the mega-rich world unveiled itself before them. The yacht's spacious interior was generously trimmed with Indonesian teak, each piece matched and varnished to perfection. A black, upright Blutner piano had been secured to the salon's main bulkhead, facing the porcelain-lined fireplace. Next to the crews' quarters, a small, clawfoot tub enhanced the nineteenth-century atmosphere of barely restrained opulence.

As the policemen worked their way from the bow, they could but wonder at the extravagance: Christofle dinner plates, blue and gold lining, with the name of the vessel baked into the enamel; again, the name woven into the main salon's Persian carpets, the monogram of de Ségur on every towel, the Llhadro figurines, their bases glued into the special motion-dampened windowed bookcases.

Working toward the stern, the policemen went about their distasteful task, prodding, unlocking cabinets, removing cushions, looking under bunks, searching the ship's stores and refrigerated wine compartment, emptying the lazarette of its sundry spare parts and rigging. All the while, the three *carabinieri* stood aimlessly on the stern deck, looking ill at ease in the plush surroundings.

One of the policemen opened the floorboards, exposing the bottom of the boat and the top of its keel. A sailor himself, he couldn't help but admire the pristine condition in which the boat was kept. It annoyed him to see that one of the keel bolts had been negligently left to rust, contrasting with the other bolts painted a dull gray. He turned the bolt, expecting the rust to come off. Instead, the bolt swiveled easily, opening a small compartment.

He called Lescop.

"What have we here?" said Lescop.

He reached down, and beneath the panel lay a small, watertight stainless-steel box. He opened the box and found an envelope, sealed, with the inscription: 'Confidential.' Under the printed red letters, two words, in the middle of the envelope: *Chimera Protocol*.

Below, a gold, blue and red emblem depicted a curious animal, with the head of a lion, body of an ox, and tail of a dragon. The men continued the search as Lescop opened the envelope. After reading the first page, he reached for the seat and sat down slowly, his face white.

"Jesus." He closed the envelope, grabbed the ship's papers and logbook, and ordered his men back to the fisherman's boat.

He then phoned Dulac. "I have something here you won't believe."

"What is it?"

"I must see you now."

That meant Lescop wasn't trusting the confidentiality of his encrypted phone.

"Get back to Paris, then," said Dulac.

"You can expect a call from the General Secretary. And Minister of State. I'm sure the captain is phoning de Ségur right now. I'll call you when I'm in Paris."

* * *

Lescop knew his life was in danger the moment de Ségur found out he had the document. He had to get back to the safety of Paris. He had to hire a plane. He ordered the driver to go to the Genoa private airport. His hot cargo singed the interior of his briefcase. At the small airport in Paris, he went to the lounge phone and called Dulac's private number.

"Meet me at the Bois de Boulogne, Southeast entrance," said Lescop, his speech quickened by panic.

* * *

"The police have the Protocol," said de Ségur.

"What?" shouted the French Minister of State.

"They searched my yacht. It's a chance in a million. It was buried beneath the keel bolts."

"Do you realize what this means?"

"Painfully."

"You must warn the others."

"I can't. My lines are tapped at Miranda and at my home. Do you have the list?"

"Yes, but it's nine o'clock. Why didn't you call earlier?"

"My captain didn't reach me until now."

"Who are the policemen? *I want names, now.*"

"A certain Lescop. He works for Dulac, at Interpol. Can you intercept them?"

"We'll see what we can do," said the Minister. "I have to try to reach *some* of the others. '*Quel merdier.*'"

The Minister didn't call the 'others' immediately. He had a more urgent call to make.

"Mr. President, it's Pierre. I'm sorry to wake you, but Interpol has gotten hold of the Chimera document. They have a copy of the Protocol."

After a short silence: "Who is aware of it?"

"We're not sure, but at least an Inspector Lescop, and possibly Inspector Dulac, maybe some of their men. We've just received word from de Ségur."

"Meet me in my office at the Élysée in half an hour," said the President of the Republic of France. "And get the General Secretary of Interpol there also."

* * *

In the darkness of the park, Daniel Lescop's hands were trembling as he fumbled for the envelope from his briefcase and handed it to Dulac.

"I don't think this document should be in our files," he said.

Dulac saw the inscription on the cover and turned to the first page.

"Again?" exclaimed Dulac.

"I'm afraid so."

Both men knew they had uncovered another 'Gladio,' a name that struck fear into anyone who remembered European history.

CHAPTER 66

As they sat down on the park bench under the light, Dulac's mind raced. The searing images of murdered shoppers' bloodied bodies in a Belgian supermarket; the crumpled-up body of Aldo Moro, ex-Prime Minister of Italy, in the red Renault; the bodies of the passengers at the Bologna train station . . . all flew vividly before his eyes.

Gladio floated back into his consciousness: During the 60s and 70s, terrorist acts and atrocities initially attributed to leftist groups such as the Red Brigades, were later discovered as being the work of Gladio, the most subversive rightist paramilitary undercover group the world had ever known. Gladio hid under the cover of false flags.

Originally organized by the US and Britain after the Second World War, Gladio drew its members from within the ranks of the 'stay behind' counter-espionage agents of Germany, Italy, and France. Gladio had grown, like the dragon Hydra of Lerna, its multiple heads across the members of NATO, unknown to the espionage services of member countries.

They were the first terrorists. They were state backed: They insured, through the propagation of the fear of communism, political stability of rightist governments.

Gladio's personnel had been recruited from paramilitary commandos, teachers, ex-CIA men, MI6 personnel, architects and lawyers. The operative cells functioned autonomously in complete secrecy.

Member states adhered to Gladio by the signing of either the Minister of State, or Minister of the Interior, often without the knowledge of the other members of the Cabinet: This helped ensure deniability, if found out.

The arsonists, bombers, and killers within each cell had trained in Britain, France and Belgium. With the breaking up of the Soviet empire, and the diminishing of the Communist threat, Gladio's mandate had shifted from the protection against communism to the protection of the member state's stability, whether a threat existed or not.

If none were present, Gladio would create it: Subversively, illegally, but with perfect, state-backed impunity.

Along with its sister organization, P-2, or Propaganda Due, it had "protected" Italy from the threat of a Communist regime. Its member countries had included France, Denmark, Italy, Belgium, the Netherlands, Germany, Greece, Portugal, Turkey and . . . Switzerland.

The Vatican had been seen as a silent sympathizer, since most of the cells were pro-Catholic.

The scandal had erupted in the late 70s, bringing down the Italian government. Other countries had passed laws banning fifth column groups such as Gladio.

However, the pressure on political organizations to keep power at all costs had tempted some governments to exercise a certain laxity concerning the enforcement of their anti-paramilitary laws. Now, Dulac felt it was hitting home.

Dulac read the preamble and first few articles of the Chimera Protocol:

Preamble: the purpose of Chimera is to ensure political stability within its member states. It shall combat threats to that stability by all means, including the creation of false flags.

Organization: Each member country shall create its network of cells, acting within its territory.
Friendly Groups may be used. Friendly Groups are listed in Annex B.

Training: Training of cell members shall be coordinated at Chimera headquarters. Training shall occur in host members France, Belgium, United Kingdom and Switzerland. Trainees shall be sent by member states at their expense.

Headquarters: Chimera headquarters shall be in Antwerp, Belgium.

Funding: Funding shall be coordinated by host member Italy. Donations shall be channeled through Miranda Group, for redistribution to member organizations, through Friendly Groups.

Adhesion to the Protocol: Member states shall adhere to this Protocol by the binding signature of either the Head of State, Minister of State, or Minister of the Interior.

Policy of deniability: Any member state which suspects an imminent breach of confidentiality of this Protocol, shall advise the other member states immediately. A breach of the confidentiality shall trigger the automatic resignation of the signing authority of the breaching member state.

Dulac flipped to Annex B, the Friendly Groups:

France: Miranda Group, H. De Ségur
Denmark: Absalon group, A. Harding
Italy: DSSA, Gino Servolo.
Belgium: SDRA 8, J Van Wouerts
Germany: BDJ-TD, N. Huber
Greece: L.O.K. Red Sheep, T. Papandolos

Austria: OWSGV H. Offenbach
Switzerland: P-26 L. Siegenthaler
Vatican: Cardinal Eugenio Volpe
Venezuela: E Gonzales
Britain: British Outing Club: Lord Bever

Religious Groups:
Opus Dei: P. Lemaitre
Pistis Sophia: Marchioness of Dorset

Dulac's eyes blurred, as he tried to digest the enormity of what he had read, and fathom its implications.

He jumped as his cell phone rang.

"Dulac."

"*Bonsoir*, this is Pierre Bétancourt, Minister of State."

"Yes, Minister."

"Where are you, presently?"

"At the Bois de Boulogne. Why?"

"The President, for whom I speak, requires that you come immediately to *l'Élysée*. You will be given a pass at the gate and escorted to the President's office. We are waiting."

Dulac knew the obvious subject of discussion. "I'll be there shortly."

* * *

"Here, take it," said Dulac, giving the envelope to Lescop.

"Why?" said Lescop, as if he'd been handed a live hand grenade.

"I'm being summoned to the President's office at the Éysée, right now."

"*Dieu.*"

"Go to the Orly train station, and leave it in a baggage locker. Phone me and leave a message with the number of the locker, and throw away the key. Oh, and call yourself some protection for tonight. See you in the morning."

* * *

Dulac sped through the perpetual Parisian traffic. He tried to reach the General Secretary, several times: busy. *Probably blocked.* He reached the guard house at the Élysée's entrance, and after a hurried identification, was escorted in by a black Peugeot. Two Secret Service agents were waiting at the door, and led him to the presidential suite, where Louis XVI furniture was reflected in the vast wall-sized mirrors.

The President of France sat facing the Minister of State and two empty chairs, awaiting their occupants.

Dulac thought the President looked smaller, more compact than he had expected.

"*Bonsoir,* Mr. Dulac; please sit down," said the President.

"Mr. President, Minister," said Dulac, nodding respectfully.

"I'm told you've been made aware of some highly confidential information," said the President.

"Possibly."

"Come, Dulac, we know your men have come across the Chimera document, aboard de Ségur's yacht. Correct?"

"Mr. President, before we discuss this matter, I request the presence of the General Secretary on the line."

"Minister, get the Secretary on the conference phone."

After a short pause: "Mr. General Secretary, Pierre Bétancourt. I'm in the office of the President. We will conference you in. We are here with the President and Mr. Dulac."

"Mr. Secretary, this is the President. We are discussing the Chimera document with Mr. Dulac."

"Which?"

"You are not aware of Chimera?"

"No, I'm not."

Silence, as the men looked at each other in discomfort. Dulac knew it was his move. If he didn't reveal the existence of Chimera, his life wasn't worth much. If he did, there was no going back. His instinct of self- preservation kicked in: "This is Dulac. I have been made aware of a document containing information on the Chimera Protocol. It looks like a repeat of Gladio."

"And where is this document?" asked the Secretary.

"In safekeeping," replied Dulac.

"Mr. Secretary," said the President, "this is a State document. Mr. Dulac will hand it over immediately."

"Mr. President, with all due respect, this is now an Interpol matter, and I require that we discuss it tomorrow, in the presence of the General Secretary," said Dulac.

"Dulac, does anyone else know of this?" said the Secretary.

"Yes, Lescop knows."

"Does he have it?"

"As I said, the document is in safekeeping."

He wanted to protect Lescop's life as well.

"Mr. Dulac, please wait outside for a moment," said the President, as he signaled the Minister to escort Dulac.

"Where does this leave us, Mr. General Secretary?"

"Mr. President, I have to see the document, but my mandate is clear: To uphold the laws of the member countries of Interpol. What is the legitimacy of this document?"

"I don't know. I've just learned of its existence tonight," lied the President.

"How embarrassing," said the Secretary.

"To put it mildly. When can you get here?"

"Say, by 6 a.m.?"

"I'll be waiting."

"Mr. Dulac, the General Secretary will be here at 6 a.m.," said the President. "Be here also. Good night. Minister, stay!"

CHAPTER 67

The last thing Dulac wanted was to be alone. He knew he would be followed out of the Élysée. He took the Benelli out of the glove compartment and tucked it inside his belt. He drove to Karen's.

"Who is it?" asked Karen sleepily over the intercom.

"It's me," replied Dulac.

She buzzed the door and he walked up the darkened staircase to the apartment.

"You look terrible," she said, smiling.

"Nowhere near how I feel."

"Again? It's getting to be a habit."

"I've just come from the Élysée, with the President and Minister of State. We've discovered another subversive paramilitary group. It's called Chimera."

"So?"

"If it becomes public, this document will bring down the government of France."

"*Holy shit.*"

"As you Americans say," he affirmed, smiling. "It's a repeat performance of 'Gladio', which brought down the Italian government in the late 70s. France is a member of Chimera."

"Where did you find it?"

"On de Ségur's yacht."

"What's the connection?"

"Miranda acts as a conduit for the money to each country's organization. Pistis Sophia and Opus Dei are also used. Worse, the Vatican is a signatory state, represented by Volpe."

"Jesus. Where is this document?"

"In safekeeping for the moment. Karen, I have to decide what to do with this, and I haven't much time. I have a meeting with the President and the General Secretary of Interpol at 6 a.m. tomorrow."

"This is incredible."

"It's all making sense now. They killed Salvador and Conti because they were threatening to expose not only the Vatican, but some or all of the member countries. They crucified them to warn the members that this is what awaited them if they broke the Code of Omerta. They had to set a horrific example, the ultimate deterrent. The plaques made reference to the mythical animal, to the Chimera, not to the Evangelists, as they wanted us to think. We were duped into believing the murders were at first a Pistis Sophia reprisal, then, a drug money-laundering matter: both false flags. They're experts at it."

"What do you mean, 'false flags'?"

"It's an old maritime warfare term: It's an accepted tactic for an enemy ship to hoist a friendly flag, in order to approach, subversively, its prey. Once the first shot is fired, the ship must lower its false flag and hoist its true colors. The German raiders used the tactic very successfully during World War II. Now, any organization committing a criminal activity and hiding under the colors of another creates a false flag. Gladio did it brilliantly."

"But I don't understand. What does Chimera fight against?"

"It depends who you ask."

"What do you mean?"

"I suspect the President will say it's to combat fundamentalists and extremist religious groups, by infiltrating, taking quick action — and, let's not forget — planting false flags. If you ask me, I'll tell you that with Gladio or Chimera, you're bypassing the legal system in the name of the supposedly greater good, the good of the State. These people have license to kill."

"And I thought the CIA was bad. More individual rights being trampled by the rights of the State."

"In a nutshell, yes." He walked to the window and looked at the darkened street below.

"Karen, I took a chance coming here. I've surely been followed. You should leave France, wait till this blows over."

"Maybe, but what about you?" She looked worried and clasped Dulac's hands.

"I'll be all right. They won't get rid of me without knowing where the document is. Besides, now the General Secretary, Lescop and some of his men know about it. They can't kill us all."

"That's comforting as hell."

"We'll see what tomorrow brings. It should be one very interesting meeting."

* * *

Dulac slept fitfully. He pored through the different scenarios. He knew he had to get the General Secretary on board. Would the Élysée try and circumvent the General Secretary? Would the Secretary suspend him in the name of the affairs of state? With the threat of a leak to the press, would they dare? Would the President resign, sacrifice himself?

Alternatively, would he give the Minister of State to the wolves? Would the whole Cabinet resign and create parliamentary chaos?

After a quick breakfast, he kissed Karen at the door.
"Wish me '*merde*,' as we say."
"You've got it."

* * *

At 6.15 a.m., the President sat smiling, open shirt, his legs crossed, relaxed, as if nothing had happened. He wasn't resigning, Dulac thought.

On his right, the Minister of State looked pale, hiding behind his dark-rimmed glasses, head bowed, staring at the table.

The General Secretary stood, shook Dulac's hand, and looked at his watch: "You're late," he said, in a chiding voice.

"Sorry, gentlemen," replied Dulac, quickly trying to assess the mood.

The President spoke: "Let's get down to business. Mr. Dulac, under normal circumstances, the document you have, its very existence, would never be revealed. Documents of state are key to the security and welfare of France. Every country has them, and guards their confidentiality fiercely. Their exposure can threaten national security, and worse, cause civil chaos. We need not remind you of all the political unrest that was created in Italy for years, after the disclosure of Gladio and Propaganda Due. Personally, I feel their disclosure was a mistake. I don't have to tell you that the potential for an economic crisis within all the member states is very, very real. We're talking here of destabilizing the whole of Western Europe."

The President paused and sipped his coffee.

"Now consider a moment, Mr. Dulac, the reason why Chimera was created. Are you aware of the growth rate of fundamentalist groups in France recently?"

"I have a rough idea, Mr. President."

"Do you? What if I told you your limited resources at Interpol don't allow you to penetrate even 1/10 of these groups?"

"I am not aware of that number, Mr. President."

"This is not a reproach," said the President turning to the General Secretary. "It's simply a fact."

Dulac knew that his next question would blow the powder keg. He lit the fuse.

"Are you saying that you're justified, Mr. President, in allowing the existence of an illegal, subversive organization because of the supposed inadequacy of the French police force?"

"My fundamental responsibility as President, Mr. Dulac, is to ensure the security of France's citizens."

"By any means?" replied Dulac, feeling increasingly alone. *Why doesn't the Secretary react?*

"No, and I disagree with your classification of Chimera as illegal and subversive. We have legal opinions to the contrary."

"What about public opinion, Mr. President?"

"Mr. Dulac, don't threaten me."

"Wouldn't think of it, sir."

"What do you intend to do with the document?"

At that moment, Dulac's cell phone rang.

"Gentlemen, please excuse me, I forgot to turn it off."

"Petrov here."

"Yes, just a minute."

Astoundingly, Dulac rose from his chair, turned away from the President and took the call.

"What is this?" said the President, incredulous, turning to the General Secretary.

The Secretary, embarrassed, hunched his shoulders in ignorance.

"We have a written confession from Oleyev," said Petrov.

"Fantastique." Dulac didn't want to even think of how Petrov had obtained it.

"Cardinal Volpe, and de Ségur, through a Swiss company named Soderca, gave him the contract."

"Will he testify in their trials?"

"He will be in prison for a long time."

"What about a rogatory commission?"

"A what?"

"Never mind," said Dulac, "I'll check into it later. Thanks, Petrov, for the call."

Dulac returned to the meeting.

"Please excuse me, gentlemen. It was Moscow."

"And?" asked the President.

"I'd like to speak to the General Secretary in private. This concerns the archbishops' murders."

"Go ahead, then," said the President.

Dulac rose and the Secretary followed him out the door.

"Oleyev confessed: De Ségur and Volpe hired him," said Dulac. "I don't have the details. I need your support in there."

"I haven't seen the document. I can't attest to its legitimacy," said the Secretary.

"I have. I can tell you that the Minister is going down. Maybe the President, also."

"Dulac, don't play God here. There's too much at stake."

"Like the lives of our citizens, perhaps?" He felt like adding: *You gutless wonder*, but bit his tongue.

"Well, yes, that also," answered the Secretary lamely.

* * *

As they returned, Dulac made up his mind: If he had to go it alone, he would.

"So, gentlemen, care to share your secrets?" said the President.

"It's really only evidentiary issues," replied the Secretary.

"Then let's get on with the matter at hand," said the President.

Dulac screwed up his nerve: "Mr. President, I will not divulge the document to the press under two conditions."

"Which are?" said the President, looking concerned.

"That the Minister of State resigns before the end of the week, and that you create a parliamentary investigative committee into Chimera."

"Only that?" queried the President sarcastically, looking in amusement at the Minister and the General Secretary.

"Dulac, you really have no idea," said the Minister of State.

"Mr. Minister, as Mr. Nixon found out, even the government isn't above the law."

"Thank you for reminding us of that, Mr. Dulac," said the President, then turning to the Secretary:

"Is that the position of Interpol?"

The Secretary fumbled for words:

"Ah, as I told Mr. Dulac, Mr. President, I haven't seen the document, so I can't really judge if such drastic measures are necessary."

Old Spineless is true to form, thought Dulac, as his stomach did a quarter turn.

"Well, then, Mr. Dulac, you seem to be playing this dangerous game here by yourself. Are you sure you know what you're getting into?" said the President.

"Mr. President, I know full well my chances are slim, but I cannot stand by and simply forget about the innocent civilians that were butchered in Italy, in Belgium, in Spain, in the name of the supposed protection of democracy. Mr. President, do what *you* must. I'll do what *I* must. There won't be blood on *my* hands."

"I see," said the President. "Then we have nothing further to discuss."

"Good day, Mr. President, gentlemen," said Dulac, as he rose to leave. "I trust you will make an honorable decision."

CHAPTER 68

"Can't you stop this madman?" shouted the Minister of State, turning to the Secretary nearly immediately after Dulac was gone

"I can get him off the case, but that won't solve your problem, will it? Can you phone the editors?"

"Are you insane?" said the Minister. "He can go to any underground newspaper, like the *Canard Déchaîné* and have us all before a judiciary inquiry in an instant."

The President finally spoke:

"Gentlemen, I've had enough of your inanities. I'm calling an emergency session of my Cabinet. That will be all."

* * *

The next day, Dulac found his table at the restaurant already occupied by Jean Vinet, ex-editor-in-chief of *Le Figaro*.

"*Bonjour,* Jean, thanks for coming," said Dulac.

As the journalist rose to meet him, Karen appeared, walking briskly toward the table.

"This is Karen Dawson, Professor of Mythology at La Sorbonne. I've asked her to join us," said Dulac, while Karen and Vinet shook hands.

Dulac ordered a bottle of Perrier.

"Jean," said Dulac, his shoulders hunched toward the center of the table, leaning closer to Vinet, "I have something, that if made public, will probably bring down the government."

"Thierry, what have you been smoking?"

"I'm not joking."

Vinet looked at Karen, who wasn't smiling.

"You are serious, my friend."

"Deadly so. I'm talking to you off the record. Do you agree?"

"I haven't much choice, if I want you to talk to me."

In the past, Vinet had lived up to his word. *A refreshing trait for a journalist*, thought Dulac.

"I was at the Quai d'Orsay, at the Elysée, yesterday. I asked for the Minister of State's resignation by the end of the week. There's probably an emergency Cabinet meeting going on as we speak."

"What the hell is all this about?" asked Vinet.

"If he resigns, I've promised not to go public. It's up to you to find out from the Minister."

"And if he doesn't?"

"Come and see me. You'll have the story of the decade."

"Who else knows?"

"Don't try, Jean."

Dulac knew he'd been followed; he hoped he'd acquired another insurance policy on his life. They had lunch and Vinet left.

"I don't have time to wait," said Dulac to Karen. "I'm going to Rome. Go to America, to your parents, anywhere. You'll be safer than here."

"If I'm thinking what you're thinking, it's going to get messy in Rome too, right?"

"Very. Lescop has pre-cleared this morning, with the Italian Public prosecutor, a warrant for the holding for questioning of Fiore and Volpe. Petrov sent a copy of Oleyev's confession and Kurganski's interrogation transcripts to the

Rome magistrate, Paolo di Martino. The magistrate has waived the need for a rogatory commission in Russia until he hears what the prelates have to say. Petrov also sent him a copy of Vasiliev's letter."

"Wow," exclaimed Karen.

CHAPTER 69

Dulac picked up Lescop at his apartment at 6 a.m. the next morning. They had agreed to meet the two Interpol officers, Delongchamps and Valdieu, at the airport. Their flight to Rome was scheduled for 7:15 a.m. Dulac didn't want to be standing waiting at the airport, a sitting duck.

"We meet Inspector Guadagni at the *Prefectura* at ten," said Lescop. "He has the warrants and the instructions."

Dulac also knew that there would be a strong chance that the news of the imminent arrests had been leaked to the Vatican, even though he had made sure that both Volpe and Fiore were present.

It was a crisp sunny morning as they flew over the Vatican. Below, Dulac could already see the disk of pollution forming over St. Peter's Basilica, like a tarnished halo. *How appropriate*, he thought. He read the morning newspapers: No hint of resignations in either *Le Monde* or *Le Figaro*. Among the policemen, the tension was palpable, as the expressionless faces of the Interpol agents belied their nervousness.

Dulac had thoughts of doubt and disbelief. But pictures of the dead archbishops flashed in his mind, giving him peace and resolve.

The state of the Vatican has two symbolic police forces and an effective one: the *Vigilanza* and the Swiss Guards are primarily decorative. The Italian police is not. When the Vatican and Italy signed the Lateran Treaty in 1929, Italy agreed to provide the constabulary forces to arrest criminals on Vatican soil, try them in Italian courts, and if they were found guilty, to imprison them in Italy. This alleviated the Vatican's need for an expensive justice and prison system.

Every year, Italian police arrested hundreds of pick-pockets, the most common criminals in the Vatican.

Dulac's taxi reached the prefecture. As he gave the instructions to Guadagni, Dulac lit his seventh Gitane of the day and paced nervously the narrow corridor at the entrance. *I can still abort the whole thing.*

Moments later, he looked outside, where two Alfa Romeos' motors hummed. Dulac and Lescop went downstairs, got in the back of the second Alfa and sat down. Ahead, Guadagni and four policemen slammed the doors and were off.

Dulac thought, *Will the prelates have been tipped off and escaped?*

The Alfas stopped in front of the Petriano entrance of the Vatican. The men exited and Guadagni showed the Swiss Guards his credentials.

"We wish to see His Excellency Archbishop Paolo Fiore and His Eminence, Cardinal Eugenio Volpe. Police business," said Guadagni, formally addressing the senior officer of the Swiss Guards.

* * *

Twenty minutes later, Dulac saw Fiore, accompanied by four Swiss Guards, striding confidently toward the entrance. Suddenly, at the sight of Dulac and the policemen, Fiore froze. For a moment, he looked nervously around, as if seeking an escape route. Then, with a look of determination, or was it fatalism, Dulac didn't know quite which, he strode slowly toward Dulac and smiled.

"Yes, Mr. Dulac?"

But Guadagni interrupted:

"Archbishop Paolo Fiore?"

"Yes?"

"It is with the greatest regret that I must inform you that I have a warrant for holding you for questioning in connection with the murders of Archbishops Salvador and Conti, and accessory to the murder of André Dessault. Other charges may follow."

At that moment, Volpe appeared, accompanied by three Swiss Guards:

"What is the meaning of this?" he asked Dulac. Before he could reply, Volpe turned to Guadagni.

"What are you doing here, Inspector?"

"We have a warrant for holding you for questioning in relation to the murders of Archbishops Salvador and Conti, and accessory to murder of André Dessault . . ."

"Absolutely ridiculous," cried Volpe, waving his right hand in dismissal.

"Not really," said Dulac. "We have confessions from Victor Oleyev, and Andrei Kurganski. Also the Marchioness of Dorset has agreed to testify for the prosecution. We also have other testimony and evidence linking you to the Chimera Protocol."

Volpe stepped back, paralyzed, speechless, staring at Dulac. His lips trembled uncontrollably. He grabbed Fiore's shoulder with his right hand.

"You, you can't arrest us. We are representatives of the Vatican. We have diplomatic immunity."

Dulac had dreaded this. He knew that legally, Volpe and Fiore had the status of diplomats. Once they were back in the Vatican, they couldn't be extradited, unless diplomatic immunity was waived. Under international law, only one person could waive that immunity: The Head of State, the Pope.

The seven Swiss Guards now moved up along Volpe and Fiore, closing ranks.

Their intentions were ominously clear. Dulac knew that there was no love lost between the Swiss Guards and the *carabinieri,* as each guarded their territory jealously. Their coexistence was at best tense; sometimes violent. As each faction's men sized up their counterpart, the situation was getting explosive. Inspector Guadagni's men started to reach for their sidearms, and the Swiss Guards dropped their halberds and reached for their nine mm pistols.

Dulac waved the policemen back.

"We'll have none of this," he said. Turning back to Volpe: "Very well; you and Monsignor Fiore are under house arrest. You'll not leave the Vatican until we resolve this. Is that clear?"

"We'll see about that," challenged Volpe.

"No, your Eminence," said Guadagni. "With all due respect if you step outside the Vatican, my men will arrest you immediately. I have no other choice."

Dulac addressed the senior Swiss Guard. "I want to speak to Cardinal Legnano. Tell him it's urgent."

Volpe and Fiore turned and walked away slowly, haphazardly, seemingly lost, changing directions twice, bumping into each other. They finally disappeared past the Piazza del Santo Uffizio.

CHAPTER 70

Dulac's cell phone rang.

"It's me," said Karen. "Did you see the news on TV?"

"No, I'm still at the Vatican. Volpe and Fiore are invoking diplomatic immunity. I'm waiting for Cardinal Legnano."

"The Minister of State has resigned. He's giving personal health problems as the reasons. The President has accepted his resignation."

"Fantastic. Any mention of Chimera, or of a parliamentary investigation?"

"No."

"Here comes Legnano. Talk to you later." He hung up.

"Mr. Dulac? What is all this about?" said Legnano.

"Your Eminence, we have evidence that Cardinal Volpe and Archbishop Fiore are involved in the murders of Archbishops Salvador and Conti. We have warrants to hold them for questioning, but they have invoked diplomatic immunity."

"Mannaggia la Miseria," exclaimed Legnano. "Come, let's talk inside." The Cardinal took Dulac by the arm, waving the Swiss Guards aside.

A small group of photographers, ever-present around St. Peter's Square, had formed nearby, awaiting the imminent confrontation between Dulac's men and the Swiss Guards. As Dulac accompanied Legnano to his office, he felt invigorated by the news from Karen. *The President of France is taking this seriously*, Dulac thought. *The last thing the President wants in his election year is a scandal the size of Gladio.*

Dulac sat down.

"Your Eminence, are you aware of Chimera?" said Dulac.

"What?"

"It's a successor to Gladio."

"Good God," exclaimed Legnano. "Again?"

"Yes. We believe Volpe, Fiore and de Ségur are behind the murders. The letter from Salvador to Conti, the anonymous donations, the killing of the Marchioness' illuminator, the funding through Miranda of Chimera, the hiring of assassins through the Russian mafia: Everything is there. It all fits."

"But what did Salvador and Conti do to deserve such a horrific fate?"

"They broke the golden rule of Chimera: Omerta. We believe they got wind of the donations through their participation in the Finance Review Committee, and worked their way upwards. They became aware of Chimera, maybe even got a copy of the Protocol."

"Protocol?"

"There is a protocol signed by the representatives of the member states, including the Vatican. Volpe signed for the Vatican. I've met with the President of France, and as you know, the French Minister of State has resigned this morning. He had signed for France."

Legnano looked away.

"I know where you are going with this, Mr. Dulac."

"I knew you would. Will you see the Holy Father? He alone can lift diplomatic immunity."

"What do you propose?"

"The same conditions I proposed to the President: If you hand over Volpe and Fiore to the Italian authorities, to be properly judged in a court of law, I won't reveal Chimera to the press. I can't guarantee it won't leak out somehow by other means, but it might give the Vatican enough time to sever itself from Chimera."

"We don't have much choice, then," said Legnano.

"My men are waiting. We need an answer today. I can't keep the lid on this forever. You saw the gaggle of journalists."

"I'll speak to the Holy Father. Please wait here."

CHAPTER 71

As Cardinal Legnano walked to the Pope's secretary's office, he realized the Holy Father already knew what he was about to tell him: Surely, Volpe and Fiore were the penitents the Holy Father had protected under the seal of confession. He had to be careful not to compromise the Pope.

Mannaggia la Miseria, what a mess, thought Legnano.

"Good morning, Monsignor," Legnano said to the secretary. "I need to see His Holiness right away. It's urgent."

"I'm sorry, he's already seeing someone."

"Cardinal Volpe?"

"I, I'm not at liberty to say."

"Yes, I know. How long will they be?"

"I have no idea. They've been in there for a while."

"I'll wait."

"But he has other appointments."

"Believe me, they'll wait."

Cardinal Legnano trussed up his cassock and sat down. He could feel the inseparable couple of destiny and history weighing heavily, bending further his osteoporosis-stricken back. He felt like a spoke in a huge wheel, set in motion by those eternal human frailties, ambition and power. At the hub lay an organization that had inherited all of Gladio's dreaded traits. At the perimeter lay dead citizens, dead archbishops, civil rights, democracy. He knew it was time to choose sides.

The door opened and the Holy Father, dressed in his plain white cassock, his expression severe, walked toward him.

"My dear Legnano," he said in a grave tone, as he showed the Cardinal inside the library.

"Please cancel my appointments for the day," the Pope instructed his secretary.

"Volpe has told me everything," said the Pontiff, looking devastated.

"You didn't know?"

Before the Pope could answer, Legnano quickly realized his indiscretion and the portent of the Pope's possible answer.

"I won't answer that question. Volpe has told me the authorities want to arrest Fiore and himself for the murders. He asked that I not waive diplomatic immunity. What is your opinion?"

"Holy Father, I have just learned of Chimera and the Vatican's participation in it this morning."

"How deeply are we involved? Are we simply sympathizers, as in Gladio?"

"No, according to Dulac, we are signatories. Your Holiness, Interpol is at the door, waiting for your answer. They have threatened to go to the press if we don't waive immunity."

"We didn't waive it in the sex cases," said the Pope.

"I know; I disagreed with that decision. Your Holiness, if the Church doesn't waive immunity, She will be seen as protecting and harboring criminals. All the more so that these men are so high in the organization. We're also talking about murder."

"Legnano, they haven't been convicted yet. Volpe says he was coerced into accepting by the Venezuelan drug cartel — Vega, is its name? He said he was merely their instrument."

"With all due respect to Cardinal Volpe, I find that hard to believe. If it were so, why would Vega not have acted directly, without the use of false flags, or for that matter, the Russian mafia? No, Volpe knew that Miranda, in which the Vatican has invested heavily, was under scrutiny by Salvador and Conti. He couldn't risk it being disclosed to the public, not only as a money-laundering operation, but more importantly, as a funder of Chimera — which would thereby disclose its existence. He also signed the document on behalf of the Vatican. Dulac says he has evidence Volpe hired the assassins."

"I see," said the Pontiff, his voice reduced to a whisper. "We must sever all ties with this Chimera."

"And with Miranda, Your Holiness, but that doesn't solve the immediate problem."

"I suppose not. What about Monsignor Fiore?"

"He was probably acting under Volpe's instructions. He's very ambitious, and has ultimate faith in Volpe. I've seen it at meetings of the Finance Committee. Also, he is under pressure to perform. His investment choices have been disastrous."

"Hence the temptation to use illicit funds," said the Pope.

"Exactly."

"Do you think he participated in the murders of the archbishops?"

The question surprised Legnano: If Fiore was one of the penitents, the Pope already knew the answer. Was the Pontiff baiting him, or had he, Legnano, been wrong in his judgment of Fiore?

"I cannot make a statement like that. But what concerns me is that Fiore was always interested in mythology. It was one of his favorite subjects at the seminar."

"Good gracious."

"And we know that Gladio's trademark was the creation of false flags."

"Like the Pistis Sofia letter."

"Unfortunately, yes."

"Are other members of this Chimera involved?"

"A trial might answer those questions."

The Holy Father rose, turned away and clasped his hands behind his back, and said: "I cannot begin to foresee the consequences of giving Volpe and Fiore to the Italian authorities."

"Holy Father, I think the consequences of not doing so are even worse."

"When does Interpol want an answer?"

"Right now. They're waiting at the entrance."

"Impossible. Tell them they will get their answer tomorrow afternoon. I have to meet with Volpe and Fiore. And with our lawyers. May the Holy Spirit give us courage, and the strength to get through this, Legnano."

"Yes, Your Holiness."

Legnano went to give Dulac the news. As he approached, he could see journalists and photographers milling about, waiting, as the Swiss Guards stood, an orderly phalanx contrasting with the mix of journalists and Dulac's men. Legnano took Dulac aside: "His Holiness requests until tomorrow afternoon, before giving his decision. He has to meet with the prelates, and with his inner council. He also has to seek legal advice."

"That's a long time. I can't guarantee there won't be a leak," replied Dulac.

"At least give us till tomorrow morning, then."

"That's more feasible. I can accept that. Give me your word that Volpe and Fiore won't leave the Vatican."

"You have my word."

CHAPTER 72

The Alfas drove away, in a throng of journalists' cries of, "Unfair, irresponsible! The people must know! At least tell us what it's about. Why didn't you get what you wanted?"

The policemen had been well prepared: *No comment*, had been the unified reply.

It would be a long night. Entering the hotel, Dulac, followed by three persistent journalists, sat down at the bar and ordered a double whiskey. As one of them tried to engage him in conversation, he turned away and gazed into empty space, lost in his thoughts.

* * *

The next morning, Dulac rose at 6 a.m. and knocked on Lescop's door.

"Meet you downstairs. The cars will be here at seven."

As they sat down in the Alfa, Dulac had a sense of foreboding. He tried to imagine the Holy See's options. *Will the Vatican bluff its way out of this, as it tried to do in the sex cases? Under the policy of deniability of Chimera, would the Vatican discredit Volpe, and deny his authority to bind it? Difficult, since he was Secretary of State, ranking immediately below the Pope.* He had witnessed how they had manipulated him during the alleged crisis of the Pistis Sofia letter, which had been a deliberate plant by Volpe and Fiore. *Could they still influence the Pope?*

They approached once again the steps of the entrance, adjacent to St. Peters Basilica, and Dulac could see the already-formed phalanx of Swiss Guards, in colorful contrast with the grayness of the day. *How ironic. The local police protecting murder suspects from arrest. Only in the Vatican. Doesn't look promising.*

The unlikely assembly formed again, as some journalists mixed with Dulac's and Guadagni's men. An hour went by. *Still no sign of Legnano.* Dulac paced back and forth, lighting Gitane after Gitane. Finally, exasperated, he signaled to the Swiss Guard.

"Can you see what's holding up Cardinal Legnano?"

The Swiss officer left in the direction of Legnano's office.

Suddenly, Legnano appeared, walking beside Fiore, whose blank, expressionless face looked straight into St. Peter's square and beyond.

"Good morning, Monsignor Legnano, Monsignor Fiore," said Dulac. "Where is Cardinal Volpe?"

"The Swiss Guard is getting him. He probably didn't sleep well," replied a somber Legnano.

Dulac knew he had won.

At that moment, a Swiss Guard erupted, walking briskly, and took Legnano aside.

Legnano signaled Dulac and Guadagni.

"Come, something is wrong, Volpe won't answer. His door's locked."

They followed the Swiss Guards and walked briskly toward Volpe's apartment.

"Cardinal Volpe?" shouted the senior officer as he knocked. No answer.

Legnano nodded to the Swiss Guards to break down the door. Three of them lunged in unison. The door broke open.

Cardinal Volpe lay askew, immobile in his uncovered bed, eyes glazed.

"Mio Dio," exclaimed Legnano, as the guard felt for a pulse and shook his head.

Cardinal Eugenio Volpe, Secretary of State of the Vatican, descendant of Alfonso ll, Duke of Ferrara, descendant of Lorenzo di Medici named the Magnificent, was dead.

CHAPTER 73

The special evening edition of the *Corriere della Sera's* head-lines roared in red letters:

> *Archbishop Paolo Fiore held for questioning in deaths of Archbishops Salvador and Conti.*

> *The Vatican today waved the diplomatic immunity of Archbishop Fiore, in relation to the deaths of Archbishops Salvador and Conti. Inspectors Thierry Dulac of Interpol and Guadagni of the Rome police, commented in brief: We are looking for possible motives, including financial issues related to the Vatican bank. Monsignor Fiore has been relieved of his duties related to the Financial Committee of the bank, pending the results of the investigation. Fiore is under house arrest at the Vatican, awaiting his preliminary inquiry."*

At Legnano's plea and insistence, Dulac and Guadagni had agreed to let the Vatican make its own coroner's inquest as to the exact causes of Volpe's death. The Vatican would also choose the date of the announcement, after the autopsy report.

Dulac had returned to Paris the following morning, and had been summoned to the Secretary's office.

"Congratulations, your team handled that well yesterday. Now I'm going to tell you something that will surprise you. Please don't take this personally, but you've been removed from the case."

"Excuse me?" said Dulac, incredulous.

"In the interest of national security."

"Really? I thought national security had been served rather well, yesterday."

"That's not the point. The President wants to postpone any further activity until after the elections. He thinks the risk of public disclosure will endanger the electoral process itself."

"And let the trail go cold. No thanks."

"It's not your choice Dulac," The Secretary's voice grew firmer under the challenge of his subaltern.

Dulac's every fiber revolted at his boss's obvious buckling under political pressure, against the essential principles of Interpol. To bring it up now would mean all-out war with the Secretary. He bit his tongue.

"I'll see what my friend at *Le Figaro* thinks of this," said Dulac.

"Don't be a bloody fool. They've already prepared total deniability of the document as a false flag planted by the Islamists. They're building up their case as we speak."

Dulac was shaken. He hadn't expected such a quick response. Obviously, the creative minds of the French government and Chimera hadn't been idle.

"And de Ségur?" he asked.

"De Ségur is nowhere to be found. According to his secretary, he was last seen at his office, late last night. The Paris police searched his house. We have his yacht in custody."

"Will you press charges?" said Dulac.

"We're still evaluating the evidence. Dulac, Lescop will take over your functions in the case. Please hand over all documents you may have in your personal possession. That includes the Chimera document."

"I don't have it."

"Don't play games, Dulac. You have access to it."

"So does he."

"Lescop?"

"Yes."

Dulac could feel the slow impact of the decision permeating his mind and body, down to the marrow. *I don't believe it: I'm damn well being fired.* It felt all the more unfair that he had broken the toughest case of his career. He wasn't about to help this Judas turn the sword in his wound.

"You have everything here." Dulac rose and walked out.

* * *

"Restaurant *Chez Anatole*," Dulac instructed the taxi driver.

Two hours later, after a *steak frites* and half a dozen Glenlivets straight up, Dulac sat at the now-deserted bar, his frustration and anger dulled by the scotch. *Let's see what Karen thinks,* he thought. As he left the bar, the evening air clung tightly to his clogged nostrils, his eyes watering from the smoke-infested room. He hailed a taxi.

After extricating himself from the taxi, Dulac tripped on the first stair of the apartment's staircase, and barely managed not to fall. *I'm completely stiff, just like in Montpelier.* He rang the bell insistently, and Karen buzzed him in.

"I've been fired, bloody fired," he yelled, stumbling up the stairs, as she stood in the doorway.

"What for?"

"Politics: The elections. I'm in the way. Volpe is dead. Those bastards let de Ségur get away. He's too close to the President and the Minister of the Interior."

He threw off his jacket, and sprawled himself onto the sofa.

"How about a scotch?"

"Maybe you've had enough."

"You're probably right. Half a scotch?" he said, measuring with his thumb and forefinger in front of a semi-closed eye.

Karen smiled and prepared the drink. He wasn't going anywhere tonight.

* * *

The next morning found Dulac in the foulest of moods. He drank the remaining pot of coffee, trying to cleanse the poison that throbbed double-time in his breast. He felt exhausted, but relieved.

I need to get away, far away from all this. The Secretary is bluffing about Chimera. I'll see Jean at the Figaro. *No, that would definitely put an end to my career, or what's left of it. Let the storm pass.*

"So what now?" asked Karen.

"Fiore will go to trial. That bastard de Ségur, I swear I'll get him. Right now, I'm going to massacre some Brahms on my piano. Care to join me?"

"Sure, after my classes this morning."

After breakfast, as Dulac melted into the amorphous crowd walking to work, he questioned his own significance. People went on to their secretaries, coworkers, coffee breaks, board meetings, malaizes and heart attacks, ignorant of his efforts, oblivious to his fight. He felt he should tell them. He sat down at the bistro. After three coffees and two croissants, he thought, *Was it really so important that they know?*

* * *

A week later, after trying unsuccessfully to drown his self-pity in a mixture of more Glenlivet and Brahms, he called Karen.

"How about a mountain trek in Canada? I hear they have great walking trails in the Rockies."

"Sounds great. When?"

"I'll clean things up at the office. How about next week?"

"I'll see if I can shift my classes."

CHAPTER 74

As the Airbus lumbered down the tarmac into take-off position, Karen gently squeezed the slender, pianistic hands, and drank the remainder of her orange juice. It had been a long time since she had shared a vacation with a man.

Dulac clasped the seat belt shut and felt the slow tightening of his muscles preparing his body for take-off. He felt happy. The happiest he had been in a long, long time.

He couldn't guess that, a few hours later . . .

EPILOGUE

Rome, Corriere della Sera, *May 3, 2005:*

> *Cardinal Eugenio Volpe, Secretary of State of the Vatican, has died in his sleep of an apparent heart attack, said the Vatican in its newspaper,* L'Osservatore Romano, *this morning. He had no previous history of heart ailments. The Holy See has named Cardinal Giuseppe Legnano to replace him.*

London's Daily Messenger, *September 21, 2005 edition:*

> *The Marchioness of Dorset, former member of the Board of Directors of Miranda Group, is serving a six-month sentence in London, after pleading guilty to attempting to smuggle 5.1M USD into Italy. Kostas Stephanopoulos, the captain of the vessel involved in the smuggling, is serving his three-year sentence in Naples, as are two of his crew members. Although sources say the Miranda Group may have been used to channel the illicit funds, no legal action has been taken against the Group at this time.*
>
> *Hughes de Ségur, ex-President and CEO of Miranda Group, for whom there is an international Interpol red flag*

arrest warrant for murder in relation to the Archbishops
Salvador and Conti assassinations, has been seen in Belize
recently. There is no extradition treaty between Belize and
France, or Italy, or Switzerland. His French lawyer says he
has no immediate plans to return to France.

Rome, Corriere della Sera, *November 2, 2005:*

After an explosive trial in Rome lasting two months,
Archbishop Paolo Fiore has been found guilty of accessory
to murder in the Salvador and Conti cases. Says he falsified
letter under South American mafia instructions, blaming
Pistis Sophia sect. He awaits sentencing.

Paris, Le Canard Déchainé, *November 29, 2005:*

Following the discovery by Jean Vinet, freelance journalist
and ex-editor of Le Figaro, *of 'Chimera,' an underground*
paramilitary organization, Severine Pontet-Dubuisson,
France's recently elected first woman President has promised
a parliamentary investigation into Chimera. Rumors point
toward the participation of the ex-President and Minister
of State.

Moscow, Pravda *January 30, 2006 edition:*

Victor Oleyev, recently convicted mafia boss, is serving his
twenty-year sentence in Irkutsk for the murders of Sergei
Vasiliev, Olga Fedova and Andre Dessault, and his role in
the murders of Archbishops Salvador and Conti. His seized
assets, including his helicopter and house in Rubliovka, have
been sold to pay his unchallenged tax assessments for the
years 1991 to 2003. An unfinished painting portraying
him as Henry VIII fetched 55,000 rubles at Christie's of
Moscow last month."

* * *

Nicola Vasilieva was on her way to Vancouver, after a short visit to her aunts in Calgary. The Airbus from Paris had stopped over in Calgary, and was nearly full, as she entered the economy class and found her way to her seat. Some of the ongoing passengers had exited the plane to stretch their legs for twenty minutes, before the plane resumed its flight.

As she sat down, she glanced at the open glossy magazine, lying on a woman's pink sweater on one of the seats beside her. It depicted snow-clad mountains of the Rockies under blue skies and a gleaming sun. *Whistler, trekking capital of Canada*, the title read.

She was about to have the surprise of her life.

THE END

ALSO BY ANDRÉ K. BABY

THIERRY DULAC THRILLERS
Book 1: DEAD BISHOPS DON'T LIE
Book 2: THE CHIMERA SANCTION

Thank you for reading this book.

If you enjoyed it please leave feedback on Amazon or Goodreads, and if there is anything we missed or you have a question about, then please get in touch. We appreciate you choosing our book.

Founded in 2014 in Shoreditch, London, we at Joffe Books pride ourselves on our history of innovative publishing. We were thrilled to be shortlisted for Independent Publisher of the Year at the British Book Awards.

www.joffebooks.com

We're very grateful to eagle-eyed readers who take the time to contact us. Please send any errors you find to corrections@joffebooks.com. We'll get them fixed ASAP.